Beyond Sandy Ridge

Nancy B. Brewer

Beyond Sandy Ridge

Nancy B. Brewer

Revised Edition 2012

Cover Design by Sean Snakenberg, Brentwood
Cover Photography by Vernon A. Brewer, Jr.

PUBLISHED BY
BRENTWOOD PUBLISHERS GROUP
4000 BEALLWOOD AVENUE
COLUMBUS, GEORGIA 31904

Books by this author

Published by Brentwood

Carolina Rain
978-1-59581-573-6

Lizzie After the War
978-1-59581-680-1

Letters from Lizzie
978-1-59581-714-3

A Doll Named Fannie
978-1-59581-569-9

Quotes and Poems in Black and White
978-1-59581-663-4

Garnet
978-1-59581-696-2

The House with the Red Light
978-1-59581-680-1

 To order additional copies of this book or other books by author: www.nancybbrewer.com

Retail orders email: msnancybnc@aol.com

*If ye have faith as small as a mustard seed,
nothing shall be impossible unto you.*

Beyond Sandy Ridge *is a work of historical fiction. It is the author's desire to give you a true sense of the times. Therefore, names of real people and places have been added. However, the storyline is imaginary. Any resemblance to any persons living or dead is purely coincidental.*

Dedication and Acknowledgements

Beyond Sandy Ridge
is dedicated
to my husband and my best friend, Vernon;
and
with respect to the past, my father, Doug;
and
with hope for the future, my daughter, Caroline.

With special thanks to
JoAnn Rish, Pat Baker and my mother, Carolyn;
and with appreciation to
Brentwood Publishing and Monica for their help and support.

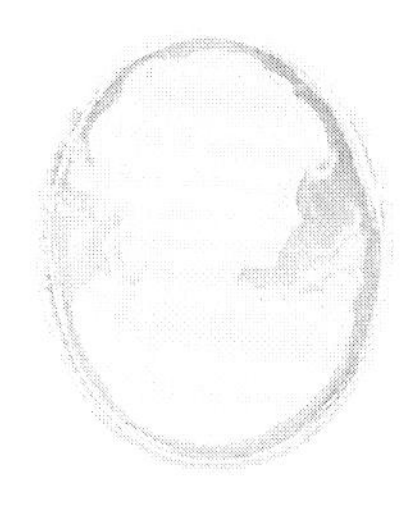

October 6, 1864

My Dear friends,

At age 18, the world lay at my feet. I was graced with a pleasant face and blessed to be born the daughter of a hardworking man. I wish all I had to share with you were the joys of life on our plantation, but much has changed since those carefree days.

Of course in 1860, I had heard the political talk. Any newspaper you chose to read clearly outlined the issues and predictions of what was to happen between the North and South. I considered it little more than parlor conversation until the war fell on our doorsteps.

At first, we thought the war would be short lived. By spring of 1862, we learned how wrong we were. There were soldiers coming into the coast of Charleston, sometimes as many as a thousand a day. Many were badly wounded. Many more were sick.

My choice to be a nurse was not a likely one for me, but with such a great need, we were all obligated to do whatever was asked of us. As Mammy always said, "You never know how strong you are until you are called upon."

The next four years became about sacrifice, hard work and pure determination. Those big drops of ***Carolina Rain*** *just kept falling. Our defeat came in the winter of 1863 when our home went up in flames, leaving us standing in the ashes of our smoldering dreams.*

With the war closing in on us, we sought refuge at my sister Sallie's home in Stanly County, North Carolina. The addition of more family was an unspoken burden on Sallie. Her husband, Ransom, was off fighting in the war and she had two children of her own to feed.

Now here I am, living in the land of tall pine trees and red dirt hills. The people here live a simple life. They do not judge you by how much money is in your purse or by the clothes you wear. Perhaps, that is why I fell in love with Joel Simpson from North Carolina.

It is a heartbreaking experience for a woman to find the man she loves cannot marry her. Desperate and lonely, I was determined to find solace in the arms of another. My wounded judgment convinced me to marry Edmond Cook. Unbeknownst to me, he was a man of questionable character. Edmond's death was tragic, but my bitter tears were softened by the blessing of our child, Victoria.

Do not try to understand love, control it or hold it.
Although love is humble, it is strong and suffers all,
And if it be true, it will always find it's way.

I am not certain if it is the nature of love or the nature of God, but love has found its way. I pray that this war is over soon and Joel and I will be together at last.

I must be strong, for these are the thinnest of times and there is nothing to rub against anything. The war has taken it's toll on the South; fortunes lost and lives forever changed.

We Southerners are a strong lot. Like our ancestors before us, we will survive. I will never lose faith. I am standing on the promise that tomorrow will be a better day.

Yours forever,
Theodosia Elizabeth Sanders

CHAPTER 1

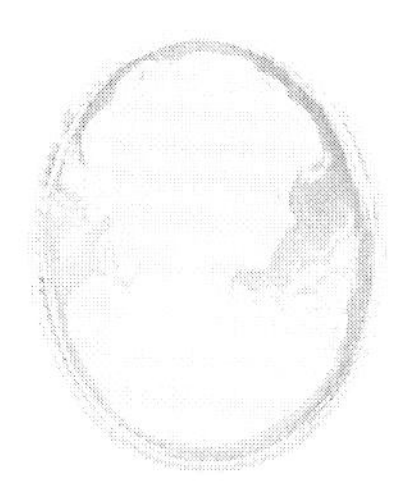

Reflection of Charleston

Thursday, October 6, 1864

My eyes are slowly forced to open as the morning sun flickers across my face.

When I arise, I am surprised to see a letter has been slipped under my bedroom door. I open the envelope and find myself smiling, recognizing the handwriting as Fannie's. My heart is warmed by the words I read.

Happy Birthday to you,
Theodosia Elizabeth Sanders.
Today you are twenty and two.
And to you I will always be true.

Dr. Fannie Holloway is one remarkable woman. I recall our first encounter. She was as confident and secure in her self-worth as any woman I had ever met. As our friendship developed, I realized she had a heart of gold. However, it is her keen mind that earned her the reputation as one of Charleston's finest doctors. This is a remarkable accomplishment for any woman, let alone a Negro woman.

It is hard to believe it has been nearly a year since we left Charleston. In my mind's eye, I often return to Sandy Ridge. I can see clearly the live oaks blowing in the wind as they stand proudly against the backdrop of the white-pillared mansion. I can smell the sweet honeysuckle blooming and the welcoming aroma of fresh-baked bread. My ears echo with the sounds of laughter and the soulful singing of the slaves working in the fields. I run my tongue over my lips remembering the taste of the salty air.

What would I give to spend one more hour with my sister Annabelle or to lay my head in Mammy's lap and let her rock away my sorrows?

I think of the fussy crinolines and the tight-fitting corset that I used to scorn. I would welcome them back, if only I could dance across those grand halls again.

My heart is bleeding. I want to cry out, but there are no ears to hear, save the pretty pages of my diary.

The ruffled dresses, petticoats and fanciful ways,
Sweet tea, fried chicken and all our Southern ways,
Are slowly fading down the river,
Like ships sailing away.

Poise and manners have gone astray,
Replaced by the rude awakening of the day,
Now listen here, fear for our dear Southland
As young souls pass and the old decay.

Yet, who will shed a tear or shout hooray?
If only I could beg or plead his stay,
Would he smile and kiss my hand,
Just once more…
For the grand old days?

The truth interrupts my thoughts; Sandy Ridge is only a memory. The slaves have all fled seeking the frontier of their freedom. The burned hull of the big house will soon tumble to the ground.

My little sister, Annabelle, trapped in the passions of youth and the urgency of our uncertain times, found herself to be an unwed mother. So assured the child she carried was a boy, she proudly chose the name, Thomas Jacob. Thomas, for her beloved and Jacob for our dear Papa. Annabelle's intuitions and her tender body failed her. She exchanged her soul for a beautiful baby girl on a stormy night, April 25, 1861.

Three years have passed and this happy little girl we call TJ is the spitting image of her mother. So much so that Papa often slips and calls her Annabelle, reminding us this darling little girl will never know her own mother. Now we can only pray fate will be kind and her father will return safely home from the Great War.

Yes, North Carolina is my home now and I am thankful to be safe, but Charleston will always be in my heart. The old memories bring tears to Mother's eyes. Therefore, we seldom speak of them.

Some memories will forever lay heavy upon my bosom. Folks know my husband, Edmond, was killed. I suppose that out of respect they do not ask questions. Once I tried to tell Papa what happened. "Lizzie, what is done is done," he said, stopping me. "It is God's job to pass judgment, not mine."

He was right. No amount of talk can change things. I found peace in believing that Edmond's death was his own fault. Even the innocence of a colored girl like Cindy Lou was worth protecting.

My whole life seems like a bittersweet dream, but here at my sister Sallie's house, everything was real. Papa's fortune was lost, Annabelle was dead and Sallie's husband, like most men, has been called to join the Confederate Army.

I ask myself, will our prayers save a chosen few or will mothers and lovers be left to cry in poetry and song?

Sweet were the times when we loiter'd,
Arm in arm on the sandy beach,
Or down the path, through the orchards.

Oh, how I remember the sound of the sea,
The smell of the blossoming tree
And the gentle touch of my lover's hand.

His voice was smooth as satin yards,
And my name forever on his lips,
Oh, what would I give for those feverish days.

But man's rage did call,
And he fights for Southern cause.
For his safe return, I can only plead.

The waves still pound against the shore,
And still doth bloom the blossom.
But, now my love sleeps forever,
Beneath his marble stone.

By day I can occupy my mind, but nighttime I am defenseless. Visions of working with Dr. Fannie in the hospital haunt my dreams. I can see the soldiers looking up at me with their dark hollow eyes and hear them calling out my name. Some nights, I awake exhausted after frightening dreams of Edmond chasing me through the woods and marshland. Still, perhaps the most disturbing are the sad faces of old friends, but never Fannie's. Just like in real life, she is always laughing and making jolly. "Ain't nothing too serious," she always says. "Even death is a joke on the old devil, if we are living for the Lord."

When they made Fannie, they broke the mold. How many times I have reflected back on the day I read this headline in the *Charleston Post*:

Appearing On Stage Tonight: Kate and Maggie Fox, World Famous Spiritualists.

Learn what is to come and reveal the unknown.

When I showed the article to Fannie, she shook her head. "No, not me, I don't fall for such foolishness. A team of wild horses could not drag me to see those girls."

It did not take a team of wild horses, but I did have to drag her tooth and nail through the door. I still laugh thinking of her bulled up sitting there with that funny little hat pulled down over her head. "You're scared aren't you Fannie?" I asked. She said no, but I could beg to differ.

Before the performance, if you wish to call it that, a gentleman introduced the girls as Modern Spiritualists. They were supposedly just simple farm girls from Western New York State. He claimed they were the greatest mystery of all time and God appointed their talents. They could predict the future, advise the lost and speak to the dearly departed. Then he lowered his voice and cautioned the audience, "If anyone be faint of heart or afraid of secrets that may be revealed, they should exit to the rear immediately."

The room was filled with whispers and folks looked around to see who might leave. If I had not placed my hand on Fannie's arm, she might have made a beeline for the door.

The curtain went up and standing before us were a pair of plain-looking girls dressed in calico dresses. As the evening proceeded, an array of people walked on stage and claimed to receive a reading. Most of them acted as if they had discovered some profound information.

The program was coming to a close when the younger of the two called out, "Wait, I have a message for a young woman by the name of Lizzie."

Fannie's mouth dropped open and she slid down in the seat. I made no effort to speak up. The girl came to the edge of the stage and peered out into the audience. She then motioned for the gentleman to help her down off the stage. I held my breath and slowly she came to my aisle. She touched me gently on the shoulder, "Are you Lizzie?" she asked.

I was sure this was some sort of trick and I laughed, but suddenly I could see a pained look of seriousness in her eyes. "Yes," I answered softly.

"I have a message for you," she said. "I am led to tell you today that someone loves and thinks of you. He wants to tell you to meet him in North Carolina."

I did not trust her and believed she was misleading me, even though she was partially right. It was true. I was in love with someone from North Carolina. And it was Joel Simpson. However, our love could never be. Joel was a man tortured by his own integrity which bound him to his estranged wife, even though she had been in an institution for over seven years. Joel unselfishly encouraged me to seek happiness without him.

Therefore, when I met Edmond, I forsook all precautions and married him. At first, it was exciting and wonderful, until the real man I married was exposed. Now Edmond lies in his grave and I suffer to keep all those foul memories buried with him.

If I had only taken the time to talk with the Fox sisters, would they have told me Joel's wife would die unexpectedly, leaving Joel free to remarry? If the future had been revealed, I would have never consented to be Edmond's wife. Yet, how empty my life would be now without my precious little Victoria. She was the reason for my suffering and now is the reason for my existence.

Now God has placed me here in North Carolina, just a few miles from the house Joel occupied before he was called to war. We were blessed to be able to seek refuge at Sallie's home after Sandy Ridge burned. Sallie welcomed us with open arms, but we all knew it was not without burden. Poor Sallie already had her hands full trying to take care of herself and her own two small children, Minerva and Noah.

More people meant less for everyone. I feel that especially applies to me. I am always the first to leave the table, even if my belly is still growling. After all, I have Victoria and I came dragging Cindy Lou along, too.

My responsibility for Cindy Lou often makes me feel I am the one enslaved. Mammy used to say, "*Som bodies' gots to do that gal's thinking for her.*"

Cindy Lou does not have the wits to plan out even a simple day's work. Left alone she will sit around all day drawing on little slates or scraps of paper. Still, I am always astonished at how she can capture the likeness of someone as real as a photographic image.

Among all of us here in North Carolina, the tension is growing. Even if we do not speak of it, it is there. Papa sleeps in his clothes on the sofa in the front room. He claims to fall asleep reading, but his Enfield rifle is always nearby. Mother reads the Bible and sleeps most of the day. Sallie tends to the children in the front room, so she can watch the road. It is my desire for my emotions to be unknown. Being exposed makes one vulnerable; introversion feels safer. Only in the pages of my journals do I allow my thoughts to escape me.

Every passing day thoughts of Joel Simpson fill my mind. In reality, we only shared a moment and a few passionate kisses, but never one night in each other's arms. Still, I knew how he would feel lying next to me, the sound of his breathing and how he would whisper my name. I knew how he would take his coffee and the way he looked in the morning light. Yes, I knew Joel as I knew myself, and one day we would be together. Even war cannot deny destiny.

For these days as Autumn 1864 comes to a close, all we can do is pray that the war will end as well. Papa says better sooner than later, or we will all be just a greasy spot upon this earth.

Since November of 1860, I have completed nine scrapbooks and I am working on number 10. I am not as careful in my applications as I was in my scrapbooks of younger years. I no longer tie pretty ribbons and place them carefully next to party invitations or tender letters. Not a single dried pansy or forget-me-not embellishes the war year pages. Nor do I attempt to properly align the news clippings on the pages. It is news, bitter news, but Papa says it is important work to keep records. I am not exactly sure how or why, but I have been appointed the family historian.

After reading Fannie's letter and placing it in the drawer with the others that I will read repeatedly, I glance over at the huge heap of newspapers lying on the floor. I do not have a writing desk here at Sally's house. I most often spread out on the floor or curl up in the chair by the window to do my work. Victoria and I share a little room. It is pleasant enough. However, it is often too warm. I always smell like a fry cook because it is actually the maid's room and is directly over the kitchen.

Originally, the room was furnished with a small iron bed, dressing table and a cedar wardrobe. Papa made it a bit more serviceable by installing a bookshelf and constructing a folding screen to divide the room. Now I can read and work on my papers as late as I please without fear that my lamp will keep Victoria awake.

It is early and the house is still. I can hear Victoria sleeping in her crib on the other side. I walk over to the bookshelf and pull out my last scrapbook with clippings of 1864. There are only eight blank pages remaining in the book. I am debating whether to begin a new scrapbook or chance that October's news will prove uneventful and eight pages would be sufficient. I am dreadfully sick of the news of battles and the frightening predictions of the War Campaigns.

Thumbing through my scrapbook, the headlines flash across the pages.

Grant promoted to commanding General of Union forces

Battle of Spotsylvania, Virginia - Union 18,000 casualties, Confederate 12,000 casualties

Confederate victory at Cold Harbor, Virginia, Confederate Victory!

Battle of Petersburg, Virginia - Confederates hold Petersburg

Oct. 1, 1864- The body of Rose O'Neal Greenhow was recovered from the sea at Fort Fisher, N.C. Mrs. Greenhow, also known as "Wild Rose," was a renowned spy for the Confederacy. The small boat in which she was escaping capsized and she met her demise being dragged to the bottom of her watery grave due to the heavy weight of the gold she was carrying on her person.

Like a cat running over my grave, an eerie thought sends a chill down my spine.

With so much tension between the North and South, how much more could this old earth stand? Perhaps it would explode and break apart at the Mason-Dixon Line, leaving all of us to fall in a fiery pit of despair.

The house is coming alive and I close my scrapbook. What a shame to waste such a lovely morning hovering over spent news or reflecting back on the glory days of Charleston. The smoky smell of something cooking on the stove is filling the room and the sun is trickling through the worn lace curtains. Walking to the window, I admire the landscape. Fall has opened beautifully.

Victoria begins to stir. I peek around the screen to eye my little daughter, now almost a year old. She is wide-awake, sitting up, playing with her toes. I pause to study her soft blonde features. People say she looks like me, but it is undeniable she has inherited her father's crystal blue eyes. I fear that one day those eyes will look up at me in discontent should she discover the truth about her father. For now, she is just a babe and as long as God gives me the strength, I aim to shelter her from the evils of this world.

"Hey there baby boo," I say cheerfully, as if I do not have a care in the world.

At once, the head full of curls turns my way. Her eyes brighten and she stretches out her buttery fat little arms for me. She loves me and I love her more.

Chapter 2

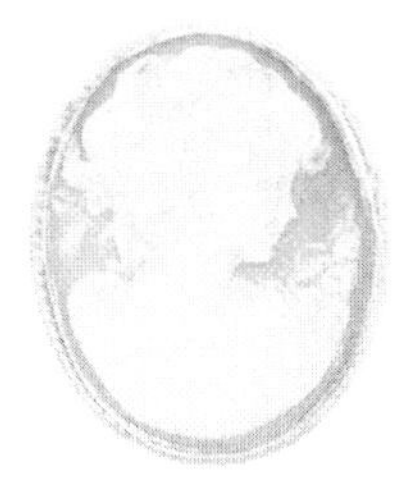

Faith, Hope and Letters

Meals are uneventful these days. No matter what it is, you are thankful. It is better than starving, so I am told. I think I miss coffee most. We have experimented with different substitutes, the latest being okra seeds. Today's breakfast consists of rice and a piece of bread fried in a bit of salt-pork grease. At least I have my memories of grand banquets and fine foods, but this is all the children have ever known. I suppose it is best not to have anything to compare.

After the meal, Papa readies to go to the Post Office. He always goes alone.

Going to the Post Office is much like a visit to the doctor; it can be either good news or bad. As 1864 is coming to a close, printed material is scarce and we depend on the letters from the front lines for news. Lord forbid Papa comes home empty-handed or worse with a letter addressed to Sallie from Ransom's commanding officer.

Once Papa is out of sight, Sallie begins to walk the

floors. At first, she attempts schooling the children, but her voice is tight and squeaky. Most mornings the children are attentive to their studies, but this morning they are fidgety and silly. I suppose intuitively they know they do not have Sallie's full attention and misbehaving is their way of gaining her focus. Sallie is quick to lose her temper and Minerva begins to cry. Witnessing the scene, Mother calmly walks to the foot of the steps and calls for Cindy Lou to take the children upstairs to play.

"Sallie, you must not take out your frustrations on the children," she says, coaxing us into the front room.

"I know Mother, but..." Sallie's voice drops off to a whisper.

For the next two hours we busy ourselves with needlework. The conversation is dull and Sallie is constantly looking out the window. I should be concentrating my prayers for Sallie. After all, Ransom is her husband and the father of her children. However, I am secretly praying that Papa returns with a letter for me from Joel.

Papa is the only one that really understands my relationship with Joel. It is here I must clarify – I have NO relationship with Joel. That is the point. One of my greatest fears is if something happens to him, no one will even know to contact me. I might spend the rest of my life waiting for the man I love to come home.

It has now been over four weeks since I received a letter from Joel. I have read the letter so often I can almost quote it by memory. Thinking of the letter, I decide to excuse myself to go upstairs. Mother looks at me oddly. Does she know? I suspect not.

Once upstairs, I take out a box from underneath my bed and open up my last letter from Joel. Before I read it, I hesitate. I stop to imagine his hand upon the paper and his eyes looking tenderly at the words. "Oh dear Lord," I pray softly. "Please grant me the favor of your blessing. Let it be soon I shall hold his hand and look into his eyes once more."

My Dearest Lizzie,

I am sorry I have not written to you as of late. I am vain enough to hope you have missed my letters. Please know I would never wish for you to worry on my behalf. I have had good reason for my lapse in writing and I trust you will excuse the shabbiness of my handwriting. I was shot in the right hand at the battle of Spotsylvania Court House, Virginia, on May 9th.

I will tell all later, but for now, here is what happened in brief: We had been into the Yankees for about two weeks and now we finally had come to a rest. That morning, we met up with them again in a grove of cedars. General Lee planned to lead us into battle himself, but the men would not budge until he took a position to the rear. The fighting was fierce, the worst I have seen as of yet. Within no time, the landscape was flattened out. I took a bullet to my hand that knocked me off my feet. There were so many bodies strewn out over the ground, I could hardly keep my footing. By the very grace of God, I managed to get myself back to camp. Since that time, I have been in the hospital here in Danville. I am due to be released tomorrow to rejoin my company. With so many killed, I do not see how either side could declare it a victory. As to what is next, they say Grant is heading for Richmond, so I reckon we will be hot on his trail.

Lizzie, with all this time in the hospital, I have done a great deal of thinking.

I had planned to hold my heart's words. Now, I must face the cold hard truth if this war does not end soon, I may not return.

Out there on the fields, a man must come to terms with his own mortality. I am not afraid of death, only of leaving this world without telling you I love you with all my heart. Lizzie, if God brings me home, I will not be too proud to beg for your hand in marriage. Just having your consent will give me the courage to go on and will serve as my shield against the enemy. If I am to die, know that your words have made me the happiest man that ever lived. Well, they are calling for me now and I must close. Please pray that the sun will soon set on this great discord.

All my love and devotion,
Joel

My consent letter had been written on the last remaining piece of fine stationery I brought with me from Charleston. I did not have a proper envelope. Instead I carefully folded the letter in a pretty piece of wallpaper and wrote his name in nice block letters. It seemed secure. Under normal circumstances there would be no problem, but the mail is not trustworthy or reliable these days. I can only pray he received it.

Once I finish reading Joel's letter, I place it back in the box for safe keeping.

My mind is filled with uneasy thoughts and I lay

across the bed and close my eyes. If only I could be like Sleeping Beauty and escape this world until my Prince Joel returned.

I feel myself drifting off to sleep, but suddenly I am brought back to consciousness by a little voice in my head, "Lizzie, be careful what you wish for."

I jump to my feet saying aloud, "Forgive me Lord."

After I come to my sanity, I am relieved it was not a premonition that woke me, but Papa arriving back home. Running to the window, I see him jump out of the carriage and hold a bundle of letters high in the air. He knows Sallie is sitting by the window waiting.

I scramble downstairs just in time to see Papa handing Sallie her letter.

Sallie takes a deep breath. Her hands are quivering and Papa must open the letter for her. I sit down next to Papa and as if he can read my mind, he shakes his head. Another week in passing and there is not a letter for me.

We wait patiently with our heads bowed for Sallie to read the letter first to herself.

Afterwards, she reads the correspondence to us. Occasionally she blushes and pauses briefly. We have become accustomed to this, knowing she is omitting little tidbits that Ransom has intended for her eyes only.

Ransom is with the 42nd North Carolina Regiment, Company H. From his letters we have learned he spent the close of 63' in Wilmington. Early 64' his brigade was taken by rail to Petersburg, where they engaged in the Battle of Cold Harbor and the Bermuda Hundred. Ransom says the worst of it is knowing that many of his childhood friends will not be coming home.

These letter-reading rituals were common in most homes; such was not the case for poor Phoebe Burris. She was a quiet woman in her early thirties who lived alone in a shack down by the Rocky River. From time to time, Papa would haul a load of wood out to her place and I would take her a small ham or a pot of stew, when we had it to spare. No matter what the weather, she was always in church on Sunday, wearing a homespun dress just like the rest of us. We feared something was wrong on Sunday, September 17; her seat was vacant. Mother suggested we ride out after church to check on her. Papa went to the door and Mother and I waited in the carriage. He knocked several times. He looked back at us puzzled and motioned he would go around back.

"Lizzie, perhaps you should try the door," Mother suggested. Agreeing, I walked up on the wooden porch and slowly turned the handle. The door appeared to be unlocked, but it was jammed. I pushed against the door with my shoulder and the door popped opened. I called out "Phoebe", but there was no answer. I remember feeling something at my feet and I looked down to discover a small grayish kitten brushing against my leg. I picked up the kitten and stepped inside. It was a still September afternoon and you can imagine my surprise when a sudden gush of cool air slammed the door behind me.

The house was dark and odorless, no fire or food cooking. I clutched the kitten to my breast, walked over to the window and pulled back the curtains. A beam of light rushed in and cast a halo over a letter lying open on the kitchen table. My first instinct was to read the letter, but I could not bring myself to reach for it. I was already intruding, but if Phoebe walked in and caught me reading her mail, my honesty would be compromised.

As I walked through the three-room house looking for clues, an eerie feeling of utter and complete sadness surrounded me. The bed was made, the chamber pot empty and the candles were burned down. The only sign that someone had been there recently was a small pot of cold beans on the stove.

It seemed like time had stood still and I found myself drawn to the letter. I dropped the kitten to the floor, sat down at the table and took up the letter.

Dear Mrs. Burris,

On September 19, 1864, Company C of the 23rd North Carolina Regiment, engaged in the battle of Winchester Virginia. It is with great regret I am writing to inform you that your husband, Private Willie James Burris, was killed in action.

I hope you will find comfort in knowing his death came swiftly and his suffering was short. Speaking for myself and the Montgomery Volunteers he was among the finest of soldiers, brave and devoted to the southern cause. You can take pride in knowing that Willie James Burris gave his all for his country.

My dear Mrs. Burris, if mere words could heal your pain I would gladly supply, but is only through God and the grace of time you will find your peace.

Respectfully yours,
Lieutenant General Jubal Anderson Early

I picked up the letter and walked outside. Papa and Mother were standing by the carriage talking. Papa was rubbing the back of his neck and shaking his head. I could tell Mother was upset too. I handed her the letter and she read it aloud to Papa. At once he exploded into a fit of rage, grabbed the letter from Mother's hand and tore it to pieces. "Damn this war!"

Papa hopped in the carriage and turned to us. "Let's go. I'll have to get someone out here to pick up the body."

"Body?" I asked.

Papa just repeated, "Let's go Lizzie, there is nothing we can do now."

Mother obeyed, but suddenly I remember the kitten. Without giving an explanation, I ran back in the house. Papa called out to me, but I did not answer. When I returned with the kitten in my arms, nothing more needed to be said. I named the kitten Phoebe. She would be a welcomed gift for my little Victoria.

Phoebe Burris's death was hard for folks to take, but not hard to understand. Jumping off Rocky River Bridge was her way of ending her despair. It was true there was plenty of despair across our Southland. Some folks hid behind false hope and faith, while others feared their own despair would consume them next.

CHAPTER 3

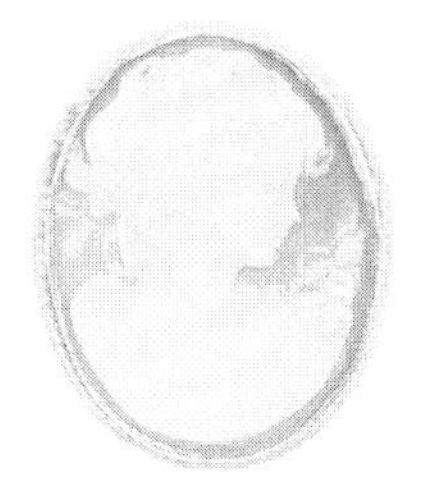

A Hard Day's Work

Papa is not a well man, at least not by my standards. He is but a shadow of his former robust self. His shoulders are bent and his beautiful head of hair is thinning, exposing a sunburned scalp. Perhaps saddest of all, the sparkle is gone from his eyes when he smiles. Instead, his eyes are hollow like a child who had once been beaten or starved for food.

It is doubtful Papa will ever be the same since he came home from the Yankee prison. We have all tried to forget those months. Even if we could, Papa's rattling cough is a constant reminder. Papa is not one to complain. Even in these hopeless times, he still says "Into every life a little rain must fall, but thank the Lord it is sweet *Carolina Rain*."

It pains us to see him doing more work than should be asked of a man half his age. With Sallie's husband Ransom gone, all the farming is left to Papa and Harper. I myself have taken up wearing trousers and helping out on the farm when necessary. Even though Papa does not like it, he says little. The vanity of the old times is a small price for food on the table. We replace our worn-out leather boots with home-made shoes with wooden soles and canvas uppers. My little

Victoria has never had a decent pair of shoes or a new dress. She lives in hand-me-downs and homespun dresses.

Thank God for Harper. Papa had gifted Sallie and Ransom with Harper and his wife Violet as a wedding gift. Once Papa owned over a hundred slaves, but between smallpox and the war, Harper, Violet and Cindy Lou are the only ones left. In many ways, they are more like family than slaves.

Some evenings, Papa comes in from the fields nearly in dead man's shoes. I have even seen him falling asleep at the supper table, but the next morning he is back to his duties at hand. Papa's strength is nothing more than shear guts and determination. He is the finest example of a man and all admire him for his courage and gentle nature. How could anyone love him more than me? If it can be so, it is Mother.

I shutter to think what Mother would do without Papa. She is gloomy enough as it is. I was not there to witness the terrible withdrawals Mother suffered after moving here and no longer able to obtain her laudanum. Sallie said it was a dreadful sight to watch. She refused to eat and expelled even a sip of water. After the third day, she curled up in the fetal position and barely spoke at all. Sallie sent for the old Indian woman who delivered her children. Again, this mysterious dark woman's herbs and ways were a blessing to our family. Mother's body was slowly freed from the poisonous addiction. Even her headaches are a thing of the past. Who would have ever thought modern medicine could prove to be so vile.

Back at Sandy Ridge before the war there was plenty of everything. Now here in North Carolina there is not plenty of anything; even the air seems tight. We must be content to live on what we can raise or grow. We try to set aside cash crops, but there is very little surplus. With Papa's fortune lost, our only dependable income is Ransom's military pay of $11 a month.

Let me remind you, our household consists of three children: Victoria, Minerva, Noah; and four adults: Sallie, Mother, Papa and myself. There are also three slaves: Cindy Lou, Harper and Violet, making up a total of 10 souls living on $11 a month.

Food prices are ever soaring: sugar is $12 a pound, wheat is $25 a bushel and flour is rising to $500 a barrel! Then there is salt, which is becoming more and more scarce. Strange how you never think of how essential something is to your existence until you do not have it. Without salt, we have little means to preserve meats and vegetables or tan hides. It is a known fact that salt is a necessary mineral to sustain good health in humans and animals. We have lost a mule and the rest of our animals are looking poorly. Speaking of health, we must take all precautions to maintain ours. What if any of us would become ill? How in God's name could we afford even one bottle of medication or tonic? I have not said a word to anyone, but my health is not at its best. I have given thought to writing of my ailments to Dr. Fannie in Charleston, but I hesitate to use a stamp unnecessarily.

It is understandable why I have secretly held on to a few gold coins – not to be a hoarder, but in respect of what is yet to be revealed. Just last week, I helped Papa bury our few valuables in a metal box down by the well. He said it was best to have more than one pair of eyes to mark the hiding spot. Just before Papa closed the lid he turned to me, "Anything else Lizzie?"

"No, nothing," I said, wondering if he knew about my gold coins.

Then he slipped off his wedding band and dropped it in

the box. It was my suggestion to plant a thorn bush over the location. Hopefully it will discourage the Yankees if they show up digging around.

In Charleston, I had the ocean for a reference point of where I was in the world. Here I feel as if I am in the middle of nowhere. The county we live in is called Stanly.

Papa and Mother are from Montgomery County just across the Yadkin River. Papa's cousin operates the ferry. When we first came here, we crossed the river to see our folks up in the hills.

Sallie and Ransom's house is west of Bear Creek in a community near Bethel Church. This area of North Carolina is considered to be a crossroad between Anson, Mecklenburg and Cabarrus counties. Twenty miles northeast is the county seat, Albemarle. The next largest city, Salisbury, is approximately 30 miles in the adjacent county of Rowan.

There is a strong sense of community here. Good neighbors like the Hinsons and Tuckers are not only a blessing, but essential to surviving in times like these.

In addition, we are thankful to have extended family living only a stone's throw up the road. Ransom's parents, Cynthia and Reuben, are both up in age. Cynthia is the better of the two, a good cook and a reliable hand for tending to the children. Mr. Huneycutt's hearing is poor, his eyesight is dim and he refuses to admit he is an old man. Since the war, he was forced to close the family dry goods store, but he still tries to maintain his farm. Just since I have been here, he has been laid up several times with a faint heart. When Papa goes out to help him, Reuben insists on paying him in some form. I know Papa does not want to be paid, but he accepts graciously. If he refused, old Reuben would be too proud to ask for help the next time.

In the house next to them lives Caroline and her husband, Robert Burris. Caroline is Ransom and Thomas' sister. She is a gentle, kind and God-fearing woman. People can say what they want, but I think Thomas made a wise decision to entrust Caroline with TJ. Even if he had not been called off to war, how would an 18-year-old boy take care of a baby? Caroline and Robert love little TJ just as much as their own little boy, Robbie. I know in my heart my dear sister, Annabelle, is smiling down from heaven on her little girl every day.

Caroline's husband, Robert, is noticeably self-conscious of his limp, and when the army rejected him, he was shamed. Caroline considered it a blessing. "Let the people talk if they want," she said. "God and I know my husband is not a coward and what anyone else thinks is of no concern of mine."

Monday, November 14, 1864

After church on Sunday, the men had decided they would have a hog killing first thing the next day. Papa said it was a tad early to hang meat, but everyone was down to the bare bones. Besides, we could not afford to feed them much longer. There were two big hogs in the pen. Papa, Robert and Mr. Huneycutt had shared the expenses of raising the pair and now they would share the meat.

It is 7 o'clock Monday morning and Mr. and Mrs. Huneycutt have arrived. I look out the window and see Harper giving instructions to Cindy Lou and Violet. Already a fire is blazing under the two large wash pots. Back on the plantation, I had seen the slaves carrying out this ritual, but today I must help.

Quickly I throw on a pair of old trousers and a woolen shirt. I run a comb through my hair and I am alarmed at the amount of hair in my hand again. I must write to Dr. Fannie just as soon as I have time. The smells from the kitchen are filling my room and I hear the voices of the men downstairs. I am crawling around on my hands and knees looking for the mate to my boot when I hear a tap at the door. "Lizzie, it's me." I recognize the voice as Mrs. Huneycutt. Not waiting for me to answer, she opens the door. "What are you doing on the floor dear?" she asks.

With one boot on and the other in my hand, I jump to my feet.

"Oh," she says laughing. "Well, I came up to tend to Victoria. You go on downstairs and get a bite to eat. Don't worry, I'll see to her when she wakes up."

I could hear Victoria stirring and I knew she was already awake.

"Go on now, before she starts crying," she teases.

I hobble downstairs and sit down on the bottom step to put on my boot.

Papa and Robert are talking in low voices in the hall. They could not see me, but I could hear their conversation.

"Jacob, we have got to make a decision – eat or pay our taxes. I have been looking for work, but I don't like the idea of going off and leaving Caroline and the children alone."

"I know what you mean, Robert. On behalf of the war efforts, I invested in Confederate bonds. Now, even if I could afford to buy more, I am afraid they will be worthless. This new money is not worth the paper it is printed on! Furthermore, there are so many counterfeit bills floating around you'd be a fool to take it. The imposed five percent levy on land and slaves is understandable, but you cannot get blood out of a turnip. Even though I said I would never do it, it looks like I might be forced to sell Harper and Violet or at least hire them out. The girl, Cindy Lou, is another issue. She is a good worker once you get her headed in the right direction. It takes patience with that one. I hate to think how she might be treated under different circumstances." Papa's voice drops off when Mother comes into the hall.

"Lizzie, you are looking lovely again," she jokes, patting me on the top of the head. "Go on in the kitchen. I have something special for you. I have finally come up with the best coffee substitute yet!"

Papa passes me by and nervously says "Yep, ground pecans and dried yams, didn't you say, Tempie?"

Mother laughs, "Is that what I said?"

In the deepest way, Papa's words have upset me. Mammy would be sad to see this day; better she is dead. The kitchen is still warm and left on the table is a single biscuit and small pot of creamed corn. On the stove, I spy the coffee pot. I take down my cup and fill it with the hot brown liquid. After just one small sip, I agreed. Mother is right; this is wonderful. This gives me a sense of renewed hope and comfort. This morning's bad news may never come to pass. Things are bound to turn around soon.

When I finish eating, I open the back door and three frisky little children greet me. Minerva is pulling TJ in a little wooden wagon and Noah is trying to pull her out, so he can have a turn.

"Aunt Lizzie!" calls out TJ. "The mens just left to go down to the barn. That colored man of yours is going to kill the hogs."

This created excitement and they all began talking at one time. "He is going to hit them on the head with a big axe, ain't he, Aunt Lizzie?" Noah looked up at me pleased to have made the announcement.

"Well I am not sure of that, but I am sure I do not want to see the deed done," I answered.

"I do," says Minerva. Uncle Robert let Robbie go, but Papa said I could not."

"Well, I think there will be plenty for you to see before the day's over. Grandma Huneycutt is upstairs with Victoria and she will be in need of some company."

In the distance, I hear a gunshot, then another. My only thought is I am thankful for the hog's sake it was a bullet and not the axe. I pulled TJ out of the wagon and opened the back door. "Go on now and give Victoria a big hug for me."

TJ and Noah go on in without a fight, but Minerva hesitates. "Let me stay and help, Aunt Lizzie. I ain't no baby."

I lean down on one knee so I can look directly into her big blue eyes. Her little cheeks are bright pink and her curly blonde hair is a rat's nest of tangled-up curls. I take out my handkerchief and wipe her runny nose, "Oh, I know you are a big girl, and Grandma Huneycutt is going to need you to take care of the children. We will send for you if we need you."

To my surprise, she reaches up with her dirty little fingers and gently strokes my face. "Aunt Lizzie, I love you," she says. "I hope I am as pretty as you when I get to be an old lady." Then she flips her little body around and into the house she goes.

I hear someone laughing and turn to see Sallie standing over me. "Old lady, we could use your help," she says, taking my hand and helping me to my feet. "Mother and I are down in the smokehouse mixing up the salt rub and getting ready to do the wrapping. Papa wants to know if you think you can stomach helping them scald the hogs and prepare the meat."

"I suppose so. How bad can it be? I am sure I've seen

worse working in the hospital." Sallie did not wait for my response and had already turned to go back to the smoke-house.

I look up to see Papa and little Robbie riding up over the hill. Little Robbie is sitting up proudly in front as Papa guides the horse pulling the two bloody pigs toward the kettles. Several makeshift tables are set up with an assortment of knives and cutlery tools. Violet and Cindy Lou seemed to be preparing for what is to be done, so I join them for my lesson in hog dressing.

I am told by Mr. Huneycutt that it is important the hog's jugular veins be cut as soon as the beast is killed. Given any time, the blood will clot and the meat will be spoiled. The little drag up the hill may have helped with the draining, but from where I am standing all I see is blood, mud and guts.

The men set about lifting up animals by way of block and tackle over the boiling pots of water. I can smell the old familiar smell of blood as they are lowered into the boiling water. Violet whispers to me, *"You's gots to scald de hide to gets the hair off."*

After this is done to Harper's satisfaction, he picks up a large butcher knife. Violet turns to me as if on cue, *"Nows itz times to getz the innards. Here grab hold of de basin."*

Together we lift up a heavy metal pan and hold it under the belly of the hanging hog. The steam from the water is wetting my hair and I begin to flush as Harper approaches with the knife. Skillfully he inserts the tip just between the legs and slices open the lower stomach of the hog. When the intestines begin to flop out into our waiting pan some of the blood and tissues splash on my face. I am just above fainting when Violet's laughter takes my mind off the site, *"Dem chittlens, sho be good later on, Miss Lizzie; you waits and seez."*

Just as sure as a surgeon, Harper knows where to end his

cut. Cindy Lou takes away the basin and we lift up the second to collect the stomach, liver and heart. When our work is done, they drop the animal to the ground and the butchering begins.

Before, we would eat only the select cuts of meat and pass on to the slaves the organs, ribs and lesser cuts of meat. Today we will use all parts of the hog and nothing will go to waste. We will use the hide for leather, the fat for cooking lard, making salves, candles and soaps. The only part that will not be eaten or used will be the blood, for Biblical reasons.

The hams will be smoked and cured. Some of the meat will be pickled such as the feet and ears. Mr. Huneycutt has spoken for the brains; he likes them fried with his eggs. A variety of sausage and liver pudding will be prepared. Then lastly, Harper and Violet show us how to use the organ meats.

By evening the butchering is done and all that is left on the front lawn of the slaughter is a big pot of fat and scraps boiling down for lard. The tiny bits of crackling meat are boiling up to a crisp in the fat. The best cuts of meat have been taken to the smokehouse, rubbed down in salt, pepper and brown sugar. Soon they will be hanging over a green wood fire to cure.

A sweet smoky smell is filling the air and the children can be detained no longer. Out the door they come, with Mrs. Huneycutt carrying baby Victoria on her hip. The moment Victoria sees me she starts to cry. It is then I realize how awful I must look. Bloodstained and smelling to high heaven, it is enough to frighten anyone away, even my own child.

Violet and Cindy Lou dip out enough of the hot cracklings and we all enjoy a surprise treat. Just when I think those poor pigs could sacrifice nothing more, Harper has one more surprise for us. He delights the children with two big balls, each made by blowing up the bladder of the pigs.

At last, the day came to a close. The men went into the barn to change out of their bloody clothes. Violet and Cindy Lou were drawing water from the well to bathe.

If it were not so cold, I would have gone down and jumped in the creek before I went in the house.

I had neglected Victoria all day and she will need to be fed and put to bed. My bath will have to wait. When I walk in the back door, Mother is waiting for me with a pot of her so-called coffee.

"I have put Victoria to bed for you," she says. "I have the water heating and your robe is hanging on the door."

I look around to see the metal tub sitting in the middle of the kitchen in front of the stove. "Thank you Mother. You are so thoughtful."

"Don't think I was just thinking of you. You have to clean up if you are going to sleep in this house tonight," she says smiling. "Now hurry up and get cleaned up. Your father will need the same treatment when he gets in."

"Mother, you might as well go on to bed. In case you do not know, Papa and the men are into the corn whiskey and he is in no hurry to come inside."

"Oh, he is, is he? Well, so be it. He has had a long hard day; we all have. I expect that is the last of the whiskey anyway. He can sleep out in the barn tonight, if he wants to. Good night Lizzie."

I pour a cup of the coffee, slip off my clothes and sink down in the nice hot water. There is not much time for things like this lately. I close my eyes and reflect back on the early days when I first met Edmond. Even though the marriage turned sour, the early months were exciting and sensual. There was rich red wine, days of laughter and nights of passionate lovemaking. Will it be like that again with Joel? The question is, will Joel come home. My thoughts are interrupted. I can hear Papa and the men laughing outside. I am glad to hear him laughing. Whiskey is good; I wish I had some.

CHAPTER 4

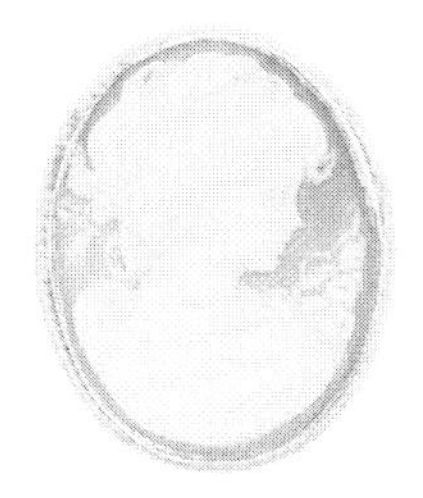

Gypsy Moth

Tuesday, November 15, 1864

Dear Fannie,

It has been awhile since my last letter. It is not because you are not in my thoughts, but stamps are hard to come by. Please say you are doing well and the medical clinic is still running full force. Your stress and workload these days at the hospital must be unimaginable. Please know you are in my daily prayers.

Guilt hangs over my head for leaving you and Charleston. If I were still there, at least I would be doing some good. Here it feels like I am just growing older by the day, waiting for something. God knows what that will be.

In your last letter, you asked about Victoria and Joel. First, let me tell you what I know the most about. Miss Victoria is healthy and growing in leaps and bounds. She is into everything and is talking up a storm, even though most of it you cannot understand. I hope that one day soon you can come for a nice long visit.

As for Joel, there is good news and no news. He has written and asked me to marry him. I wrote him with my consent, but I have not heard back from him in over a month.

If you are able, please write. We get little news here and we want to know what is going on in Charleston. I hope you will not think of me as selfish, but there is another reason for this letter today. Fannie, I am not feeling well and have all sorts of minor complaints. It is a puzzle that possibly you can solve.

First, I am no longer having my monthly. Now, don't you dare get any ideas in your head. There is not the slightest opportunity for anything here other than work. Next, I go to bed tired, but sleep does not come. I have very little appetite and suffer with leg cramps and sore muscles in my neck and back. However, most distressing is my hair is dry, brittle, and falling out by handfuls. Lastly, my skin is red and angry.

You see, I am a small mess. I must rid myself of this big dark cloud that hangs over my head. If Joel comes home and finds me in such a state, he is likely to change his mind about me. There are no pharmacies here, but we are plenty rich with herbs. I will not worry, for I have the utmost confidence in you. With that grand statement, my dear, I will close and wait patiently to hear from you.

Affectionately,
Lizzie

Papa will be leaving for the Post Office soon. With no time to tarry, I hurry down the stairs. Sallie informs me Papa is sick in bed with a sudden illness. "No mail today," she says, looking forlorn.

Mother speaks up, "Well that is what he gets. It is time old men know their limits. Mr. Huneycutt is sick too. After the hog killing they all stayed up half the night drinking and playing cards. I suppose when they got too drunk to come in the house they just laid down with the cows. Your Father came in this morning about daylight and Robert drove Rueben home. I think most of his illness is self-induced. Anyway, he is not up to going anywhere today, not even the Post Office."

"I can go to the Post Office," I announce.

"Lizzie do not be silly. I will not hear of it," Mother insists.

"I know the way and Harper and Violet could ride with me. Mother you know in Charleston I went wherever I pleased, alone."

"Well, that was only because I was not there to stop you."

"Please Mother, Lizzie is used to this kind of thing," Sallie begs.

Papa's voice comes from the hall. "Lizzie if you drive, I'll ride."

"Jacob!" Mother shouts. "You are better off in bed."

"I'll be alright once I get something in my belly and a cup of your coffee.

The mail is important and these girls should not have to pay for my sins."

Mother is too mad to answer and storms upstairs. Sallie looks at me and we try not to laugh. Just for a moment in the dim morning light, I see my Sallie again – a halo of butternut curls falling softly around her face, that familiar impish grin and the sparkle in her big blue eyes. It is almost like old times. I close my eyes and pray,

Dear Lord, thank you for this glimmer of hope. Yet, I know reality is evil and ever pressing. It is my best friend and my worst enemy. My reality is vain and demands my attention, whether I like it or not.

When I open my eyes, Sallie is now standing by the window. The sparkle is gone, her eyes are distant and her face is aging with worry. Before I have much time to reflect, Papa bounces into the room. He is smiling and talking in a voice louder than normal.

The theatrics are not working. He is as pale as a ghost.

Shortly afterwards we are on the road to Albemarle. I realize Papa is asleep. I struggle to reach the blanket in the back and toss it across his shoulders. He should have stayed home, but perhaps the fresh air will cure his drinking sickness.

Ralph, our old horse, is slow. If he travels much more than five miles, he will come to a halt on his own. Today is no exception, just 45 minutes into the ride he stops alongside the creek.

The jolt wakes Papa and he looks up. "This is his spot. He stops here every single time. Rest assured he will not budge until he has a long cool drink and a belly full of sweet grass."

"Maybe that's what he thinks he is suppose to do," I laugh.

"Well, while we are stopped, did you bring us something to eat?" Papa asks.

"Of course," I reply, digging into the basket in the back seat.

After a little refreshment, I am happy to see Papa's coloring is back to normal. We sit on the roadside and talk for a while. It is a pleasant morning, not very cool for mid-November. With the warm sun shining on my face, I decide to lie back on the dried grass and close my eyes. I could easily drift off to sleep listening to the birds singing and the creek running behind me.

The solace is wonderful until Papa shouts out "Damn gypsy moths! The fellow who thought it was a good idea to bring these things over on the boat is a bigger fool than I am. Well, I bet he was a Yankee too! Now these crop-eaters have migrated all over the South." With these words he crushes an innocent moth in his bare hands.

"Papa, I agree with you. They are a nuisance, but I must disappoint you a bit. The scientist that brought them here was a Frenchman, not a Yankee.

"Frenchman, Yankee, it is all the same to me." He pretends to be angry, but I know he is of good nature. He jumps to his feet and climbs into the driver's seat.

Hiding his smile, he calls out, "Let's go Lizzie. Daylight is burning."

As the road opens up toward Albemarle, Papa begins to whistle. I am happy to see he is back to his old self. I find it peculiar that my mind drifts back to thoughts of the gypsy moths. They were taken from their home by the 'hand of man' and placed in an unnatural world. Yet, now the 'hand of man' wants only to destroy them. Of what crimes are they guilty? They did not ask to come here. They are only trying to survive. Is this not the basic instinct of all creatures great and small?

We arrive in Albemarle just a little past noon. This town sits upon a high hill with the Court House being the highest point. Poor old Ralph is dawdling. The incline is difficult for an old horse, more so for one that is not so richly fed. Papa stops the carriage in front of the Post Office and leaps out. "Only a minute, Liz," he calls back.

I know Papa's minutes. We all do. "Papa! I am going to walk down the street for a bit."

"Well...," he hesitates looking up and down the street. Yet before he agrees or disagrees, a man calls to him from the doorway of the Post Office. "Come to see me, have you Jacob?"

When Papa turns his back, I escape and make a beeline down the street. He will find me; after all, there are only a few stores in which to browse. I never look back and dart into the first open door. It is a dry goods store of sorts, but I am disappointed to find there is very little to my fancy in this or any of the other stores. I should have known the shops would be nothing like the ones in Charleston. The thrill is over quickly.

I head back toward the carriage in a somber mood. Something catches my eye in the alley and I hear music. I see a brightly colored covered wagon with two large gray horses hitched behind the Post Office. There is a dark-haired young man sitting on a little stool out front. His back is turned to me and a small crowd surrounds him. I bravely take a few steps in the direction of the music. There is a young girl playing an unusual instrument and the tune is foreign. I watch as a old woman in brightly colored clothing steps out of the wagon. Soon, two local ladies step out behind her. One opens her purse and hands the mysterious woman money.

"Gypsies!" I find myself saying aloud. I had only read about their kind and was not sure they even existed.

I pause, feeling almost intoxicated by their music. If Papa were standing here, he would take my arm and walk me quickly back to the carriage. Here for the first time in many months was something exciting! I look up the alley to see if Papa is in sight. "There are townsfolks standing around, so it must be safe to investigate," I say to myself, walking briskly toward the festivities.

Once among the crowd, I see the young man is painting a portrait of a little girl. It is a striking resemblance of her likeness. I must have lost track of time while standing there watching his skilled brush masterfully stroke the canvas. In fact, Papa startled me when he tapped me on the shoulder. I jumped back in defense and embarrassed myself by knocking over the artist's little table. The paint splattered on the ground and all over the hem of my skirt.

The young man rose and turned to face me. Perhaps it is the unexpected attention or his handsomeness, but I begin to feel faint. "I...I am so sorry for upsetting your paints," I apologize.

He smiles and looks at my skirt, *"The paint is of no concern, but your attire I am much sad for. I must owe you."* He speaks in broken English and the origin of his dialect is unfamiliar.

Papa is helping him upright the table when we hear a man's voice breaking through the crowd. "So there you are! You no-good thieving Gypsies. This is no place for the likes of you. I am ordering you to pack up and get out of this town right now!"

With those words, the barrel-chested man, obviously the sheriff, commences to flap his arms at the people.

"Go home folks! The show is over."

In seconds, the streets are clear and Papa and I are left standing alone with the Gypsies. We are all lost for words, until the old woman steps out of the wagon, "Antonio! *What is happen here? Are you responsible for this young woman's dress?"*

"Yes, Bunica. I am afraid I be the guilty one."

Clearly displeased, she comes forward to get a better look at me. Taking up the hem of my dress, she begins to rant and rave in her native language. Antonio smiles at me sheepishly. I get the feeling he is used to this. Letting go of my dress, she collects herself and turns to Papa. "*We will make right. Antonio will paint. He paints beautiful your daughter."*

Antonio begins shaking his head. *"Yes, lovely lady. I paint your portrait. It will be my greatest masterpiece."*

"No, that is alright," I reply.

Papa catches my hand. "Lizzie, don't respond in haste," he whispers, eyeing the nearly finished portrait of the little girl. "The man has talent. We have such few luxuries these days. I say we take him up on his offer."

Papa arranged for Antonio and his band of Gypsies to follow us home. He agrees to let them camp out until the painting is done, providing there are no complaints.

Heading back down the road, Papa starts laughing. "Your dear mother is going to be fit to be tied, when she sees us come rolling up. You know, I don't like to upset her, but this is going to be priceless." I agreed with Papa, but I was not sure I wanted to be in the same room or even in the same house while he explained it to her.

I was right – inviting a gypsy family home was not one of Papa's most popular deeds. We had never heard Mother speak a word about Gypsies. Now suddenly, she is an expert on them. She has Sallie scared to death they are going to steal the children and Cindy Lou and Violet fear they will put a hex on all of us. Papa assures Sallie that he will personally make sure the children are safe and at the first sign of any misbehavior he will send the Gypsies packing.

Before evening falls, Cindy Lou, Harper and Violet are wearing little leather pouches around their necks. "Mojo" is what Mammy used to call those little bags of herbs and bones. We have seen these many times before, but you just do not ask questions. The Negroes are a secretive lot when it comes to their superstitions.

Mother thought she could tactfully warn little Minerva and Noah not to go outside where the Gypsies are camping. Now, both the children and Sallie are scared to go to sleep. Thankfully, Victoria is too young for this foolishness. The debate is still in full force when Victoria and I head upstairs for bed. At the top of the steps, I pause and look down at Papa. He winks at me. Poor Papa, he is going to pull a hard night getting this crowd to settle down.

....

Just after breakfast the next morning, there is a gentle knock at the front door. Minerva peeks out the window and at once screams out, "Run! The Gypsy man is coming for us!"

Just as she runs by, Papa grabs the back of her collar. "Enough of this young lady. Nothing is going to happen to anyone!"

Sallie is standing in the hall grasping her throat and Mother grabs up Noah.

"Now this is all just a bunch of nonsense," Papa says quietly. We are all going to act as if we have some sense around here. Lizzie is going to get her portrait painted and we are going to be nice to these folks. Have I made myself clear?"

All heads nod except Mother's. "Tempie?" Papa asks.

"Well, I will not stir the pot, Jacob, but you better keep an eye out. I have read about the Gypsies," she adds in defense.

"Tempie, those were fairy tales," Papa says, and makes an attempt to give Mother a little kiss on the cheek. She pulls away and Papa smiles at her amusedly. "Now, if everyone will have a seat, I am going to invite this young man in."

Sallie, the children and Mother all crunch together on the sofa. Papa opens the door and I hear his voice, *"Mr..., I am afraid we did not get your name."*

"Sanders, Jacob Sanders," Papa replies in an uncomfortable, loud voice.

Antonio walks in, removes his cap and his black glossy hair falls across his forehead. His dark eyes scan over the room in amazement as if he has just stepped into a mansion. *"So fine a home you have here, Mr. Jacob."*

"Thank you. Let me introduce my family," Papa begins. "This is my daughter Sallie, her two children and my wife, Tempie. I think you have met Lizzie."

"Ah, Dizzy," he repeats, bowing down before me.

The mispronunciation of my name delights the children and the uncontrollable laughing begins. Even Mother and Sallie have smirks on their faces.

Antonio looks embarrassed. *"Do I say something wrong?"*

Papa pats him on the back. "No I think you are more right than us. Just for the record, it is Lizzie, not Dizzy. Dizzy means crazy."

"Loco?" Antonio asks.

Papa nods his head yes.

"It is I who is loco. Miss Lizzie, a thousand pardons."

"I think the parlor room here will be good for you to

set up," Papa speaks up, clearing the air. "There is a nice light coming in from the window, and if need be, I can bring in a lamp. Best of all, we can close out these little monkeys here," he jokes, looking at the children. They are accustomed to his teasing and Mother and Sallie take the hint.

They gather up the children and close the door behind them.

"Most perfect. We will begin shortly, yes?" Antonio asks, turning to me.

Suddenly aware of my appearance, I run my hand through my hair and stroke over my old gray flannel dress. I am hardly the object of a masterpiece.

Antonio must have read my mind. *"Miss Lizzie, Antonio paints you in the finest dress you can ever dream. I see in my eye for you blue velvet, no? Mr. Jacob, with your permission, may I ask Miss Lizzie to bare her shoulders a wee bit? A beautiful face is better framed by a graceful neck and a pair of lovely shoulders."*

Papa looks over at me and tilts his head to the side as if he is the artist.

"Yes, yes, I see what you mean. I think the man has a point Lizzie. What do you say?"

Antonio is clearly undressing me with his eyes and I can feel my face turning red.

He steps closer to me and looks directly into my face as if he is going to kiss me. *"And perhaps, you should pin your hair up like so."* He reaches out and lifts my hair off my neck. Then he whirls around and announces he will be back in half an hour to begin his work. I turn to the window and watch him walking briskly back to his wagon.

Papa gives the fire a couple of good pokes. "Go on, Lizzie and get ready. Your mother will take care of Victoria.

You remember when Mr. Devoe came to paint Mother. It takes time for these things. That was a magnificent painting of your Mother. I would give anything to see it just one more time, but it went up in smoke just like everything else at Sandy Ridge."

Papa looks for a moment as if he might cry and excuses himself from the room. I stand there reflecting back on what he has just said. Once Papa could afford almost anything, even the services of a well-known French artist. Maybe in a small way, he can relive those days, even if it is a Gypsy artist this time.

The thought gives me a new outlook on the painting and I rush upstairs to prepare. The door is open to my room and Mother is dressing Victoria. The moment she sees me, she reaches for me and starts to cry. Mother scolds her. "Victoria, you are such a mommy's girl. Mommy can't take you right now."

Mother sits her back down on the bed and works on the business of putting on her shoes. Victoria is quiet, but her blue eyes full of tears are intensely watching me dig through my trunk for something to wear. After both shoes are on, Mother lifts Victoria and says, "Tell Mommy bye-bye."

"Bye-bye, Mommy," Victoria says in a weak little voice.

I take her in my arms and she lays her head on my chest. She is my evidence that there is still goodness on this earth. "Listen to me, Miss Vicki. Can you be sweet and play with Grandmother for a little while today? "

Mother takes her from my arms and looks at me harshly. "You better watch yourself, Theodosia. Those kinds of men have a way with women. I have read about that too."

I am laughing when she closes the door even though she might be right.

There is something strangely alluring about this man. He is a fit figure of a man with well-portioned features and straight teeth. Yes, he is a handsome man, in a common sort of way. However, it is his eyes which seduce me, like black shiny mirrors looking into my soul. They say Gypsies know all, the past and the future. "Silly," I say aloud. "Just plain silly."

I turn back to the trunk and sort through a few of my old dresses I have pulled out. Glaring up at me is the blue silk gown I wore at my 18th birthday party. I stroke the faded material in remembrance of that day. This material sure caused a hellish fight between Sallie and me. On the day Ransom brought it to me, he also came to ask Sallie to marry him. Sallie was so sure Ransom had come to court me that she ran off to Aunt Sara's. If she had not finally listened to reason, she and Ransom would not be married today. Oh, but that seems like a lifetime ago. Sallie and Ransom have two children now and I am 22, a widow with a baby of my own. I am sure Sallie has long forgotten about this old dress.

With a little effort, I am still able to fasten the dress. It will do. Sitting down in front of the mirror, I frown at my dry brittle hair. Combing it is a dread lately. A handful always comes out and today is no exception. Before I came to North Carolina, my hair was so thick it was an effort to pin up; now it is much easier. Perhaps I will wear it pinned up more often. The room is filled with sunlight and my reflection is clear in the mirror. Funny thing, people can lie to you – you can even deceive yourself, but the mirror never lies. Sallie is not the only one these hard times have taken its toll on.

Before stepping out in the cold hall, I cover my bare shoulder with my old woolen everyday shawl. It is a misfit look and appropriate for how I feel. Opening the door, I look right and left. With a little luck no one will see me sneak into the parlor.

My footsteps are quiet, but Sallie meets me at the bottom of the steps.

"Oh hello, Sallie," I say cheerfully, trying to ease by her.

She steps her foot in front of me so that I cannot pass. She pauses for a moment and gives me a big sister look. Without warning she lifts up my shawl. "Oh, I see what you are hiding, that old dress! I was hoping it had burned."

She had not forgotten about that day. "Sallie, if you like we can burn it together when I am through with the sitting."

"No, let's keep it around. Seeing it reminds me of Sandy Ridge. A lot has changed since then, except you Lizzie; you are still just as beautiful." Sally opens her arms wide to embrace me and her fresh tears wet my face.

Down the hall, Papa is braced against the doorway of the parlor. He is dressed in his work clothes and his tall lanky body is curtained across the entrance. Seeing me approaching, he bows to me and steps back. Papa is trying to be comical, but he only succeeds in adding to my embarrassment. Antonio is waiting with his blank canvas and tray of paints. "*Please come sit,*" he instructs, pointing to the little stool in front.

Although the room is nice and warm, I pull my shawl up tightly around my shoulders before I sit down. Antonio takes his place behind the easel. "*I am ready, Miss Lizzie.*"

I am self-conscious of where to place my hands and how to hold my head. Antonio calls out again, "*Miss Lizzie, I am ready.*"

Papa clears his throat, "Lizzie, the shawl."

"Oh yes, of course," I answer. Now, I have Antonio's

full attention. I can feel the heat of his dark eyes upon me as I unwrap myself before him.

On day one of the sitting, Antonio is studious to his work. He talks in short sentences and his face is expressionless, like someone in a trance. He is looking at me, but only as his subject of study. For the next few hours we exchange very little eye contact. He is not interested in what I might be thinking or concerned of my comfort. My eyes are free to wander over his person. His hands are smooth, but he appears strong and fit for labor. There is an air of vanity in his manners and dress, evident by his open collar exposing his masculine chest. The room is warm and I can smell the soft musky smell of his clothes.

I am a person capable of being patient. However, after this length of time he should know anyone would need a break. My back is aching and my throat is parched.

There is a knock at the front door and we hear voices in the hall. Shortly the parlor door opens and in steps a pretty young girl with matching features of Antonio. Her costume is old world and her dark hair is tied up with a bright-colored scarf. She feels me staring at her and lowers her eyes to speak. *"Antonio, Bunica has prepared a masa for all."*

"Multumesc, Zina," Antonio responds. Standing to his feet, he pats the girl on the shoulder. *"Miss Lizzie, I introduce to you my sister, Zina. She speaks English not so good, but she will be learning. Zina comes to tell me Bunica, or grandmother as you say, has prepared a meal for all. We would be most pleased to have your family join us."*

I am at a loss for words by this sudden invitation. "Oh, no, I do not want to impose and besides my household is fasting today. President Davis has declared this day, November 16, as a day of prayer for our troops."

Before I could say another word, Papa walks in through the front door. His timing has always been uncanny. Antonio is quick to invite him and much to my surprise Papa is quick to accept for the two of us.

"I will let Bunica know to expect two?" Zina asks.

"Yes, tell your Grandmother it will be an honor. We will join you shortly," Papa answers.

The girl smiles as if she has understood and goes to inform the grandmother. Antonio makes haste to close his work. As soon as he turns his back, I poke Papa.

He smiles. He loves to get the best of me. "Lizzie, go change your clothes. We must not keep Bunica waiting," pronouncing the word as if he was a Gypsy himself.

Making my exit out the door, I look back at Papa and stick my tongue out at him. Secretly, I am excited to be doing something out of the ordinary. Papa and I are alike in that respect. We both like adventure. Eating a meal with the Gypsies is certainly going to be an adventure.

It is almost dark when Papa and I start across the lot to visit with our campers.

In the distance, we can see Antonio stirring a pot over the fire. Papa stops and takes hold of my arm. "Lizzie, let me tell you what I know of these people. They are called Roma or Nomadic folk. When I was a boy, there were some Gypsies that came through here. Three or four wagons of them camped out near our place for a whole summer. They sold all sorts of wares and did odd jobs for people. They didn't bother anything that I knew of, but a lot of people were afraid of them. My brother and I would sneak off just after dark and go spy on them. It was exciting listening to their music and watching them dance. I can still remember the smell of that food cooking. It was on one of those nights we met her. We were watching from up on the hill when the next thing I knew, a big stick cracked me on the head. I jumped up and there she stood. A little mess of a sort. A girl about my age with long dark hair and big black eyes. Her name was Rosa and that was the beginning of our friendship. That summer, my brother and I practically became Gypsies. We were down at that Gypsy camp anytime we could slip away. I remember taking Rosa home with us one day. Mother fed her supper, told her about Jesus and gave her a little Bible. Then one day, we went to see Rosa and they were all gone. I have often wondered what happened to that little girl."

"Papa is this a true story?" I asked in amazement. We all knew Papa liked to exaggerate his tales a bit.

"Why, Lizzie, I can't believe you would ask such a thing," he says, giving me a little nudge forward. We both are laughing when we walk up to the camp. It is always good to be with Papa. He is not just my father, he is my friend.

From the moment I step in the wagon, I am spell bound. The grandmother kisses us on the cheek and welcomes us into her rolling home as though we are family. On a small folding table covered with a lace tablecloth, an impressive looking meal is set before us.

When the last bowl is placed on the table, Bunica takes a seat at the head of the table. *"We say gratie,"* and she bows her head. I can only understand a few words of the prayer, "Jesus Christ" and "Amen." Later I was to learn their native tongue was Romanian.

When we lift our heads, I look at Papa. He is looking at the grandmother inquisitively, but simply says, "Amen."

"Let us eat!" Antonio declares.

The exotic aroma of all the strange foods fills the air. I am famished, but I hesitate to partake. Antonio takes on the job of translating and advising us on what we will be eating.

The composition of the food seems of little concern to Papa. His plate is full of this mystery food and he is obviously enjoying it. He enjoys it more once Antonio fills our glasses with *tuica*, a sweet plum wine.

The soup or *ciorba* is a sweet and tangy broth with tender pieces of pork tripe. The bread, *polenta,* is very much the same as cornbread The dish called *sarmale,* to my understanding, is a stuffed cabbage. The pickled eggs and pigs feet are not for me, but I found most tasty the sheep milk cheese, or *byndza*.

During the meal, Papa seems to be drawn to every word the grandmother says.

At last, he can contain himself no longer. "Tell me how your family came to be Christians?"

Tears fill the eyes of the old woman and she was unable to speak. Antonio became her voice. "*My dear mother, God rest her soul. She was responsible for bringing the word of Jesus Christ to many of the Gypsies. She followed the Christian faith since a very young child.*"

My heart is pounding when Papa asks, "And what was your mother's name?"

"Rosa," Antonio answers.

Papa's voice was tight, when he turned to the Grandmother. "Do you remember me? I was the little boy that came to play with Rosa when you were here many years ago."

The grandmother takes a long hard look at Papa. Her little hands are trembling as she reaches into her pocket and produces a small black Bible. In her broken English, she looks at him with soulful eyes. "*The Kingdom of Heaven is like a grain of mustard seed, which a man sowed in his field.*"

Papa and I walk back to the house that night in silence.

There were no words needed; we had witnessed a miracle.

I undress by the moonlight, but before I slip into the bed, I drop to my knees,

Dear Lord, With the faith of a mustard seed one little girl moved mountains. Forgive me Lord, but I fear I have not had the faith to move even the mustard seed. Please help me to understand that all is in your hands. Amen.

Lying in bed, I am drifting off to sleep when suddenly I remember something very important. The painting of Mother was not in the house when Sandy Ridge burned! I had taken it for safekeeping to Fannie's house. I will keep this a secret until I find a way to get it delivered to North Carolina.

CHAPTER 5

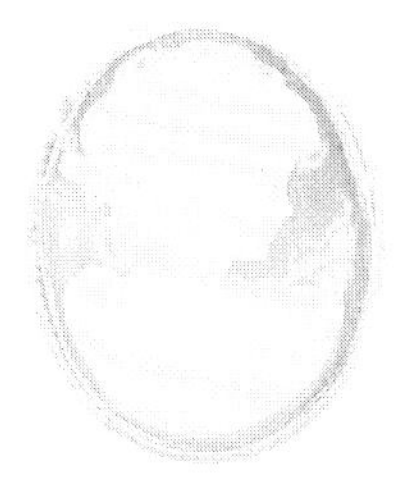

Never Say Good-bye

Saturday, November 19, 1864

Day four of the painting is coming to a close. Antonio informs me he will no longer require me to sit for him. He claims my face will forever be imprinted in his mind. Three days ago this would have been good news, but today I am oddly sad.

We have become friends in a strange sort of way. He tells me about the places he has been and recites his poetry as he works. Antonio is what one might call a hopeless romantic, painting the world through rose-colored glasses. He has trained his eyes to see only beauty. His work brings him great joy.

I would say Antonio and I are near in age, but his youth has not been interrupted.

There is much to envy about a lifestyle free of worry or fears. His motto, "A Gypsy is never in one place long enough to own it's grief."

Just yesterday I stood at the window and watched him run across the field like a young deer. He is thin and agile. I think he will be forever young. He cannot be enticed by money or worldly goods; he desires nothing. I wonder if it is possible to escape the clinches of despair, or would despair become the hunter and reclaim me as its prisoner.

The clock strikes five. Right on time, Bunica and Zina arrive. Mother has invited them for our Saturday night supper. Papa's story warmed Sallie and Mother's hearts and eased everyone's fears. Well, almost everyone. The slaves are still wearing their little Mojos around their necks.

With all the time Mother has spent visiting with the Gypsies, she may now be able to write a book. She tells Papa they are just so fascinating. I suppose Mother is bored and this little distraction has been good for her. Mother is the first to invite our guests to the table. Antonio carries the lead of the conversation at the table and promises to provide us an evening of entertainment following the meal.

As soon as the plates are cleared, under Antonio's direction the dining room table is pushed up against the wall and the chairs are placed in a large circle. Once the room is arranged to his liking, he steps into the hall and returns stroking his guitar.

The music is fast and lively and Zina enters the circle dancing. Antonio begins to sing and Bunica encourages us to clap hands. Zina is dancing in circles and the motions are like none I have ever seen. She is smiling seductively and her hips are swaying. Mother covers her eyes with her hands as if she is embarrassed, but I am sure she is enjoying the show. Moving closer to Papa, Zina invites him to join her. Mother's eyes are wide open now! Papa attempts the dance motions, which comes as a great delight to all, especially the children.

Before the night comes to an end, we all have a try at this exotic dancing.

Sallie and I hold hands and dance around the circle like children. "What would they think of us in Charleston now?" she asked.

"I don't know, Sallie, and I could not care the least," I answer in a loud-enough voice that catches an approving nod from Papa.

It was well past the children's bedtime when the Gypsies left to go back to their wagon. I have the easy task. Victoria is already asleep on the sofa. I lift her up without waking her and carry her upstairs. Sallie's children are still wild with excitement. It will be a chore to get those two in bed tonight.

The next day when we come home from church, Zina and Bunica are sitting on the front porch. This morning I did not see Antonio and I question if something is wrong.

"*No, No, Miss Lizzie*," Zina was quick to explain. "*Antonio flushes us out of the wagon. He wishes to work alone, so he finishes painting.*"

"*Yes,*" says Bunica. "*We now come to heal you.*"

"*Miss Lizzie. You not so well,*" Zina says, taking hold of my shoulder and looking deeply into my eyes. Very gently, she touches my throat and closes her eyes.

Bunica turns and looks at Mother. "*Zina heals, her hands anointed by God.*"

Mother looks at Papa and then nods her head, "Come inside where it is warm."

I am confused. Does Mother know something about this? I have not told a soul of my strange ailments. How does Zina know?

Sallie and her children are bundled up and waiting for Papa to take them to the Huneycutt's. It is their Sunday ritual to visit with their grandparents after church.

However, this Sunday Sallie stayed home to allow the children to sleep in. I expect she was saving herself the embarrassment of presenting cranky children.

As soon as the door opens, the children run to climb in the carriage and Sallie follows. Just before Papa turns to leave, he whispers to Mother, "Would you like me to come back early?"

"Everything is fine, Jacob. Now go on and get out of here," she teases.

"Now, isn't this nice to have the house to ourselves," Mother says, looking around uneasily. "I'll put out a little something for us to eat while you ladies chat."

Mother disappears through the kitchen door. I look over at Zina and her head is bowed as if she is praying. Slowly she lifts her head and looks at me. "*Miss Lizzie, I have gift of sight, I see and know things others do not. Perhaps it be curse or blessing, but it is real. I believe something in your past is choking you, like a noose around your throat. It is holding your body prisoner. I have prepared special medicine.*"

She reaches in her pocket and hands me a little bag of powder *"Take under your tongue three times a day."*

Her voice is as soft as a bubbling brook and there is an undeniable holiness surrounding her. Something about her seems so pure and honest.

Mother comes back with a tray of cheese and bread and places it on the table in front of us. I am surprised to learn Mother is taking Zina's medicine as well.

"Go ahead, soon is better," Bunica says encouragingly.

Opening the little bag, I take a pinch of the brown powder and place it under my tongue. It tastes like roasted corn. "What is this?" I ask.

Zina hesitates. "*The Adam's apple of a pig. Not to worry, very good for you.*"

Before they left, Zina made me promise to take her strange medicine as she directed. I agreed, well, at least until I receive word from Dr. Fannie. She would know best.

....

Monday morning, November 21, I arise after sleeping soundly all night. Shortly before noon, Antonio knocks on the door with the painting wrapped in newspapers. The whole family is eager to see the final portrait. Antonio sets his masterpiece up on the easel and Papa is given the honor of the unveiling. As the newspapers fall to the floor, before us is the most astonishing painting any of us have ever seen.

Mother gasps and Papa has tears in his eyes. "It is amazing," was Papa first remarks. "How can we ever repay you?"

"You have paid me more than you will ever know. It has been my honor." Antonio pauses for a moment and wipes his eyes. His face is tense and he is searching for the right words to say *"Good-bye is not in our vocabulary. We trust in the circle of life and if God be willing, someday our paths will cross again."* With those words he pauses briefly to admire the painting. Then he spins around and looks at me and our eyes meet for the last time. He tips his hat to Papa and walks out the door.

I run to the window and I see his wagon is out front waiting for him. My heart is pounding and tears fill my eyes. My first instinct is to run after him, but Papa catches my arm. "Lizzie, it is their way."

Papa and I watch as the wagon fades down the drive. When we turn around, we are alone. Papa understands. Antonio was my friend and I will miss him. I look over at the painting. "Cover it up, Papa, at least for today."

Papa gathers the newspapers off the floor with every intention of honoring my request, until he sees it is a recent copy of the Carolina Watchman. Unfolding the paper, he sits down in the chair by the window.

"Lizzie, take a look at this. It is an advertisement from Saltville, Virginia. They are calling for men to haul wagonloads of wood up there to burn in the furnaces. It says they pay out partially in salt and the rest in Confederate currency. They are pulling over 4,000 barrels a day out of those mines. With the railroads down, they need help hauling the salt out. A wagonload of salt would be a blessing to the folks around here."

I could see the wheels turning in Papa's head. "No Papa! Saltville is a hotbed right now, even I know that. Since the Union did not get their hands on the mines in October, common sense tells you they will be back. The last thing you need is to get caught up there in the middle of a battle!"

Papa folded the newspaper and placed it in his coat pocket. "Now Lizzie, don't get your feathers in an uproar. I am not about to take any risk. You know me."

"I do know you and that's the problem." I called out to him as he walked out the front door.

....

The next day finds me lonely and confused. Papa and I have decided to store my portrait until I have a home of my own, if and when that might be.

It is only November and I am wishing for spring. This is a monotonous time of year; the trees are bare and the days are gray. It is too cool now for much doings outside and there are no visitors.

There seemed to have been an abundance of things to fill my days before, but now I walk the halls without a purpose. With Antonio here, my mind had been so distracted that I barely thought of Joel. Now all I can do is think of Joel. I know I am poor company and I am neglecting Victoria. It is a sin to be so gloomy and I pray God will help me be more cheerful.

The one good thing is my health seems to be improved. I am sleeping soundly and my complaints are lessening. Mother and I both agree Zina's medicine has been most helpful.

It is Tuesday and Papa is leaving today for the Post Office. He has asked me to ride with him again this week. I think not. It is too damp and cold. I will spend the afternoon in the parlor waiting.

Papa returns late afternoon and as always, he holds the letters up high in the air so Sallie will see he has mail. Sallie takes a deep breath and resituates herself on her chair. She is smiling as if she is mocking me. I am sure she is not, but it makes me angry. Does anyone care that I have not received a letter from Joel or anyone else for that manner?

Papa is soaking wet when he comes in the house and Mother insists he put on dry clothes at once. He is a bit reluctant to follow her advice, but he hands her the letters and a small package and goes upstairs. Mother comes into the parlor and looks at me first. "Lizzie, there are two letters for you today. One is from Dr. Fannie and the other appears to be from Joel Simpson."

She continued to sort through the mail, handing Sallie her letter and announcing there were several letters for Papa and for her a package and a letter from her friend Mary. I am hearing her words, but in my mind I am tearing open the letter that Joel has sent.

I try to remain patient until Papa comes downstairs. Sallie goes first as always. She reads the letter to herself before she reads it aloud. It is good news, Ransom is safe and getting some well-deserved rest. His regiment has been sent north of the James River near Fort Harrison. They have built their winter quarters along Darby Town Road and at present it is peaceful there.

Opening letters is a bit like Christmas; you must wait for everyone to take their turn. Mother has her letter open, she puts on her spectacles and stands up by the window and begins to read:

Dear Tempie,

I am sure you know by now, Jacob was wise to seek refugee in North Carolina. I do not know how much news you are able to receive, so I will tell you what I know.

The Union has re-elected Lincoln, much as we predicted. Since General Grant's armies in Virginia continues to be in a stalemate against Robert E. Lee's army, Lincoln has turned loose on us the devil himself, General William T. Sherman. He has already shown the depth of his wickedness. Thousands have already fallen victims of his strategies of 'Total War' and 'Scorched Earth.'

He even defiles God, while the whole South was observing a day of prayer; he left Atlanta in a blaze of flames. Ordering his men to cut the last telegraph wire that linked him to his superiors in the North. I fear he has become a power on his own, unregulated by government or God.

He has turned his own men into beast, forcing them to live off the land, stealing and killing for food and supplies. He orders his troops to burn everything in his path, and destroys entire cities. He blesses his disciples for murdering innocent civilians and destroying livestock.

We are all afraid of his next target. He is known to lead his troops to areas where he can seize and destroy the most. He is surely to destroy all of Charleston right down to the last cotton gin and railway.

They say his army is over 65,000 strong and he is joined by thousands of former slaves who march along behind him, as if he is their great savior. They have been redeemed all right, burned out of their homes with nowhere else to go.

James insisted I go to the cottage in Columbia and I have been here since July.

We have had frequent guest, including a visit by President Jefferson Davis. Lately my days have been divided, partly at the hospital and partly visiting with Mrs. Preston. She has been so despaired since her son, Willie, was killed in the Battle of Atlanta. Even though there is not much to be gay about these days, I must say, I much prefer my visits with Mrs. Preston in her beautiful garden, than to the horrors of hospital work.

I am sending you a little gift which is nearly as dear to me as you are. It is a fan that President Davis gave me. Perhaps it will serve as remembrance of me, should we not see each other again. I know I should not speak of sad endings, but in this day and time we must live every day as if it were our last.

Land and sea may separate us, but we shall meet again in heaven,

Mary

After Mother's letter, the fact that I have letters to read is unimportant. The conversation flows to the issues of the war. I bite back the tears, but I am unsuccessful. Mother jumps up immediately and puts her arms around me. "Lizzie, I know this is frightening news, but we will get through this together."

"I know Mother, I know," I whisper as I stroke the pair of envelops in my hand.

Papa is in tune with my emotions. "Lizzie, now let's hear your letters! Good news I am sure."

I feel a warm feeling in my heart and I wipe my eyes. "Maybe we have all heard enough news for today. Perhaps I will read my letters in my room."

"Aye, a secret love letter?" Sallie asks.

"Well, let's at least hear from Dr. Fannie," Mother insists.

Opening the letter, I scan over the words quickly. It is clear it will reveal my medical concerns to everyone. I look nervously at Mother, who motions for me to begin reading:

Dear Lizzie,

The clinic is still running and the number of children that come increases daily. Simon and Millie have come back on their own accord. As a freed col-

ored, Simon had hoped to find work on his own, but jobs are scarce. Some of the Negroes are now saying they were better off as slaves. Many have run off to join the Union army or to work on the railroads. Even though times are hard, Simon and Millie say they will never forget what you did for them, especially since Millie is now expecting a baby. Lizzie, their baby will be born free and that is something you can be proud of.

Now, to the business of your sickness. I am nearly certain your problem is glandular, mainly having to do with a gland in your neck, called the Thyroid. Do you recall studying this in any of my medical books?

This disorder can present an array of problems, all of which you have described.

I am sad to say I am seeing an increase in numbers of cases with Thyroid deficiency.

There are a number of factors which contribute to this disorder: It may start with poor nutrition and a diet lacking necessary minerals, especially iodine or salt. At fault also, is stress, both emotional and physical, and lastly imbalances occurring in the postpartum period following pregnancy. I believe you are dealing with all of these.

The condition, although somewhat serious, can be controlled once these issues are resolved. It will take several months of therapy to regulate and restore your health.

Therefore you must be patient and follow my guidelines as closely as you can.

Getting enough iodine in your diet is difficult for all of us here in the South.

However, there are foods that are rich in iodine naturally such as, fish, eggs, cheese, milk, strawberries, potatoes, fruits and green leafy vegetables. Eat of these freely. Sugar is not good for this condition, but I imagine there is a shortage of it as well.

So, here are my recommendations:

Try as best you can to improve your diet. Drink plenty of fresh water to flush toxins. Employ someone in your household to administrate massage on the back of your neck twice a day and apply hot and cold compresses to your throat. Cindy Lou should serve you well for such treatments.

Physical activity is also a key to recovery. Partake in at least thirty minutes of physical activity daily. Early morning walks in the fresh air will be most agreeable and on days when the weather will not permit, stair walking is excellent.

This condition is often associated with melancholy. The added exercise will help, but rest and relaxation is also needed. May I suggest picnics by the river bank or soaking in a hot tub. I have heard there are a number of mineral springs in your area. If you can find their location, bathing and drinking of the water would be most helpful.

Along with the above, here are some herbal suggestions:

2 tsp. honey and apple cider vinegar in hot water daily.

Rosemary tea: for nerves as needed

Lemon balm tea: A cup a day -

Thyme tea: to regulate menstrual flow

The last thing I would like you to acquire is a compound made from the thyroid gland of the pig. If you are unable to prepare it yourself, perhaps you could consult with the Indian woman who delivered Sallie's children.

Once the condition is stable, your menstrual cycles with resume and the hair loss will stop.

I know I have given you plenty to keep you busy. If lack of iodine is the culprit, I suggest your family consider these remedies to safeguard their health as well.

Lizzie, do not worry. By Spring, things will be looking up. Please write me and let me know of your progress.

With love,
Fannie.

When I finished the letter, you could have heard a pin drop. The silence was broken when Sallie asked, "Lizzie is your hair falling out?"

"Yes," I answered.

Sallie runs her hands though her hair and produces a handful of loose hair.

Papa hit the wall with his fist. "Damn war. What else will it cost us?"

Mother's voice is calm. "Jacob, we can make these changes and everything will be fine."

Papa collects himself and comes over and kisses me on top of the head. "Of course we will. Ladies, I am sorry to have lost my temper." Then in a playful tone he asks, "Supper ready?"

I am not sure if Papa really believes everything would be alright, but somehow I do. I will always believe the paint spilling on me was not just an accident, but God's way of bringing Zina to us with her medicine.

Spring is certain to bring a change, but for now I have a letter to read. A letter from the man I love and one day soon to be my husband.

CHAPTER 6

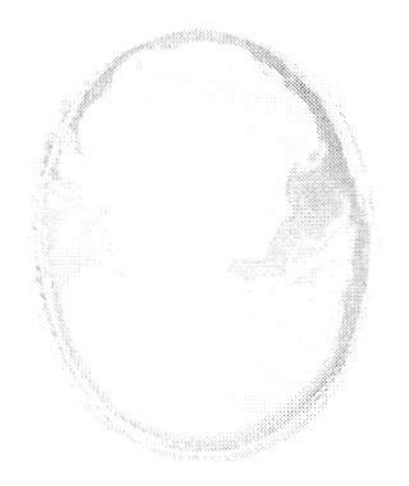

Apple Brandy

Papa has been in a grave mood since we received word from Charleston. He went into town again yesterday and came home late with a handful of newspapers. I recognized this old look of seriousness on his face.

Even though today is Thanksgiving, two men have already been by this morning to speak with him in private. Many Southerners questioned Lincoln's endorsement to establish the fourth Thursday of November as a national day of prayer. National being the key word, is his only motive to keep the Union together? Mother feels a day of thanks and prayer can only be beneficial for both North and South. Our family will come together for an evening meal.

Papa remains in hibernation for the balance of the day. When the house is full of voices, he makes his appearance. His face looks weighted and his eyes are weak. I look at Mother in question. She gave me a slight nod and closed her eyes for a second. I know her signals all too well. Even if something is wrong, we are to pretend it is not.

The meal is readied and we take our seats. In the dining room, the eight adults will be seated: Ransom's parents, Caroline and Robert, Sallie, Papa, Mother and myself. In the kitchen, there are five hungry children: TJ, Robbie, Minerva, Noah and Victoria. Cindy Lou and Violet will see to the feeding of the children. Afterwards, they will take their plates out back and enjoy their meal with Harper.

In Charleston, we would have richly prepared the table for all, but now the responsibility is a combined effort. We are fortunate it was Papa's luck to shoot a wild turkey. We also have potatoes, beans and beets.

Once the meal is laid before us, Papa stands to give thanks,

> *"Blessed be our Heavenly Father from whom all blessings flow. Help us not to forget Your undying mercy even in times such as these. Let us be thankful for our family and the food upon our table. Be with those who are alone, hungry and suffering. There are many empty chairs at our dining tables today. Some wait for their loved ones to return. Yet, many of our Southern sons are now in your keeping. Let us not forget no matter how great or small we are, we need You. In this world, the unexpected is certain. Are we to question why You would allow typhoid to claim the lives of Abraham Lincoln's innocent son or our dear Annabelle? Or most recently, the tragic death of our own president Davis' baby boy? No! It is not for us to question, but rejoice in the glory of Your will. Help us to be cheerful and faithful with the assurance that one day we will see them again in heaven. But, most of all Lord, we pray for peace. Peace for our Southland and the Northern borders as well. May we remain strong, healthy and brave in order to do Your will, not ours. Finally, we ask that Your mighty shield be there to*

protect Ransom, Thomas and our dear friend, Joel Simpson. We ask these things in Your Holy Name, Amen.

After the prayer, Mother makes a well-received announcement, "Even though flour is rationed, apples are not. The trees grow and bear fruit even in spite of the war. In preparing for the meal, we realized we would have to make a decision, apple pie or bread. So, we decided to let the children make the decision. Apple pie it will be!"

Papa adds his comment, "Those apples make pretty good brandy too, gentlemen."

All enjoyed the meal and the pie. The men waste no time once their plates are empty sneaking down the hall for a taste of Papa's brandy. Before Papa closes the parlor door, I overhear him say, "Old Lincoln ordered over 50,000 turkey pies to be sent out to his troops, while our boys are lucky to have a piece of stale bread. Well, I think we have all had a belly full of Mr. Lincoln!"

I was not the only one who overheard. Sallie was clearing the table and the plate in her hand dropped and shattered on the floor. In her haste to collect the broken pieces, she cut her finger. She begins to cry as if it is a deep wound, but we know it is not her finger that is badly wounded. It is her heart. She is thinking of Ransom on this day.

Mrs. Huneycutt lifts Sallie to her feet and takes her out to attend to her finger. The rest of us continue working without talking.

When they return, the ladies' conversation turns to the Gypsies. Both Caroline and Mrs. Huneycutt are eager to hear all the details. They are astounded with my telling of Zina's medicine and how her diagnosis matched Dr. Fannie's. Mother just has to share her expertise on the subject. "Well, if you ask me, this whole health issue started when my girls gave up the notion of wearing a corset. A stout backbone is essential to health and it is certain a woman's backbone is far too weak to support her."

I am happy when at last the day is over and the house is silent. I have retired to my room and Victoria is sleeping. Opening the drawer by my bed, I start to take out Joel's letter to read again. I have done the same every night since it arrived. I am startled by a tap at my door and slip the letter back in the drawer.

I fully expect to see Mother at the door, but it is Papa instead. He is grinning at me sheepishly and offers me a drink. Only one whiff lets me know it is some of his apple brandy. Papa knows Mother would not approve, but he says strong drink once in awhile is good for the constitution. "Can I talk to you, Lizzie?" he asks softly.

I widen the door and he takes a seat in the little cane-bottom chair by the fire. He drops a pile of newspapers on the floor for my scrapbooking. He holds his head in his hands for a moment giving way to the seriousness of his words. "Lizzie, I am ashamed to say I have fallen behind on the news. At one point, I thought we were tucked away from everything here in North Carolina. I just kept hoping the war would end and we could just start over. Now I realize there is nowhere to hide and I was wrong. These are hard times and likely to get worse. Yet, how can I complain, if I am just sitting back and watching it happen?"

I feel my face flush. I fear what Papa's next words might be. Turning the cup up, I take a sip of the brandy. It runs warm into the pit of my stomach. Slowly I sit down on the bed in front of him. Our knees are touching. "Papa you have done all you can. What else could you do, especially here?"

"Lizzie, after I got the news from Charleston, I spent the last couple of days meeting with some of the local men. Governor Vance's recent notice warns that not only are we in danger of a Union invasion, but subject to raids of lawless deserters from both sides who are lurking in the swamps and mountains. These men are stealing, pillaging and even murdering people. The Governor is encouraging men to establish military forces at home to help protect the citizens. Even though the military age has been extended to 55, if I were to join the army now, they would send me home in March when I turn 56. That being said, I have only one choice to serve and that is to join the Home Guard."

Not really knowing what this might mean, I ask, "By Home Guard, you mean you will be staying at home?"

"Mostly yes, Lizzie. We are the police of sorts protecting the local people. However, I must confess there is one mission in the works. If enough men can be raised, we are planning a trip to Saltville, Virginia. We hope to bring home several wagonloads of salt. "

"Papa, I saw this coming, but it is Mother who will be blind-sided. It is going to be hard on her if you leave."

"Papa laughed. "No Lizzie, I am sure it is going to be the hardest on you. You will be left dealing with your mother. At best, I will only be gone a couple of weeks. Timing is everything here and you of all people can attest for the need of salt."

He stands up to leave and reaches in his pocket. "Oh I almost forgot. I got this for you at the druggist. He says it works miracles. "

Reaching for it, I read the label, *"Burnett's Cocoaine an elegant preparation for dressing the hair and restoring hair loss. It is not a made of heavy animal fats such bear grease and lard with offensive odors, but oil of Coco-Nut. It is most agreeable and cooling in nature and is perfect for the ladies toilet. It can also be used to soften skin and penetrates rapidly without leaving a greasy residue. It is highly recommend because its ingredients are those in Cocaine. It has long been the secret of the natives of Eastern sea islands for luxuriance and abundance of beautiful hair."*

I thank him for his gift and he shakes his head and slips out the door. Holding the product in my hand, I read the instruction and apply it to my scalp. Papa is always considerate of my needs, but I fear the product was way too expensive. Wiping my hand free of the oil, I open the drawer and take out Joel's letter.

November 1864

Dearest Lizzie,

It was the finest of days when I received your letter. I feel like no harm can come to me now that I have such joy in my heart. I have told everyone who will listen we are getting married. Have you told your family or are you keeping it a secret? I am sure you know best. If it is not dear in cost, could you send me a little photo of yourself and a lock of your hair? It would please me greatly.

Our last battle on October 19, at Cedar Creek, Virginia, is proof that the Confederacy is loosing its footing here in the Shenandoah Valley. General Gordon had plans to surprise the Yankee encampment down by the river. We marched most of the night down the mountain by way of an old narrow pig's path. Just about sunrise, we crossed the river.

They were easy picking and we took prisoners still in their nightclothes. However, the fighting turned on us when Yankee General Sheridan and his troops showed up. By that time, we were worn down and outnumbered. Some of us were able to fall back before they cut off our escape route; hundreds like my friend, James Basinger, were captured. Now the Union has made a hero out of Sheridan and Old Lincoln has been re-elected. I suppose we will stay in the Valley and be moving up toward Petersburg for the winter. I cannot say for sure, as things change here quickly.

I witnessed something here the other day I hope to never see again. One of the other brigades brought in this fellow as a deserter. They marched him up and laid him across his coffin. Twelve men aimed and fired, but six of their guns were loaded only with powder. Afterwards the doctor pronounced him dead and they buried him. I reckon it is one thing to die an honorable death, but none of us want to die like that.

Lizzie, I must tell you a secret which I even hate to put in writing. I am not confident we will win this war. If you would see how our troops are beat down and the numbers killed, you would agree. It is most likely poor going for the Union troops too.

I will stop with the bad news. Please write and let me know you and your family are well. I bet your baby girl is growing up now. I have not been sick once, but the wound on my hand was still open and running. One of the boys told me to pour some whiskey over it. It seemed like a waste of good whiskey to me, but after a couple of days, it healed over. You might try it if any of you get a wound.

Well my darling I will close and get back to my duties. Do not fret for me for my heart is light and looking forward to the day when I hold your fine form in my arms again. I dream of our home and a couple of children who are pretty like you.

With all my love,
Joel

CHAPTER 7

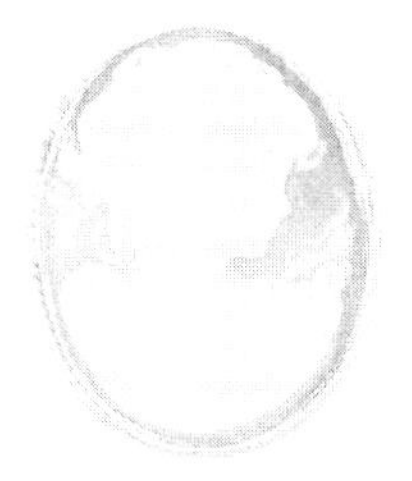

Frogs and Princess

My pistol is cold in my hand. "Ready, Aim, Fire!" Papa shouts. The bullet leaves my barrel and hits the target dead center. "Good girl," Papa says, looking around at Mother and Sallie. "At least one of you remembers what I taught you."

He is disappointed Mother does not even remember how to load the gun and Sallie is too timid to pull the trigger. Nor do they remember simple things, like to lock the doors at night. Papa makes it clear; while he is away, they should rely on my judgment.

Papa is placing a great deal of confidence in me lately. I suppose his reasoning is I have run my own household. If you ask me, it is the blind leading the blind, but what else can he do? He contracted Harper out to the government to cut wood. Papa thought it was a good idea at the time. The work has slowed on the farm and Harper could be home on Sundays. Now Papa wishes he could revoke Harper's contract.

Yes, it is official. Papa will be leaving tomorrow for Saltville. It is wearing heavy on his heart leaving a household of women alone.

Mother was uncharacteristically calm as Papa outlined the details of his plans.

This makes me a bit suspicious of the herbal tea Mother is drinking daily. Papa explained there would be 12 men from the Home Guard and six wagons caravanning together. They figure it will take them about nine or 10 days to get to Saltville. If they can make it by Sunday, December 12, they could load up on Monday. With a little luck, he will be home before Christmas with the salt and a purse of money.

....

It is still dark when I awake the next morning, but a soft covering of newly fallen snow illuminates the ground. The fire has gone out during the night and I can see my breath in the room. I quickly peek in on Victoria. She is snug and warm under her blanket. Thankfully, children sleep much warmer than adults do. I light the fire and dress to go downstairs.

Mother and Papa are in the kitchen. Papa is eating and Mother is drinking her tea.

It appears she has been up for hours packing food for Papa's journey. I wonder what is in that tea?

"Papa looks at his watch. "They will be here for me shortly. Lizzie, are you going to the barn with me?"

Stuffing a boiled egg in my mouth, I follow him out into the fresh air. The moment I step out the door I am mystified by the tranquility of this sparkling blanket of snow. It is as if we are the last souls on earth. Not a sound to be heard; even the wind is still. I stop and look to the heavens. Tiny grains of snow pelt my face. "Feels like salt, does it not Papa?

Papa pauses and looks up for a moment. "I wish it was, Lizzie," he says, turning and walking toward the barn.

I am frozen watching his figure from the back, as if he is part of a painting. Am I lost in a memory or a vision of something yet to be?

As soon as I walk in the barn, I smell the sweet hay Papa has just tossed over to the cow. He sees she is satisfied and then turns and looks at the old horse. "Good thing you were not drafted to go on this trip."

On a hook next to the stall is a red wool blanket. Papa takes it down and with tender hands places it over Ralph. "Liz, best keep the old man covered up on days like this. He ain't got much meat on his bones. If he gets a chill, he will be down for the count. He and I are 'bout in the same boat," he jokes, looking back at me.

I laugh, but it is only to keep from crying. Papa was right; he was a bag of bones just like Ralph. It is a cold day for a man his age to start on such a long, hard trip. I would have gone in his place, if he had asked. I would do almost anything for Papa, yet he asks very little.

We feed up the rest of the animals, Papa milks the cow and I gather up a few eggs. We are just across the lot when I see a man riding up. It is light now and the peaceful serenity is spoiled. Papa walks forward to meet the intruder and I start for the house. "Wait Lizzie. I want you to meet this man."

I fumble with the eggs in my hand, finally stuffing them into the pockets of my apron.

"Hey, Sanders!" the man calls out. "I got the maps from John." He dismounts his horse and steps over in front of us.

"Lizzie, this is Mr. Green Simpson. He is with the Home Guard. Mr. Simpson, this is my daughter, Lizzie."

"Please to meet you Miss Lizzie. I reckon your pa told you I would be by every evening to check on you ladies. "

"As a matter of fact, no," I said, looking at Papa strangely.

"Well, that's my job. Some of us have to stay here to take care of the home front.

Don't you worry, Mr. Sanders, about your women folk. I can assure you if these ladies need anything at all, I'll have enough men out here to take on a small army."

Papa does not have time to return his comment before we see a wagon coming up the drive. "Well, here they are, right on time," Papa says, forcing a smile. "Got to get my gear, sure don't want to hold up this operation."

Mr. Simpson extends his hand to Papa. "Good luck there fellow. You take care and don't you worry about this place while you are gone."

I hear the driver halting the horses and the wagon comes to a stop. Calling out in an exaggerated deep voice Papa shouts, "Be right out, Sid!"

Mr. Simpson lumbers over to the wagon and Papa and I go inside. The household is awake. Mother is feeding Victoria and Sallie is trying to keep the children from being underfoot. Papa's mood seems to have lifted, and he is whistling as he gathers up his things.

Noah sees him packing and begins pulling at his pants leg. Papa is too preoccupied to notice until Noah cries out, "Papa, don't go!"

He stops and picks him up, "Listen here little man, you be a good boy and take care of your mommy while I am gone. When I get back it will be time for Santa Claus!"

"Santa Claus! Will he bring us presents?" he asked excitedly.

"I expect so," Papa says, looking at Mother for her approval.

Mother and Sallie both shake their heads to agree. Minerva and Noah begin running through the house as if it is Christmas morning. When Mr. Simpson comes to the door for Papa, I think the children were fully expecting to see Santa Claus. They are only briefly disappointed, for now they have discovered the snow.

Papa pushes through to the front door and steps outside with the men. In just a few seconds, he is back for several boxes of matches. Having a warm fire at night is an important thing on a trip like this.

By eight o'clock Papa is gone and the household has settled down to its normal routine. Mother is sewing and Sallie has started the children's lessons. I sit down at the end of the table and pull Victoria on my lap. Her little hands are greedy for everything in reach on the table. I give her a pencil of her own and her game is to drop it repeatedly for me to pick up. She is enjoying making me do her work and the children think it is humorous. In addition to this distraction, the children are begging to play in the snow.

Sallie is becoming increasingly frustrated. Even though Minerva is only four and Noah soon to be three, she takes her teaching seriously. Sallie sent off for a series of books by a Professor R.J. Foster. His theory is early education is essential to a child's development. He insists that gaining discipline over the mind at an early age is the key to a brilliant mind. Therefore, poor Sallie worries herself daily trying to teach her two toddlers to read and write. Mother and I secretly think it is pointless at such a young age. However, it does serve to give a sense of order to the day and keeps Sallie's mind occupied and off her worries.

By 10 o'clock, Sallie gives in to the children. Victoria is getting sleepy and begins to nuzzle at my breast and rub her eyes. She has just had her first birthday and I would still be nursing her if my milk had not dried. Sallie nursed her children well over a year. I am convinced Sallie is more fit for bearing children than me. If I have any doubt, Sallie will be quick to remind me.

Sallie gears the children up for a romp in the snow and I take Victoria up for her nap. She takes her bottle, but is fussy and fights sleep. The milk does not suit her lately and I fear the cow is drying up too. After finally getting her to sleep, I am carefully closing the door when I see Mother rushing down the hall. In a voice louder than necessary she calls out, "Lizzie you have a caller."

Before I can make much of an inquiry, our voices wake Victoria. Her crying drowns us out and Mother gives me a gentle push down the hall. She goes in to settle Victoria.

This is a rare event for me to have a caller. But on such a cold day, it must be very important. At the foot of the stairs, I barely escape a collision with Cindy Lou. Eyeing over the tray she is carrying, I realize how deeply our old Charleston etiquette is ingrained in all of us. I am sad to see a dented tin coffee pot filled with Mother's substitute coffee, mismatched cups and a small bowl of roasted pecans. So unacceptable. In Charleston, there would have been a silver tea service, fine china and a plate of assorted sweets.

I entered the room to see an elderly woman seated on the edge of the sofa. Seeing me, she pops to her feet as if paying homage to the queen. "Miss...Mrs... Theodosia?" she asks, not sure how to address me.

I hesitate briefly. I am no longer a Miss, but Mrs. does not seem fitting either. When I came to North Carolina alone with a baby, word spread I was widowed. I would not have even validated that marriage if it were not for Victoria. Clearing my throat, I extend my hand to the woman. "Please call me Lizzie."

She shakes my hand nervously, "Well Lizzie, I am Martha Tucker. I would be pleased if you just call me

Martha. I suspect you are a wondering why I am here. Some of us ladies at the church have been talking."

I must have raised my eyebrows at her words and she feared she was on the verge of offending me. "Oh no, Miss Lizzie. Please do not take me wrong. It is just we have all been admiring your fine manners. You dress and act like a real fancy lady. I reckon a girl learns all those ways down there in Charleston."

I am stunned. Looking down at my old dress and feeling across my hair, I wonder how she can think such a thing. "Please have a seat, Martha." I say directing her to the sofa. "Will you join me for a cup of Mother's special recipe? It tastes very closely to real coffee." Martha takes a seat, smoothes out her skirt and makes an odd little noise in her throat.

I pour the coffee and she takes up her cup. She extends her pinky out awkwardly as she drinks. After a very loud sip, she sets the cup back in its saucer. "Lizzie, I know you don't know me and it is bold of me to ask a favor. However, it is not so much for myself, but on behalf of my two nieces. You see, they recently have come to live with me. Sweet girls they are, but they ain't got a lick of raising. Their ma died when they were just babes and their pa raised them. When he joined the Army, you would have thought he would have made arrangements for them two girls. No, he left them to fend for themselves. "

"Oh, that is awful," I insert, being attentive.

"And do you know what those girls did then?" She asks, leaning forward so that we must be face to face. Her hair is tightly knotted and her complexion is pale with a yellowish tint. Her nose and chin appear to meet and when she speaks, a few bottom teeth protrude over her top lip.

"Oh no, Martha, I have not the slightest of ideas."

"Just guess," she says, employing my mind more.

"Well, I suppose they came to live with you?"

"No!" she thunders. "They rigged themselves up like men and joined the army. It was over six months before anyone knew the better. When the Captain found them out, he sent them home to the next of kin. Now I got these two girls on my hands. I am old and can hardly support myself. The way I see it, unless I can get them married off, I am bound to them from now on. I have been trying to teach them the domestic skills. It ain't been no easy chore. I truly believe I could make a wife out of a burly Negro man quicker."

Martha pauses. She looks over her glasses at me and makes that little noise in her throat again. This whole thing is so unexpected, like a fiction story from a book. No longer being able to control myself, I burst into laughter. She looks at me with surprise, but as they say, laughter is contagious. Within seconds, she is laughing too.

Our laughter gains the attention of Cindy Lou working in the hall. Fearing I have finally lost my mind, she pokes her head in the door. "*Miss Lizzie, cans I's getz yo any thang?*"

Trying to regain myself, I respond, "No thank you, Cindy Lou. We are fine."

Cindy Lou looks at me and then at Martha suspiciously. "*Yous be sho to calls me if yous needs me, Miss Lizzie.*"

Cindy Lou's interruption was enough for us to regain our former selves. I fold my hands in my lap politely and wait to see what else Martha has to say.

Martha is still smiling when she begins. "It is quite humorous. Sort of like asking you to turn my little frogs into princesses. My dear Lizzie, after meeting you today I am even more convinced. You are the one for the job. I have no money to offer you for your services. But, as one Christian woman to another, can you find it in your heart to share some of your fancy ways with these poor downtrodden girls?"

I ponder briefly over what she has asked and the long boring winter ahead.

I decide there is little to consider. "I accept the challenge! It will be my pleasure to help your nieces."

Martha jumps to her feet with excitement and gives me a big hug. "Thank you, thank you! Now, I must warn you, you have your work cut out."

"I understand. When shall we start, Martha?"

"The sooner the better, these things take time. The war could be over any day now and my little birds must be perched and ready when the boys get home. There are plenty of young ladies waiting in line. You, of course, being their biggest competition."

"I am flattered, but not to worry about me. I am engaged to be married once the war is over." I can hardly believe the words came out of my mouth. I had not told a soul, not even Papa. Now, here I have let the cat out of the bag, to a complete stranger.

Cindy Lou has slipped back in the room on pretense of refilling the pot, but I know she is eavesdropping. Next out of Martha's mouth comes a question, which I was totally unprepared. "Miss Lizzie, was your late husband killed in the war?"

I look quickly at Cindy Lou and our eyes meet. She knows what comes out of my mouth next is a lie. "Oh, yes. He was killed in the war."

"Poor girl," Martha says, looking at me compassionately. Cindy Lou is quick to gather the tray and remove herself from the room.

I walk Martha to the door and make arrangements for the girls' first lesson tomorrow morning at 10 o'clock. When the door opens, the sun reaches out to me, and I am fooled into thinking the temperature has risen. It has not. Pulling my shawl up around my shoulders, I step back inside. I pause to rest my back against the cold hard door. Martha's question troubles me. Would she be so quick for me to train her girls if she knew the truth?

I can hear Cindy Lou in the kitchen. She also knows what happened that day.

It has been over a year and it was the day Victoria was born. It was around noon when I heard the scream from downstairs. Being heavy with child, I was forced to take the stairs slowly. Once I opened the door to Edmond's office, the horror was in progress. Anyone would have stopped him. The fire poker was the first thing that found its way into my hand. Cindy Lou and I fled, leaving Edmond lying face down on the floor. The last thing I remember about that day before Victoria was born was knocking on Dr. Fannie's door. It was not until two days later I learned he was dead. Cindy Lou never spoke of her rape or Edmond's death. Just like me, she keeps it locked inside.

The rest of the afternoon was uneventful. I believe Sallie and Mother felt rejected Martha had chosen me for the etiquette teacher. I assure Mother and Sallie I will be calling on them for advice.

With the house being cold and the promise of more snow, everyone was early to bed. While Papa and Harper are away, Cindy Lou and Violet are sleeping in the children's room. The children do not mind sleeping with Sallie and we can conserve on firewood.

Once the house is still, I sort through my old school books. I am hoping to plan a lesson for my new students.

Back in Charleston, Sallie and I attended Madame Talvande's French School for young ladies. It functioned as both a finishing school and an academy for serious studies, such as mathematics, history, composition and grammar, astronomy, botany and natural sciences. All young ladies were taught elementary French, needlework, oil painting and drawing. The "finishing out' classes consisted of music, dance, singing and social graces.

Sallie and I were day students at ages 12 and 13, but in our senior year we became boarders. Mother felt it was a good experience for a 14 year-old girl.

I shared a room with 10 other girls, on the third floor overlooking the river.

I can still hear Madame Talvande say, "Exposure girls is the best teacher."

Included in our 'polite education' were carefully planned social events, dinners, dances and trips to the theater.

Reading was encouraged, but only to the Bible and approved literature. Fiction novels were forbidden, which only served to make them more enticing. A Jane Austen novel would secretly be passed from reader to reader, until it met the ill fate of being confiscated.

Madame Talvande always preached to her students the importance of making a favorable first impression. So, I decide this is where I will begin my instructions with Martha's nieces in the morning.

I figure three or four lessons should be sufficient. After all, they will most likely not be entertaining royalty or even Charleston socialites. How hard will it be to impress a herd of North Carolina boys coming home from the war?

After two hours of preparing, it is after midnight and my eyes are getting tired. I review my notes:

Making proper introductions
Sitting and standing poses
The art of polite conversation
Appropriate dress, gloves, fans, foot and headgear
Hygiene and arranging the hair in the latest becoming fashion.

I blow out the light and think over my lesson plan. Around noon, I will have Cindy Lou bring in a high tea. It will be nothing like the ones in Charleston, but I am sure we can scrape together a little something. This will give me a good idea of their dining skills and where to start the next lesson.

Just before I drift off to sleep, I pray,

Dear Lord,

It is not for me to question Your ways. I only pray You will soon have enough soldiers in Your heavenly army and this war will end. Please be with my father and the others on their way to Saltville and bring them home safely. I ask that You watch over and protect Joel, Ransom and his little brother, Thomas. I pray that one day soon we will all be together again. I do not pray for myself, for I trust You already know my greatest needs, my fears and desires.

Chapter 8

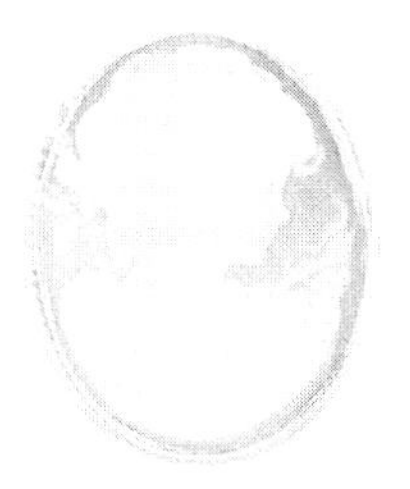

Hannah Jane and Betty Jo

It is half past 10 and Martha and the girls are late. This morning I was up at dawn to allow time to pay extra attention to my attire and prepare the parlor. How foolish of me to have insisted Sallie teach the children upstairs. If the girls do not show, there is certainly no need for privacy.

I read over my notes patiently until the clock strikes 11. Looking out the window one last time, I decide it is time for a brisk walk. Dr. Fannie insists on it. I must not be neglectful of my health.

Before I can work my way upstairs to change, we hear the carriage approaching. I hurriedly return to my seat and arrange myself in the chair. I feel almost like Madame Talvande preparing to meet her students on orientation day.

From my chair, I am in full view of the window and can see the carriage has parked out front. Cindy Lou is to my right, standing in the hall by the door. We wait, but the carriage sits still. Not a sign of life is emerging. Perhaps 10 minutes pass and still no one steps out. Cindy Lou cuts her eyes my way. *"You 'pose there ain't no bodies in there?"*

The carriage could not have gotten here on its own. I step over by the window and pull the lace curtain back to get a clearer view. Thinking they may be waiting for us to invite them in, I ask Cindy Lou to open the door and step outside on the porch.

After a few minutes of standing out in the cold, Cindy Lou starts to shiver. I am just on the verge of going out there myself when the carriage door opens. Martha steps out and behind her is the first girl. She is tall and thin and wearing a bonnet pulled down forcefully over her head. I expect to see the next sister step out, but it must be someone else. As the trio make their way toward the house, the last passenger spits a plug of tobacco out on the ground. Cindy Lou opens the door and I hear them exchanging words in the hall.

Martha is the first to surface through the parlor door. "Miss Lizzie, please forgive us for being tardy. You know it is not easy for ladies to travel alone and my nieces here...," she says, extending her tone out into the hall. "They did so want to make a favorable impression. Is this not so, Hannah Jane?"

Several seconds lapse and the bonnet girl enters the room. She does not look up, making it impossible for me to see her face. I offer them both a seat. Hannah Jane sits down on the sofa and folds her arms across her chest, but Martha walks back out in the hall. In a strained voice, I hear her say, "Now Betty Jo, lets not keep Miss Lizzie waiting."

Martha comes back in and sits down next to Hannah Jane. She looks out in the hall again and gives me a very nervous and toothless grin. Then without making a sound, the person in the hall slips through the door and leans against the wall. I suspect they saw me gasp. If this was

Betty Jo, she was certainly more boy than girl. She or he (which will remain to be seen) is wearing ill-fitting trousers, an old slouch hat and a pair of broken-down brogans. Martha motions at the seat next to her. This person plops down and crosses their legs in the same fashion as a man.

"Well here we are. Girls, let Miss Lizzie get a good look at you. Remember we are here for her help." Martha is speaking sweetly, but I can tell she is irritated.

Hannah Jane goes first, pulling her bonnet off and revealing her cropped-off red hair. I was expecting to see the same once the slouch hat came off the next one. However, much to my surprise underneath was a beautiful head of auburn hair reaching way past the shoulders. This creature, of which I had questioned its sex, is certainly a young woman. I am stunned. Her face is as finely proportioned as I have ever seen.

The word "Angelic" slipped out of my mouth before I regained my senses.

Martha looks pleased to have shocked me. She then reaches over and forces up the chin of Hannah Jane. I find she is nearly equal to the beauty of Betty Jo.

"See here, Miss Lizzie. If we can polish these girls up a bit, we might just have a couple of diamonds in the rough," Martha says, looking to me for approval.

Almost forgetting they are human beings, we study over the two girls. I suddenly realize it must be degrading to be put in such a light. I stand to my feet, attempt to welcome and shake their hands. Hannah Jane's handshake is limp and sticky. When I extend my hand to Betty Jo, she does not respond, but I hold my ground. Martha clears her throat signaling for her to be cooperative. Her small rough hand takes hold of mine. Her grip is so firm I am afraid she has broken the bones in my hand. I try not to flinch, but by her smile she knows what she has done.

I sit back down and rub across my bruised hand. "Well, ladies," I begin. "Let me make an educated guess. It is not exactly your choice to be here today. Although your aunt may have your best interest at heart, changing one's impression is not an easy task. If you do not welcome such a change, I am afraid my time and yours will be spent in vain."

Martha looks back and forth at the girls fearing the deal will fall through. The room is silent until Hannah Jane looks at her sister. *"Jo, I spect if Pa was here, he'd say we ought to listin to this here lady."*

Betty Jo pushes her hair out of her eyes and scuffles her feet on the floor. *"Wells, I reckons we could give it a try."*

"Wonderful!" shouts Martha.

Wonderful is hardly a word I can use to describe my feelings. I realize there is not an ounce of refinement in the two of them put together. It has taken all morning just to get through introductions and make polite conversation. Even still, I feel I am making a little progress. My enthusiasm is dampened when Betty Jo takes out her pocketknife to clean the dirt under her nails, explaining she had to shovel manure yesterday. Then all hope is lost when Hannah Jane says she has to go to the pot, describing her condition as the runs.

Mother has walked by several times to look out the front door; giving the appearance she is expecting someone. I know she is not. She is spying. Finally I call out to her. "Mother, please come in and meet Betty Jo and Hannah Jane."

Mother walks in and introduces herself with all the grace and fashion of her Charleston ways. It is a speck overdone, but I am sure she is using herself as an example for the students. I will not tell her that her gentle hint was pointless. It is more likely going to take a sledgehammer to knock manners into these girls.

Realizing it is almost two o'clock, I forgive the rest of my lesson plan and call for Cindy Lou to bring out the high tea. She has been waiting and is quick to return with the refreshments. She sets the tray down on the table by the window, pulls the curtains to block the afternoon sun and slips out the door.

Everything about this tea is sociably incorrect. A high tea is served around five or six in the afternoon and is sustainable enough to be considered a meal. The hour is right for an afternoon or low tea, but we have missed the noon meal and lighter finger food would hardly be satisfying. Next, we do not have any real tea, flour or sugar for sweets. Set before us is a light meal of boiled eggs, cheese, pickles and some dried apples. I could call it a high or a low tea and my guests would know not the difference.

I must say I have never witnessed such crimes in dining, with the exception of watching pigs eating from a trough. The gulping and talking with their mouths full was mild in comparison to Betty Jo's encore. After she blew her nose on a fine linen napkin, Mother took a sudden headache and excused herself.

At last, the visit is finally over. I knew Martha would ask and I am prepared for her question. "Lizzie, I fear we have exhausted your patience today. Will you see the girls again?"

"I still have a wee bit of patience left," I answer and wink at Martha. "If the girls will promise me they will work on what we have learned. Then, if Monday agrees, we will take up where we left off."

To my surprise, the girls look pleased. Hannah Jane slapped Betty Jo on the back. *"We gonna work real hard, ain't we Betty Jo?"*

Betty Jo was a little more reluctant to respond. *"I'll give it a go, but I ain't gonna give up my tabacky."*

"Well, where I come from, ladies do not chew tobacco," I answer, firmly. "However, if you can afford tobacco at today's prices, I say keep it up."

Everyone laughs except Betty Jo, who knows she is the brunt of my little joke. We all know it is doubtful she can afford tobacco and the problem will be solved.

After they leave, the house falls back to normal. When we take the evening meal, I am expecting Sallie and Mother to inquire about my day. Not a single question arises at dinner or even after the children go to bed. The three of us spend a quiet night reading and working on our needlework. Mother is the first to retire. She bundles up her work and places it under her chair. Standing to her feet, she yawns. "Well, all I can say to you, Lizzie, those two are going to be hard to polish off."

....

It has been well over a week since Papa left for Saltville. Just as promised, Mr. Green Simpson has been by every afternoon. Finally, yesterday we were able to convince him his daily visits are not necessary. We are managing fairly well and Harper is here on Sundays to chop wood and take care of the heavy duties.

Mr. Simpson hesitated, but fearing he may be imposing agreed. Before leaving, he insisted on being responsible for delivering our mail on Fridays.

We have not heard from Papa, but we did not expect to. The trip is such a rush and he most likely has little time to write. By now, hopefully, they may be loaded and on their way home. I pray Papa is getting enough rest and the weather has not been too severe.

It is Monday morning and the girls are due back for their second lesson today. I scheduled them to arrive at one o'clock, allowing me plenty of time for my chores. I dress in my old work clothes and run a comb through my hair. I am pleased it is no longer falling out. I will write to Dr. Fannie soon. She will be happy to know my complaints are improving. Some mornings I am successful in slipping out and getting my chores done before Victoria awakes, but today my rustling awakes her. I must tend to my motherly duties first before going to the barn.

With Victoria in my arms, I go downstairs to the kitchen. Mother looks up at the two of us. "Let me have her Lizzie. Cindy Lou is waiting for you in the barn."

Walking out in the cold to the barn, I ask myself, "Why is Sallie incapable of barn duties?" Somehow, all the manual labor is passed off to Cindy Lou and me. If Mother was not here to take care of Victoria, I do not know what we would do.

I hear Cindy Lou's voice as soon as I walk in the barn. *"Getz up, old man!"* At first, I do not see her, and then I see the top of her head bobbing around in the horse stall.

Quickly I rush to see what is wrong. Pulling back the stall door, I see Ralph lying on the ground. Cindy Lou is pulling on his rope with all her might, trying to get him to his feet. She looks up at me, her dark eyes are misting from the cold and her hair is hanging down in her eyes. We both know if a horse goes down, it is not a good thing, especially on a cold day like today.

"Step aside," I instruct, and kneel down next to Ralph's head. I have been around horses all my life and I know the signs of a sick horse. Gently I lift up his lips. His gums are pale and yellowish. Next I examine his eyes, finding they are dull and caked with mucous. I run my hand over his flank. He is abnormally hot, suggesting a fever. Lastly, I lay my head against his chest, his heart is beating rapidly and his breathing is labored.

"I thang hes gots the colick," Cindy Lou says.

I suspect this is not just a colicky horse. This horse is going to die unless we do something fast. Reaching for the bridle, I encourage him to hold his head up. With a great deal of coaxing, I am able to get him to drink a little water from a bucket. Carefully I push his legs under him and eventually with much struggle, we pull him to his feet.

As soon as he is standing, his bowels break loose; manure splatters all over my pants and boots. The odor is foul and Cindy Lou starts gagging as if she may vomit. "Stop it!" I shout at her. "Go and get a rake and some fresh straw. We have to dry this place out."

She hurries away, glad to have any job away from the smell. While she is gone, I dip a rag in the bucket and wash his eyes and face. The horse, noble and strong is one of God's finest creations. How sad it is. Poor Ralph is now totally dependent on a weak creature like me. I believe a horse can sense our emotions and never have I felt this more true. Ralph is speaking to me with his eyes. He knows he is dying.

We clean out the stall and put down fresh straw. He eats a bit of oats and takes some water. After brushing him down and covering him with a dry blanket, I close the stall door. I wish Joel were here; he would know what to do.

Cindy Lou milks the cow and I gather up the eggs. Before we leave, I give Ralph a pat on the neck, "You're going to be alright there, boy." But he knows I am lying.

My stomach is growling when I step out in the fresh air. We have been too long in the barn and I am afraid we have missed breakfast. Still, we must close up the barn. A draft would prove deadly for Ralph. The wind is fighting us as we force the large hollow door closed. I must dig my heels in the dirt and press my back against the door so Cindy Lou can secure the bolts.

Just as she shoves the last bolt down, I see a cloud of dust coming up from the main road. My first thought, Papa is home. No, that is impossible so soon. Walking cautiously toward the house, I see a dozen or more men riding up the road. As the dust starts to settle, I see they are soldiers. Soldiers in blue uniforms. "Yankees!" I find myself screaming out.

Cindy Lou runs toward the house, even though I call out for her to wait. By the time I reach the house, everyone is in a panic. Mother hands over Victoria to Cindy Lou and tells her to take all the children upstairs and hide in the hall closet. Minerva grabs up the kitten and starts to cry for her mother. Mother takes hold of her shoulders and gives her a hardy shake. "Listen to me! You are to go with Cindy Lou right this very minute and I had better not hear a peep out of any of you. Do you understand me?"

The children are not accustomed to such harsh talk and their feelings are hurt. They follow Cindy Lou upstairs without saying another word.

"Maybe they will not turn down our drive." Sallie is hopeful.

"If they do, they will be looking for valuables and food," Mother says.

After the children go upstairs, we have to take action. This is not the time for panic. Violet is sent to the smokehouse to hide the hams. Sallie runs to lock the doors and I go for my pistol. I consider it almost useless against so many, but it is the best we can do.

We wait in the parlor and pray. It is too late to hide. My heart is beating in my throat as we hear the horses coming up the drive. They come to a halt right outside the window. We see several of the men dismount and I place my hand on the pistol in my pocket. The Captain motions for the men to go around to the back of the house. We hear footsteps on the porch. We know he is coming to the door, yet Sallie screams when we hear him knock. I quickly cover her mouth with my trembling hand. We exchange a look, before the next knock comes to the door. "I'll go," I say, standing to my feet.

Mother nods her head and I walk slowly to the door. Taking a deep breath as if it might be my last, I open the door just wide enough to see his face.

"Good morning Ma'am. I am Captain Woodward. I am sorry to trouble you on such a cold day, but my men are badly in need of food and water. If you would be so kind to offer us what you can spare, I assure you no harm will come to you or your family."

I look directly into his eyes. He is a handsome man with a red beard and gentle blue eyes. His words are polite and he seems sincere, but he is a Yankee and I should not trust him. "Wait here, sir," I say, and softly close and lock the door.

Trying to stay calm, I find Mother and Sallie sitting side by side on the sofa. "Mother, the Captain says they only want food. I don't know why, but I think he is telling the truth."

Mother looks at Sallie. "What about those jars of potato soup? We might have enough dried apples and some pickled eggs."

Sallie nods her head and I am sent to deliver the message to Captain Woodward. He is sitting on the front porch steps with his hat in his hand. When he sees me, he jumps to his feet at once. He places his hat back on his head and turns squarely to face me. He is humble and not at all aggressive. Odd how in such serious situations there is often a bit of humor. I wonder what he is thinking, seeing me standing there with fresh manure splattered all over the front of my pants and boots. Perhaps the odor is the reason he appears more intimidated by me than I am of him.

Whatever be the reason, I am thankful he accepts our offer. He asks if we will prepare the food and serve it to his men on the porch. I agree and he immediately turns to face his men. "Gentleman, this kind lady has invited us to dinner." His announcement receives a roar of cheers from the men. "Let me make myself perfectly clear," he continues. "You are to treat these ladies with the same respect as your mother. You are not to take anything that is not offered to you, nor are you to leave anything on these premises. Are there any questions?" He pauses and looks over the faces of the men. "Very well, you may dismount and take ease."

Mother and Sallie have overheard and they are steady at the task of making the soup. I run up quickly to check on the children. When I open the closet door, Victoria and Noah are asleep curled up in Cindy Lou's lap, but Minerva is wide-eyed and holding onto the kitten. "It is going to be alright," I whisper. "Best stay quiet and out of sight. I will come for you when they leave." Cindy Lou shakes her head and pulls Minerva closer and I close the door softly. From the upstairs window, I scan over the back lot hoping to see some sign of Violet. All is still.

We waste no time in getting food ready for the men. The sooner we get them fed, the sooner they will be gone. Sallie is afraid to go on the porch, but Mother scolds her and she picks up a pot and follows us.

When we step out on the porch, we see the men resting on the ground. As soon as they notice the food is being spread out, they begin to sit up. Their faces are gaunt and I can tell they are truly hungry. The Bible says, 'Love thy enemy.' Yet, what makes these men our enemies? They are only doing what they think is their job. Sad how the government can choose our enemies for us.

They stand in line for us to fill their bowls without looking directly into our faces. We are hopeful the visit will go without incidence, until we hear a commotion coming from around the house. We turn to see two of the soldiers struggling to hold on to someone who is jerking, kicking and screaming profanities. With much difficulty, they drag their victim up before the Captain. As they force the victim down to his knees, a large Bowie knife drops out of his pants onto the ground. The man with the bloody lip speaks up, "Sir, a couple of my boys were missing and I went to look for them. I found this fellow had them gagged and tied up down behind the smokehouse."

"Is that so?" the Captain questions. "And where are those men now?"

"Sergeant Rodgers is bringing them around now. Sir."

The Captain looks puzzled. "Let's hear your side of the story," he says, extending his hand out to the man on his knees. The fellow jerks back in resentment and his hat falls to the ground. The Captain puts his hands on his hips and you hear the men start to laugh. This rough and tough fellow is Betty Jo!

"So, you are the one that tied up our men?" he asks.

"I reckons I did, but theys lucky I did not just run my knife right through them for stealin!"

"Stealing?" the Captain says, turning to look directly at the untied men who have just returned.

"Yes sir, theys was a trying to load up the meat in the smokehouse. I snuck up behind them and took them down. Like I say, theys lucky I did not slit their throats like a couple of old hogs," says Betty Jo proudly.

Betty Jo dusts herself off and flashes a mean glare over to the men who had captured her. Captain Woodward walks over and speaks privately to another officer. Then in a voice loud enough to wake the dead he shouts out, "Prepare to saddle up men! We leave this place in five minutes!"

All eyes but mine are on the Captain's slow stride as he approaches us. I am cautiously watching Betty Jo who has collected her knife and slipped over the banister at the end of the porch.

Captain Woodward removes his hat and lowers his voice to address us, "Ladies. I do not know who this young woman may be, but I am afraid that she is a better soldier than some of my own. I gave you my word and I am saddened to say a few of my men have shamed me in your presence. I assure you, I will deal with them regarding their actions. I hope you will accept my apologies and my sincere appreciation for your hospitality."

He places his hat back on his head and pauses briefly before he steps on the porch and looks at Betty Jo. He shakes his head and tips his hat to her. He is leaving with a full belly and a story to tell of the little beauty that took down two of his own soldiers.

Within minutes, the lot is clear and they are descending down the road. Mother runs upstairs for the children. We are relieved to find that Hannah Jane and Violet are safe and hiding in the woods.

When Mother comes downstairs with the children,

Minerva is crying hysterically. Sallie runs and gathers her up in her arms, but all we can make out through her tears is "The kitten, the kitten."

Minerva only wanted to hold the little kitten close and protect it. She was not the enemy. She was only doing what she thought was her job. How do we explain to her how fragile life can be or how easy life can slip through your fingertips?

CHAPTER 9

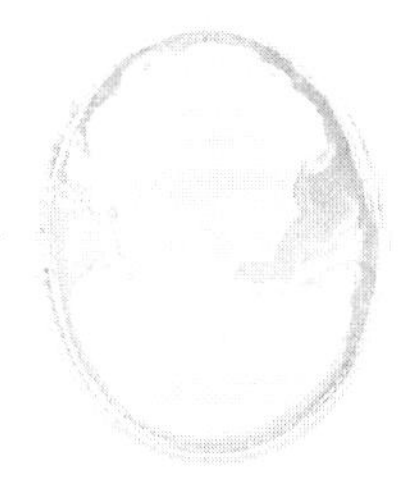

Christmas Eve 1864

Saturday, December 24, 1864

My Dearest Joel,

As I am writing this letter, I pray it reaches your hands. I have not a gift to send or even a fancy card. I only hope you will accept my Christmas wish filled with my devoted love. Just months ago I would have added, "Until the war is over and we are together again." Now the world is turned upside down and it seems even the ministers are losing faith. The old folks say it is the end of time. If General Sherman has his way, it soon will be the end of our South.

Darling, with all that you are suffering, I should not write to you with discouraging news; however, I think you need to know what has happened here.

First part of December, Papa was one of twelve men who went to Saltville, Virginia to haul back salt. Early Monday morning on December 19, Sid Whitley came knocking on our door. Since he was one of the men who had gone to Saltville, we knew something must be wrong.

We all took the news hard when we learned Papa came down with pneumonia and was not able to make the trip back home. The hospitals were all full, but the doctor was able to find a boarding house to take care of Papa.

Mother was headstrong on going to Saltville immediately. Mr. Whitley tried to explain to her that most of the railways were down. He offered to drive her, but she insisted it would take too long. So, Mr. Whitley and Mother took the train out of Salisbury later that same day. He said they would go as far as they could by train, then if need be they would rent a carriage to go the distance. We are expecting a telegram from her any day now, to let us know she has arrived and with news about Papa.

This is sure going to be a lonely Christmas. I would just pretend it was another day, if it were not for the children. I suppose it will make little differ to them if their presents are all hand-made.

It is seven o'clock in the morning as I write to you. When I close this letter, I will be going out to feed the animals. Last night we had snow, this is the second one this month.

Please write as much and as often as you can. As soon as I have more news, I will send it your way. My dear, I am sealing this letter with a tender kiss from my own true lips. I pray God will watch over you and soon this war will come to an end.

With all my love,
Lizzie

Since Papa has been gone, Friday has been the day Mr. Simpson delivers our mail and picks up the outgoing. He did not come yesterday. Since it is Christmas Eve, possibly his wife has baked us a little cake or something and he will be by today.

I had also planned to write a letter to Dr. Fannie this morning until Cindy Lou knocked on the door to take care of Victoria. Best to take care of my chores and leave Fannie's letter for my midmorning project. I dress quickly and head downstairs.

It is evident how much things have changed here in North Carolina, even how we view ourselves. As I pass through the kitchen, Sallie and Violet are sitting side by side eating breakfast at the table. We are masters of none here and if Cindy Lou, Violet or Harper wanted to leave, we would not stop them.

When I step out into the morning air, the snowy white carpet spread out before me gives a strange sensation of déjà vu. It is as if time has been rewound to the morning Papa left for Saltville. The silence is both peaceful and unsettling. I lift up my eyes to the gray sky and the snow falls on my tear-streaked face. "Salt," I recall saying to Papa.

Papa was a risk taker, but only when the odds were in his favor. I sense he knew that morning the odds were stacked up against him. Yet, in these desperate times, one does not always have the luxury of picking and choosing their battles.

"Dear Lord, put your arms around Papa and make him whole again. I pray Mother will soon be by his side to love and comfort him. Amen"

A sudden gust of wind gains my attention as the old oak tree empties its limbs on the path in front of me. The downpour of snow blinds my path. Although I am only steps from the house, I am not sure from which direction I came. The wind stops and for a brief moment I think I see two people walking toward me, "Papa, Mother," I cry out. I run foolishly ahead, only to stumble and fall, twisting my ankle. I stand to my feet and brush away the cold wet snow. I realize I am alone. There is no one here. I must have been dreaming, even though I am wide awake.

I crush through the snow feeling twinges of pain in my ankle. My boots are worn thin and my feet are cold and wet. I am wishing for Charleston. As an exercise to keep my mind off the cold, I think of the good times, Sandy Ridge, Mammy and food, always food. Papa's smiling face flashes in my mind and I can almost hear Mother's laughter.

It is my every morning practice, as soon as I enter the barn, to first glance toward Ralph's stall. He is not standing today. In the cold of the night he has died.

It is emotional for any living creature you have cared for to die, but losing our only horse is a serious consequence. We are now cut off from the rest of the world. Ralph was slow transportation, but now what if something happens or someone takes sick? We are now at the mercy of our own two feet.

I finish my work at the barn and decide to spare Sallie with the news of Ralph's death, at least today. When Mr. Simpson arrives, I will ask if he can help me dispose of poor Ralph. However, if he is not here soon, I suspect he will wait until Monday. Just as well, Joel would not have received the letter until way past Christmas anyway.

After I put Victoria down for her morning nap, I stretch out on the soft velvet sofa with a book. It is warm and cozy in this small parlor. The crackling sound of the fire and the woolen over my knees is a great comfort. I feel guilty thinking of those who do not have even these simple pleasures this morning.

I read over a few pages and fold the book over my chest. Perhaps I will not trouble Mr. Simpson about the horse. The odor will not be bad in cold weather like this.

I just will not look in the stall until Harper gets home. We will deal with it after Christmas.

I must have drifted off to sleep and did not hear the carriage coming up the drive. I see it is Mr. Simpson. I think to myself that this is odd; he normally comes by horse.

To add to the strangeness he has two women passengers. He jumps out of the carriage and stares down the drive. My curiosity is sprung. I walk to the window to see a second carriage has followed him. I recognize this rig as Mr. and Mrs. Huneycutt's.

They commence to get out the carriage. Mrs. Huneycutt is the first to look up at the house. I see her face and a shiver runs down my spine. This is no social visit. Something is wrong, terribly wrong.

Sallie is in the dining room having school with the children. When they hear voices, they spill into the hall in anticipation. At her first glance, I may have looked comical standing there with my hands clasped together.

Sallie smiles at me and in a teasing tone ask, "Who is it?"

Now our eyes meet. The smile slowly fades from her face. "Cindy Lou! Violet! I shout out, without taking my eyes off Sallie.

Cindy Lou comes running downstairs and Violet out from the kitchen. *"Whatz in de world is wrong, Miss Lizzie?"* asks Violet.

"Moe Yankees?" Cindy Lou whispers.

"No, we have guests. Cindy Lou. Take the children upstairs to play and Violet please bring some sort of refreshments."

I open the door not waiting for them to knock. Mr. Simpson speaks first. "Good evening, Miss Lizzie. We are sorry to barge in on you on Christmas Eve, but I am afraid it is important."

I step away from the door and let the group enter the house.

"Papa? Ransom?" Sallie asks, grabbing hold of Mrs. Huneycutt.

"Let's all go in and sit down," Mr. Simpson says, directing the others into the parlor. I stand by the door watching them crowd in and take a seat. They are wearing long faces with downcast eyes. My head begins to feel light and there is high-pitched ringing in my ears. Mr. Huneycutt recognizes I am just before fainting and takes hold of my arm and places me in a chair. Sallie sits next to Mrs. Huneycutt and takes hold of her hand tightly.

All faces are on Mr. Simpson, who is holding a small envelope in his hand. I can see the writing on the front, South-West Telegram Company. He clears his throat and then he takes to the center of the room. "This is my wife, Ruby, and her sister, Estelle. I reckon you know by now we have come with bad news, girls. When I picked up Sid Whitley's telegram, I felt like I best not come over here alone. If you are ready, I will read the telegram now. Sallie and I nod our heads.

To: Green Simpson-Stanly County, NC

From: Sid Whitley Saltville, Va.

Sad turn of events. Took train almost to Saltville. Rented Buggy. Bad roads and heavy rain. Buggy flipped in rain-swollen creek. Fast water. I could not save Mrs. Sanders. Went on to Saltville. Jacob had passed the same day. Have made temporary arrangements for both bodies. Will return late Christmas Eve. Break news to girls. I will come straight with the details. Sid Whitley.

Mr. Simpson, handed me the telegram, but my hand was too weak to hold it and it fell to the floor. I see their faces and their mouths are moving, but I am stone deaf. Sallie begins to vomit onto the floor and Cindy Lou is weeping in the hall. Mr. Simpson's wife is holding on to me, as I struggle to stand. I free from her grip and run out of the room into the hall. Cindy Lou tries to stop me, but I escape out the front door. The porch steps are icy and in my haste, I fall onto my back into the cold wet snow. I am happy for the pain. It frees my crying.

Within seconds, Mr. Huneycutt is standing over me. I reject his attempt to help me to my feet. I am more capable than he. I express my desire to be alone and clamber to my feet. I walk slowly toward the barn, but after a few steps I bring myself to a halt. The dead horse will be there to witness my sorrow. I am surrounded by death. I feel my body collapsing and the world goes black.

I am unaware of the time when I awake in my bed. Perhaps it is morning and this has all been just a bad dream. Sitting up in my bed, I realize my back is aching and drying on the chair next to the fire are my wet clothes. This is not a dream. I am trapped in the reality.

Pulling the covers back, I see that someone, possibly Cindy Lou, has dressed me in my flannel nightgown. My robe is at the foot of the bed and I tremble as I slip it on. I can hear voices below in the kitchen and the smell of food cooking. My stomach begins to growl and I am hollow inside.

I must go downstairs to be reacquainted with the news. My feet are leaded and it seems like a mile between each step. When I appear in the kitchen, I see Sid Whitley has arrived. Cindy Lou's face is swollen from crying, but she is preparing a meal.

Mr. Whitley looks up and I can see he is suffering for words. "Miss Lizzie, I want you to know I did all I could."

He makes an endeavor to say more, but he begins sobbing and the words are lost.

Mr. Simpson and his wife are sitting next to him at the table. Mr. Simpson jumps up and pulls out a chair for me. As soon as I sit down, Cindy Lou sits a bowl of soup in front of me. I shake my head, but she pushes it toward me. *"Yous gonna needs yo strength."*

"Yes, Lizzie, she is right," Mr. Simpson says. "There is much to decide upon quickly. I wish it did not have to fall upon your shoulders, but your sister Sallie is in no shape to reason."

"Where are Sallie and the children?" I ask him.

"Mr. and Mrs. Huneycutt took Sallie and the children to their house. They called a doctor out to give her something to help settle her down. They will take care of the children, until Sallie can get herself together."

"And Victoria, where is she?" suddenly realizing I have nearly forgotten about my own child.

"Dontz you worry one bits, bouts yous baby, Miss Lizzie," Cindy Lou says, stroking my hair. *"Violet is taking real good care of her."*

Mr. Whitley lifts his head. "I am so sorry to fall apart on you like this, Miss Lizzie. It is just this is an awful sad thing and I reckon I am to blame. I just have to tell you what happened that day."

I look at the poor broken man sitting before me. His hands are dirty and his clothes are soiled. He has had a long hard trip home carrying such a heavy burden. "I understand, Mr. Whitley, and perhaps it will give me some peace too. Let me get myself dressed and we will talk in the parlor." I gather myself up and turn to Cindy Lou before going upstairs. "Brandy, please, if there is any left."

A half-hour or more passes before I am dressed and ready to meet them downstairs. Mr. and Mrs. Simpson, the sister Estelle and Mr. Whitley are patiently waiting for me. Mr. Whitley is sitting by the window drinking a glass of brandy. I walk in and pour a glass for myself. After I empty my second glass, I find the courage to speak. "Please Mr. Whitley. I want to know what happen." My voice is strange and unlike my own.

The brief silence and the brandy seem to have helped Mr. Whitley collect his thoughts. In a strong and steady voice he begins. "The train took us up through Virginia, but on the outskirts of Saltville the railways were down and everything was in a panic. We were to find out the Union now occupies Saltville and General Stoneman's troops had blown up the mines. All of us passengers were stranded.

One fellow was local and took off on foot. He later returned with a wagon. The passengers loaded up, hoping to find transportation and lodging. He loaned us a rig so we could go into town to see Jacob. By this time it is almost dark and raining something awful. I swear there was no way to tell the road was flooded out. The buggy slid off into the creek and turned over. The current was so swift that I wound up about a mile down the road. At last, I was able to pull myself to shore. I ran desperately up and down the stream looking for your mother, but it was daylight before I found her. If it is any comfort to you, I spect she was kilt right away when her head hit a big rock."

"Mr. Whitley, what happened to my mother's body?" I ask, realizing the funeral and burial arrangements would fall to me.

"Miss Lizzie, when I got to Saltville I found that your father had passed too. The innkeeper had already sent his body to a Mr. Morrison, the undertaker there in Saltville. So I took your mother's body there too."

It took all the strength I had to speak. "Thank you very much, Mr. Whitley. I know this has been as hard on you as it has on us. Did you discuss the cost or arrangements with Mr. Morrison?"

"Yes Ma'am. I did. You have several options to consider. Cost and time being the foremost factors. I am afraid the details are not pleasant ones. Green and I talked about this while you were upstairs. This is a bad thing, sure enough a bad thing. Under the circumstances, we will do our best to handle it for you if you wish."

I look across at the others in the room. In a time like this, it is family one needs, not the faces of strangers looking back at you. Mrs. Simpson has said nothing since I entered the room, but she is now drawn on to speak. "My dear Lizzie, I certainly do not mean to minimize your pain and suffering. Just like you, I have seen some difficulties in my life. I know when we lost our son, Roy, it was overwhelming. Folks offered to take care of the final arrangements for us, but I am forever grateful we handled it ourselves. It gives a person closure, if you know what I mean."

"Yes, I do know what you mean," I answer her sincerely. "I buried my husband, as you know. I would prefer to do what I can on my own."

"Very well dear," Mrs. Simpson says, reaching across to take my hand. "I want you to know we will help you any way we can."

Strangely enough, even though I had just met her less than two hours ago, I knew that was a promise I could count on. Feeling a little courage and strength from her words, I turn to Mr. Whitley again. "Now tell me what is pending."

Mr. Whitley takes a deep breath. "Well, it is understandable these days folks are not willing to take much of a chance. The undertaker is no exception. He has two bodies to take care of and he wants to be paid. I was able to persuade him to hold out the bodies until I spoke to the family. However, according to him preserving the dead these days ain't cheap. He says he is running low on embalming fluids and mercury and arsenic have tripled in cost since the war began. If we can get the money to him right away, he will prepare the bodies and hire a Negro man to bring the bodies to North Carolina."

"And if we cannot?" I ask.

To this question Mr. Whitley shifts in his seat. "He assured me he would do the decent thing. He will have to put them both in the same coffin and bury them in a public lot."

"Public lot, do you mean the pauper cemetery? I ask, feeling as if I already know the answer.

"Yes," he answers softly.

"No, Mr. Whitley! I cannot let them be buried among the criminals and unknown. Give me a day or two and I will come up with the money somehow."

"Lizzie, it is Christmas Eve. Tomorrow is Christmas and things like this cannot wait. Perhaps the best thing would be let him bury them. Come spring things might be different and you can have them exhumed and brought back here."

"What are his charges?" I ask in a demanding tone.

Mr. Whitley reaches in his pocket and takes out an envelope with the words, Morrison *and Son, Undertakers and Cabinet Makers*. I brace myself and shake my head for him to proceed.

He places his spectacles on his nose. "First let me say, I did my best to negotiate with this man. But, I ain't never had much use for men who make their living off other people's sorrow. I suppose somebody has to do it, but they don't have to take advantage of folks. For two pine coffins he is asking a $150 and for preparing the bodies another $100. Lastly, the cost of delivery from Saltville to North Carolina is $75. For a grand total of $325."

Mr. Simpson jumps up. "Highway robbery! I sure as hell would not pay that weasel that kind of money."

Mrs. Simpson takes Mr. Simpson's hand and encourages him to sit back down. "Darling, we must not try to influence her in her decision."

The room is silent. I stand to my feet. "Excuse me for a moment." I go directly upstairs and open the bottom drawer of my dresser. Carefully hidden since the day I came here from Charleston is a velvet drawstring bag. The contents are all there: three gold nuggets, four semi-precious stones and six silver coins. This was my emergency relief. I think briefly about what Papa would say to me. He would say it is not a sound reason and that it is better not spent. Yet, what would Papa do? We shared a special bond. We were both stubborn and determined.

For the first time since the news was dropped, I find myself smiling when I walk back in the room. I hand the little bag to Mr. Whitley. He opens it cautiously and empties the contents onto the table. "Well, Miss Lizzie, I think this should be enough to satisfy the fee and then some. My son-in-law operates the telegraph office. I will ask him to open up tomorrow long enough to send a message to Mr. Morrison."

After I agree, the sisters engage me in conversation about planning the wake. They both are talking at once and my head begins to spin. One will send the announcement to the papers. The other will notify the neighbors and the church. Arrangements must be made for the food and at least two ladies must be here around the clock: one to sit with me and another to greet and attend the visitors as they arrive.

"Now Miss Lizzie, don't you worry about a thing. Estelle and I are very good at this kind of thing. Anytime there is a death, folks know to call on us," Mrs. Simpson says, feeling rather proud of herself.

Now I understand why they are here; they thrive on this sort of thing. Maybe they should be undertakers themselves. I am sure they mean well, but nothing would please them more than to witness me break down in hysterics. When I explain I will not require a sitter, they are clearly disappointed.

It has been a long day and I am beyond exhaustion. I have not seen Victoria since early morning and by now,

Violet has put her to bed. I am just above asking them to please leave when Mr. Whitley announces he must go home. It sets off a chain reaction and they all resolve to go home.

Not wishing them to change their minds, I quickly jump to my feet. "Yes, please go home to your families. After all, it is Christmas Eve."

Cindy Lou's ways are as familiar to me as my own. I know she is anxious for them to leave also. Within seconds, she is on the spot and escorts them out the door.

Once we are alone, she comes quietly and sits on the floor at my feet. She lays her sweet head in my lap and we cry. We have lost our parents and nothing will ever be the same for either one of us again.

CHAPTER 10

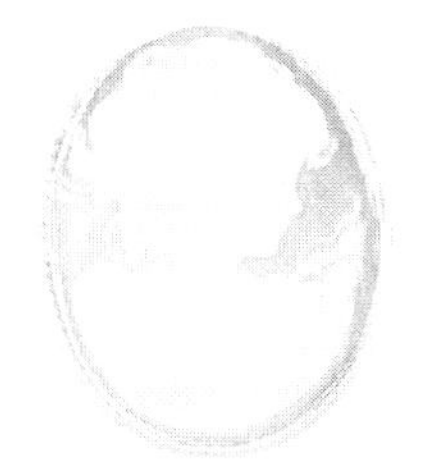

Laughter From Heaven

I am surprised to see it is 11 o'clock when I awake the next morning. My head is pounding. What I would not give for a cup of real coffee, but that is only wishful thinking.

My mind is full of cobwebs and moving in a thousand directions. The events of yesterday have left me living a nightmare. Even though I do not wish to remember, I must. I lay quietly looking up at the ceiling as I make my best effort to recap what happened. I recall the words, the faces, the stale perfume and the pungent odor that filled the room as the contents of Sallie's stomach splattered onto the rug.

I was thankful for the comfort of Cindy Lou and Violet. The loss of Mother and Papa for them is perhaps double fold, for they bear my sorrow too. I am their best friend and now, in many ways, I am their mother.

It is Christmas morning and there is no joy in this household and perhaps shall never be again. Standing to my feet and looking in the mirror, I see a tired old woman looking back at me. I dress and attempt to comb my hair and the comb is full of hair again. My body is aching with the old complaints. The medicine that Zina gave me is all gone.

Dear Lord, I am too low to raise my head. The hole in my heart is deep and the strength pours from my veins like water. If ever I was humble in your sight, this be the day. Help me find the courage among these ruins. Help me provide, protect and salvage a life worth living for Victoria. Amen.

Arriving downstairs, I see the house is working alive with do-gooders. I barely know any of their faces, much less their names. A table with an assortment of food is set out in the hall and Sallie's voice is coming from the parlor. The people look at me strangely as I push my way past them in search of Sallie.

She is dressed in black and politely sitting in the mist of a swarm of women. I make an attempt to gain her attention. However, when I spy Victoria in the arms of a woman I do not know, my priority is to reclaim my child. Mrs. Simpson intercepts me. "There you are sweetheart. We are so glad you were able to rest. It is so important at times like this. Come along. Let's get you something to eat."

She forcefully begins escorting me along and introducing me to the other intruders. The anger bubbles up in my throat and finds its way into the room. "Mrs. Simpson, will you please just let go of me! I want to speak to my sister and I want my baby!"

The activity stops and there is dead silence. Everyone turns and looks at me. I am a total mess, my hair is unkempt and my clothes are wrinkled. Victoria sees me and starts to cry. I walk silently over to the lady and take back my baby. As I walk out of the room, I hear Mrs. Simpson say, "Poor girl, she is still in shock."

Shock, my ass, I think to myself. This is pure madness and I will have no part of this. These people are having a hayday over our sorrow. For God's sake, it is Christmas. You would think they would have something better to do. I do not need their false condolences.

No one dares to stop me as I make my way down the hall and disappear through the kitchen door. Cindy Lou is waiting on the other side. I can plainly read her mind. She is just as unraveled as I am, but an outburst from her would be even more unacceptable.

Slowly I sit down at the table with the children. Little Noah looks up at me innocently. "Aunt Lizzie, did you know Papa and Mamaw have gone to heaven?"

Cindy Lou scolds him. *"Hush yous mouth."*

Noah looks down at his plate and starts to cry.

"Yes, I did. Isn't it wonderful they are spending Christmas with Jesus this year?" My words must have impressed him. He nods his pretty little head and turns back to his food. A good meal is rare these days and he is glad the ladies have delivered it. He has no idea the price it has cost us.

Cindy Lou prepares a plate for me and takes the children upstairs. I am feeling remorseful for being so disrespectful. A full belly is a comfort at times like this. I am debating on the agony of returning to the scene to apologize, until I hear a knock at the back door. Walking to the door, I pull back the curtain and see the back of someone's head. When the door opens, she turns to face me. It is Betty Jo, in her old attire and brogans.

"Won't you please come in," I say politely and force a smile.

Betty Jo, points to her feet, which are covered in mud.

"I's just wonts to let you know, that there situation down yonder in the barn ... well it is all taken care of."

"What situation?" I ask, absent-mindedly.

She leans forward a bit and whispers, *"That horse of your'n."*

"Oh, I had forgotten! How did you know?"

"Came up to see bouts helpin out with the chores and I smelt him as soon as I walked in the barn."

At that moment something inside me changed. She made me laugh. I wanted her to stay; perhaps I needed her to stay. "Come in Betty Jo and get something to eat."

"No ma'am, *I best not track up your floors. I am knee deep in it, if you know what I mean."*

"I do know what you mean," I answer honestly. "Just pull off your boots on the stoop and come on in. I'll fix you a plate."

As I watch her lean figure struggle with the removal of her boots, I wonder why our paths have crossed. She comes in, plops down in the chair and commences to eat as if she has not eaten in days. After she has had her fill, she turns and looks at me. *"Here's how I got it figured. We need fer you to keep on schooling us and you gonna need a hired hand. Except you ain't got no money and we ain't neither. Me and Hannah Jane want to make you a deal. We'll help you keep this place a runnin in exchange for them there lady lessons."*

"Betty Jo, I could not possibly let you do that!"

"*You have to Lizzie. Just look how far I have already come.*" She awkwardly wipes her lips with her napkin, emulating her refined table manners. *"I swear I will give up the tobacco and I will try my best to stop cussing."*

I look at her face. I am reminded of what I said the first time I saw her, Angelic. She is honest, simple and straight forward, not like most women I know.

"Deal?" she asks, with a serious look.

"Deal," I answer.

She smiles and gathers up her hair at the back of her neck like mine. She sees in me what she hopes to be, but perhaps I see in her what I would like to be. I would be doing her a great injustice to change her much. "Just a little spit and polish," like Mammy used to say, will serve her well.

Sallie comes through the kitchen and for the first time, I am astonished at how much she looks like Mother. She is wearing the same hairstyle and demure smile. I believe she is even in Mother's dress. "Lizzie, Mr. Whitley and Mr. Simpson have come to speak about the arrangements. Shall I send them in?"

"Yes, let us see what they have to say," I reply, as she glides out the door.

I am expecting her to return with them, but they come in the kitchen alone. I am hurt she does not care enough to even listen and mad she is making me bear the cross alone. I think briefly back to Sallie – the smile, the look. It is Mother's alright, and her medicine.

Mr. Whitley looks briefly over at Betty Jo, unsure if he should talk freely in front of her. Betty Jo stands to leave, but I ask her to stay. I do not want to be alone.

"We sent the telegram and we have his responses," begins Mr. Whitley. "As it turns out, Mr. Morrison is willing to bargain with you for your purse. He is coming himself. He says he will prepare the bodies. His man will drive the coach halfway. Then he will transport the bodies by train to Salisbury. We are to meet him on Tuesday at the train station around noon. I was thinking Green and I would take a separate wagon up and haul the coffins to the cemetery. You should plan on having a graveside service on Wednesday the 28. Does this sound reasonable to you?"

"Yes, but I do not have transportation to the train station. Our horse has died."

Before anyone could comment, Betty Jo quickly volunteered to be my driver.

"Very well," Mr. Whitley agrees. "I have spoken to the minister. He will be by this evening to talk with you and your sister. Lastly, be giving some thought to the headstones."

....

Tuesday, December 27, 1864

Since the day I turned 18, October 6, 1860, I feel like a princess who has been bewitched by an evil spell. Mother read the fairy tales of the brothers Grimm to me and now I am lost within their pages. The golden goose has died, my prince turned into a frog, the Kingdom is lost, everyone has turned into stone and I am locked in the tower. Will Prince Charming ride up on his great white horse and save me? Unfortunately, this is not a fairy tale and a happy ending is optional.

Betty Jo is here to take me to the train station. Sallie has refused to go with us, saying the children need her at a time like this. Yes, they need help running around the house like wild animals, while she walks around in a daze. I swear she is getting more and more like Mother every day. She has refused to discuss the headstones or the service. It is for damn sure she has no earthly idea how all this is being paid. I know I should not judge her too harshly. She is coping the best she can. She has always been this way, steady and grounded and never wanting to make waves. Papa used to call his girls earth, wind and fire. Sallie being the earth and dear little Annabelle the wind and I was Papa's fiery one. I only wonder how Annabelle would have taken all this if she were alive.

Now Papa and Mother are with her.

Betty Jo is driving an old-fashion buggy that belongs to her Aunt Martha. In Charleston, a girl would rather walk than be seen in a rig such as this. This is not Charleston and I am thankful on a cold morning to have a friend and a ride.

When we arrive at the train station, I see Mr. Simpson and Mr. Whitley are waiting. We are the only folks waiting for a train today and the station manager allows us to wait inside. After a two-hour delay, Mr. Whitley says, "Let's all go home. Mr. Morrison is a resourceful man and he will find a way to get here."

"By resourceful you mean greedy, do you not Mr. Whitley?"

His lips turn up a bit in a half smile, but he makes no reply. He walks over to the wood stove and begins putting on his gloves that he had laid out to dry. In the distance, we hear a train whistle. The station manager runs out saying, "Right on Time!"

Betty Jo and I wait inside as the train comes to a halt. We see our men talking to a conductor who is giving them instructions. When a few passengers begin to disembark, we walk out in the open. I can hear the conductor's words have an angry tone and Mr. Whitley is taking the brunt of it.

Mr. Simpson sees us approaching and runs up to meet us. "Don't worry, Miss Lizzie, just a little mix-up. Sid will take care of it. You ladies wait here for Mr. Morrison while I get the wagon." He pats me on the shoulder and takes off in a fast trot toward the wagon.

"Wait," I call out. "How will I know him?"

"You will, just wait," he shouts back, without breaking stride.

The train's business must be mainly cargo. So far, we

have only seen about a half-dozen passengers step off the train. The last two were businessmen and obviously not looking for anyone. Betty Jo points to a man jumping out of the last car on the end. *"I bets that theres him. The varmint is too cheap to buy a ticket."*

We watch the man as he brushes the straw off his black tailcoat and places a stovepipe hat on his head. He picks up his stride, hoping to give the appearance of a gentleman. He is tall and thin and prances toward us like a shameful woman or a fancy horse. He tips his hat to a man sitting on a bench and the man turns his head quickly.

"Not the kind of fellow you want in the trenches with you," Betty Jo remarks.

The man stops to engage in conversation with the conductor and Mr. Whitley. He begins talking and flinging his hands around. Several times, he attempts to touch Mr. Whitley's arm as if they are friends. Even though it is apparent the other two men are angry, Mr. Morrison walks away laughing. When Mr. Simpson arrives with the wagon, they begin to load the coffins. The fact that both men have tied their handkerchiefs around their nose and mouth raises cause for my concern.

The undertaker is making a beeline toward us. I am an easy target, he assumes, the mourning daughter dressed in black. As he approaches us, I smell him. I recall the odor from Edmond's funeral. It is a stench you never forget: death and embalming chemicals.

He extends his hand to me, but I pretend not to notice. "Miss Sanders, I presume?"

I answer him in a tone of authority, "You are correct, Mr. Morrison."

He eyes me up and down my frame in a degrading manner, "If I had known I would be doing business with such a beautiful young woman, I would have worn my best suit."

"Let's get this unpleasantry over as quickly as possible, Mr. Morrison."

"Yes, of course my dearie. Mr. Whitley tells me you have some valuables you wish to trade for my services. Shall we take a little lookie?"

I glimpse around to see if anyone is watching. Only Betty Jo was in sight and even she was keeping her distance. Maybe to let us talk in private, but most likely to escape his smell. When I empty the contents of the purse into my gloved hand, his eyes light up. I can tell he could hardly wait to get his hands on the loot.

"Your fee is $325. Is this correct, Mr. Morrison?"

"Of course you realize that was only an estimate, Miss Sanders. My train ticket was much more than I anticipated and of course, the cost of embalming fluids has gone up since the original quote. I am afraid we are looking at $425."

I turn to see if Betty Jo had overheard and apparently she has, for she is hitting her fist in her hand. I am slightly overwhelmed and thankful to see Mr. Whitley approaching. I raise my hand to him and he picks up his pace to join us. Mr. Morrison does not seem pleased.

"Mr. Whitley, I think we have a bit of a misunderstanding here. I believe you told me the bill was $325, but now I am to understand it is $425."

"Mr. Morrison, do you not have any honor? I have with me the original quote here in writing," Mr. Whitley says, pulling out the bill.

"My dear man, if you will look at the bottom of the invoice you will see in plain print that that invoice was only good for a period of 24 hours."

Mr. Whitley and I look closely at the bill. In the tiniest

of print, which for many would require a spyglass, was the 24 hour clause. We have no recourse but to deal with his new figure.

I open the negotiations. "Very well, Mr. Morrison. I have here three gold nuggets, four semiprecious stones and six silver coins. Of which one gold nugget, the semi-precious stones, – *excluding the ruby,* – and one of the silver coins will more than satisfy your fees."

"Miss Sanders, surely you jest. That will hardly cover my train fare."

"Alright, let's try this again: two gold nuggets, the semi-precious stones *excluding the ruby* and three silver coins."

"May I see the jewels again, Miss Sanders?"

I open my hand wide and he picks up the ruby and holds up to the light, "Miss Sanders I am afraid your offer is not good enough."

"Very well, everything in the purse *excluding the ruby*," I answer firmly.

Mr. Whitley takes hold of my arm and asks to speak to me in private. I shake my head and continue to stare at Mr. Morrison.

"I want that ruby, Miss Sanders, and I will not settle without it," he says looking at me like a spoiled little child.

"The ruby will be very hard for me to part with, Mr. Morrison. It was a gift from my late husband. He was privateer by trade, you know. He traveled all the world dealing with Kings and Queens. There is hardly any price I can put on its value."

I slowly start to put the ruby back in the purse, but he catches my hand. "Miss Sanders, you owe me a great deal of money! I am demanding to be paid my worth. I propose that ruby and three silver coins."

I pull back my hand and count out three coins. "Very

well, Mr. Morrison, if you insist on taking advantage of my situation, then I have no choice." I hand over the ruby and the coins. He grabs them from my hand, tips his hat and takes off for the train in a dead run.

"Shall we go back to the house, Betty Jo?" I say cheerfully. Mr. Whitley and Betty Jo look at me confused. "I am no fool, Mr. Whitley. You and I both know Mr. Morrison did not use a drop of embalming fluid on the bodies. I have no doubt he just threw my poor parent's bodies in those pine boxes and nailed them shut. The only peace I have is knowing that Papa is in heaven right now laughing himself silly. I figured three silver coins was a fair price for the two pine coffins. Mr. Morrison said he wanted to be paid his worth and that too was a fair request. The question in my mind was what was he worth? I decided he was worth just as much as the ruby. They are both worthless!"

CHAPTER 11

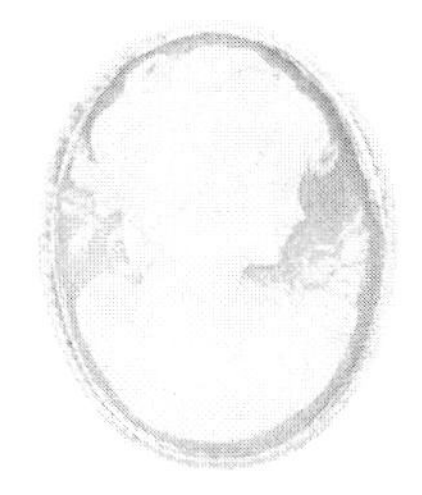

A Day To Commit To Memory

Wednesday, January 22, 1865

It is a bit of a surprise to hear Hannah Jane is getting married. After all, it has only been three weeks since they met. A funeral is hardly an event one expects to meet a future mate, but for a lonely young minister and a girl eager to get married, it is as good as any. I suppose it is true something good comes out of everything.

Martha is scattering the news all over town, "one down and one to go." She has been most complimentary of my teaching skills. I must admit *polishing up* Hannah Jane is a far easier job than with Betty Jo. Hannah Jane is softer and more naturally inclined to feminine ideas. Betty Jo, on the other hand, is a breed all to her own and that is what I like about her.

The real Sallie has returned and her portrayal of Mother has disappeared. She claims to have little recall of what transpired after finding out the news of Mother and Papa's death. God only knows what the doctor gave her. However, the medication has run out and she now must face the reality on her on accord. Just as it was for Mother, reality has always been hard for Sallie. Reflecting back, I will always believe God spared Mother the agony of Papa's death.

We are doing all we can to help Sallie put the pieces together. Today Betty Jo will drive us to the gravesite for the first time since the funeral. It is my desire to go, but also my dread. I have no idea what effect it will have on Sallie's fragile emotional state.

Today is unlike the scene one might conjure up when reading a novel of two lonely sisters visiting the graves of their fallen parents. Nothing about this day has the feeling of mourning or despair. It is encouragingly warm for the season, the sun is shining, the sky is clear and the birds are singing.

Betty Jo came early this morning and my chores were eased by the pleasure of her company. While sitting out in the carriage waiting for Sallie, I pretend not to notice she has a plug of tobacco in her jaw. We are both dressed in trousers and our heads are bare. I have grown to love the wind in my hair and this no-frills freedom.

Even Sallie herself seems in rather rare form this morning. She jumps in the carriage with zeal and her cheeks are rosy in the cool morning air. The carriage ride is not at all objectionable. Betty Jo is far more intelligent than one would first give to her credit. She is well versed and has managed to keep abreast of the war news. She informed us Sherman had overtaken Savannah and offered it to Lincoln as a Christmas gift. She warned us of Sherman's threat on the Carolinas, but today she has good news. The federal's attack on Fort Fisher on Christmas Eve was a failure. General Grant ruled it Butler's blunder and relieved him of his command. I am sure Sallie finds the news a relief. In Ransom's last letter, his regiment was on their way to the coast of North Carolina. However, the most encouraging news Betty Jo shares with us today is the possibility of a peace proposal.

Betty Jo turns the conversation to Hannah Jane and her marriage. *"I don't know why Hannah Jane just has to have herself a husband! We was a managing just dandy before the war. What does she think that little weaseling man can do fer her? He ain't got enough breath in him to chop a cord of wood. Well, I reckon he can pray fer her while she does the work."*

She then begins putting on a show for us, pretending to be Mr. Herman Furr preaching for Hannah. *"Praise the Lord! Chop that dar wood. Praise the Lord! Hoe us a row and milk dem cows. Praise the Lord! Wash dem clothes, feed dem young'uns and scrub dem floors. Amen!"*

We are laughing so hard we temporarily forget where we are heading. The road forks and we turn down the dirt road to the cemetery. We are solemn again. The road is narrow and we are forced to pull to the side to let a buggy pass carrying Mr. and Mrs. Hurlocker, who buried their only son last week.

Betty Jo parks the carriage next to the church. My eyes scan over the landscape. At the edge of the woods we see a doe and pair of fawns. Straight ahead is a big willow tree and oddly enough it has already started to bud with green. One could mistake this day as early spring. I have always found cemeteries intriguing. Perhaps it is the peaceful silence or the untold stories lying in the ground.

The wind begins to pick up as we walk across the lot toward the unsettled graves. I find myself wishing I had some cover for my head and pull my collar up around my neck. Sallie presses forward; her look is serious. She has only one mission, to see the graves of Mother and Papa.

Once she arrives at the site, she kneels down on the ground. She strokes the headstones as gently as if she were stroking their faces. "Lizzie, this is how it was meant to be, don't you see?" Her blue eyes are full of tears, but she is smiling. Her expression is as bright as a newborn Christian.

"We have to trust it was, Sallie."

"No Lizzie, it was! Papa and Mother were true soul mates. They were born for each other. Make no mistake that their departing this earth on the same day was divine providence."

I am dazed by Sallie's epiphany. It is so obvious, so simple, but not a single soul has made this association. Betty Jo steps up to the stones and reads aloud, "Jacob L. Sanders born March 5, 1809 died December 22, 1864 and Temperance Morris Sanders born March 5, 1809 died December 22, 1864."

We pause and look at the graves for one last time. "We love you," Sallie whispers.

It is an emotional walk back to the carriage, but much has changed with this visit. No longer are hearts heavy and sad, but happy and rejoicing for a beautiful love that not even death can sever. We will miss them, but they are in a far better place.

Betty Jo has promised to take us to the Post Office and afterwards we are invited to Aunt Martha's for lunch. We are not put out at all when she informs us she will be making several necessary stops along the way.

We are in no hurry today. Cindy Lou and Violet are capable of caring for the children. Mr. Huneycutt is expected to stop by this afternoon to fix the barn door. Without a doubt Mrs. Huneycutt will tag along to visit with the children. We are free to explore the countryside and relax in the sunshine.

For someone who has recently located in this community, Betty Jo knows something about everybody. We are delighted with her bits of gossip and her knowledge of worldly news. Some of it is so fantastic I wonder if she is making it up. Nevertheless, we are spellbound by her stories.

When we arrive at the Post Office, we discover that Betty Jo is picking up mail for a least a half-dozen other families. The postmaster recognizes me and quickly hands me our bundle of mail. Thumbing through it, I see several letters from Charleston, most likely letters of condolences. There is a letter from Ransom for Sallie and two letters for me, from Dr. Fannie and Joel.

As soon as we get back in the carriage, Sallie rips open her letter. Her ear-piercing scream causes Betty Jo to pull the rig to a halt. She is waving her hands over her face and gasping for breath.

"What is it?" I shout at her, expecting the worst. Several seconds pass before she is able to speak, "Ransom says he may be getting a furlough! In view of what has happened here, Colonel Brown has agreed to send a request to General Kirkland for an approval."

"Sallie, did Ransom say it is certain he is coming home?" I ask, trying to calm her down. My question insulted her and she folded up the letter and stuffed it in her purse. "Sallie, let's not get too excited. These things take time and with war nothing is certain." She turns her head away from me signaling she has nothing further to say on the subject.

Betty Jo pulls the carriage back on the road and we proceed. After a mile or so, Sallie's mood is restored and she is talking freely about when Ransom comes home. This time I do not attempt to discourage her, but join in her enthusiasm. Betty Jo makes several stops to deliver mail at some of the farms along the road. Each stop she brings out an assortment of letters, newspapers and magazines and throws them in the back. I am curious, but I refrain from asking any questions.

This is our first visit at Martha's house. She has been a widow for many years and I am expecting to see the house and grounds a reflection of such. Yet, all is well kept. We walk up on the porch and the front door is unlocked, Betty Jo calls out, "Hello, we are here!"

After entering the house, Betty Jo points for us to have a seat in the room on the left. The house has a musty smell of old wood or dusty linens, but it is clean and tidy. The furnishings are humble, but serviceable. The discreet little repairs to the wallpaper, a broken windowpane and a patch on the old armchair tell me this old house has seen some living. Sallie sits down and takes out the letter to review it again. I prefer to remain standing and wander over to the bookshelves and ponder over the titles. The room has a collective sort of decor of both old and modern. I like it here and the smells from the kitchen add to my appreciation of a real home.

We are to wait only for a short time before we hear Martha's heavy footsteps in the hall. She comes in the room in full gusto with a big smile on her face. "So glad to see you girls," and wipes her hands on her apron. "I know you little birds must be starving. Come, let's put something in your gullet."

Hannah Jane is now standing in the doorway with a pan in her hand. "*I made some fresh biscuits. We ain't got no honey, but we gots some fresh butter.*"

"Sounds good to me," I respond, jumping to my feet.

Sallie and I start toward the kitchen, but Betty Jo catches my arm and holds me back a bit. *"Just to gives you a word of advice. You might as well swallow a cannon ball as one of dem biscuits of Hannah Jane."*

I smile back at her and we walk in together as if nothing was said. Once we take our seats, the biscuit pan is passed. I politely make a comment about watching my waistline, but Sallie takes two. Betty Jo giggles. Our bowls are filled with what proves to be delicious leg of pork stew. Sallie butters up her biscuit and takes a big bite. Hannah Jane watches her, carefully waiting for her response. Sallie chews and chews and with the aid of a big drink of water she is at last able to speak. "Mmm, well you are quite the biscuit maker, Hannah Jane."

Betty Jo responds, *"You gots that right!"*

Hannah Jane does not take the remark too kindly. *"Well, you know Mr. Herman is so thin, he needs him a wife a cookin fer him. He says so himself."*

"Yep and afters a couple of three months of your vittles there'll be nothin left of him but the bare bones," Betty Jo says in a cutting tone.

In a flash, Hannah Jane's old ways come to the surface. She jumps to her feet and gives Betty Jo a shove, nearly knocking her out of the chair. *"Why if I had not done turned myself into a lady, I'd take you outside and mash your ass flat."*

Martha grabs hold of Hannah Jane, but it is not without incident. There are a few quick punches exchanged before Hannah Jane finally sits down. Martha demands they both apologize to us. We accept graciously, trying to hide our smiles. Even though Martha's disciplinary action was certainly necessary, she puts her hand to her mouth and leaves the room. I have a strong feeling she finds the girl's brash behavior amusing also.

When she returns, she has a treat for each of us: a baked sweet potato sprinkled with a bit of cinnamon.

After the meal, Martha invites us to see the dress she is working on for Hannah Jane's wedding. We follow her out in the hall. She turns the ceramic handle to the door leading upstairs. It is stuck and she must pull upon the door until it springs open. She laughs as if she has accomplished a noble feat, hikes up her skirt and starts up the steep steps. One by one we make our way up the enclosed narrow stairwell. The handrail is well worn and is evidence of its need.

At the top of the landing, the space is divided into two large unfinished rooms. One side is obviously Betty Jo and Hannah Jane's sleeping quarters. On the other side is a work area with a loom, spinning wheel and a sewing machine.

Sallie pulls her shawl up around her shoulders. Even though the sun is streaming through the large windows, it is cold and drafty in the loft. Betty Jo goes to the woodstove and throws in a couple of logs, while Martha directs our attention to the dress mannequin displaying a partially finished bodice. On the long cutting table is a copy of Peterson's Ladies Magazine, January to June, 1864.

Martha picks up the book and opens it to page 286. "It says here this bodice added to an old skirt makes a stylish and ladylike costume. The article goes on to explain, in times like this, being conservative is not just a slight consideration. How true this is.

When I saw the pattern called for it to be made up in white, I then reckoned it was just meant to be. I had just enough nice flour sack material to make it. I am in the process of cutting down my black velvet skirt to fit Hannah and there will be enough left over to make a waist piece just like the one in the magazine. "I think this is going to be lovely for a simple wedding. What do you girls think?"

It is beginning to warm up in the room and Sallie steps over to the mannequin and examines the piece. "Lizzie, Martha is quite the seamstress," she states, looking at me sincerely.

"Yes, of course," I respond, slowly. "But I have my reserves on the appropriateness of the attire. A white bodice is most commonly considered underpinning and not for show. I suppose a white body worn under a vest or sporting jacket would be fitting, but worn alone with only a sash or waist piece, I have my doubts. Martha, may I see the magazine?"

Martha hands me the magazine, Sallie and I read over the article. There it is in black and white and Peterson's Magazine is certainly a reliable source. Sallie nods her head and I agree.

Sallie lays the book on the table. She asks Hannah Jane if she has given thought to what type of headdress she will wear. Sallie takes over the conversation as if she is the expert on weddings. Martha and Hannah Jane are holding on to her every word.

I stand back feeling like an outsider and recall the day Mother and Sallie were planning Sallie's wedding. I am happy to have Betty Jo interrupt my thoughts. *"Come outs to the barn with me, Lizzie. I want to show you somethang."*

We leave them to their planning and head for the barn. First Betty Jo stops to collect the stack of papers and letters she stored in the back of the carriage. *"I wants you to see my workshop,"* she says in a rather coy voice. She stops outside the barn door and peers at me. *"Fer you come in here, yous gots to swear not to say nothin bouts this to nobody. Do you hear me, Lizzie?"*

By the look on her face, I am fully expecting to see a liquor still or a dead body hanging by the rafters, but I agree. Once inside the barn I see there are newspapers stacked up nearly to the ceiling and boxes filled with letters, bills and pamphlets. On a long flat table are rows of frames about the size of a piece of writing paper.

She picks up a letter off the table and reads. "*My Dearest Aunt Rose. I am writing to ask if you would consider taking in my oldest daughter, Helen, for approximately a period of nine months.*" She laughs and picks up another letter. *"I am sorry sister that I did not come to see you on Sunday, but I have been suffering with a terrible case of the piles."*

She tosses letters around reading bits and pieces of personal information from each, until I stop her and ask, "Betty Jo, are you reading other people's personal mail?

"Well, some of it sort of jumps off the paper at me. If they didn't want nobody to know this stuff, they should not have given it to me."

"Betty Jo, just *why* are you collecting all these newspapers and mail?"

"It is business and a purty damn good one. I takes their old papers and turns dem into new paper. Then I sells the paper right back to dem."

For the next 30 minutes or so, Betty Jo explains her process. She soaks the papers in turpentine to remove the ink and then makes the paper into a paste, remolds it into the frames, and lets it dry. Some of the papers are a true work of art with added dried flowers and botanicals.

Even though I have no inspiration of doing such, Betty Jo makes me promise not to steal her trade secret. I agree, only if she promises not to gossip to anyone about what she reads in letters except me, I tease.

It is late in the day when we leave Martha's house. Sallie has agreed to help with the wedding, which is planned to take place following church service the Sunday before Valentine's Day. Mr. Herman Furr has no idea what he is up against. Hannah Jane is hardly the role model for a preacher's wife. It will be interesting to see if he can hold on to both his religion and this little hellcat from the mountains.

All and all this has been a day to commit to memory, visiting the graves and good news from Ransom. I am pleased with the arrangement Betty Jo and I have made. She will first pass the recent newspapers to me and I will clip the headlines for my scrapbooking. Like an old habit, a fleeting thought runs through my head. "I must tell Papa about Betty Jo..." I am quickly reminded. I find it hard to bite back the tears.

Supper is waiting when we return and the evening goes by slow. I am anxious to be alone and cozy up to the fire to read the newspapers and most of all the two letters waiting for me in my purse.

At last, the house is still and Victoria is asleep. By the nice warm fire, I undress and slip into my flannel nightgown. Back in Charleston, Mammy would have cut this thing up for rags. But here, even if it is thin and full of pinholes, it is a comfort tonight. I wash my face, brush my hair and braid it back for sleep. Looking at my brush, it appears a little less hair is falling out. We now have plenty of salt, thanks to the trip to Saltville. Perhaps our health is to benefit, but what a price those blocks of salt have cost.

My first desire is to read my two letters. Fannie would understand if I read Joel's letter first. I carefully open Joel's letter, run it across my lips and visualize kissing the hand that wrote the letter.

My Dearest Flower of the South,

Words cannot describe the pain and sorrow I felt when I read your letter. It is not for us to question God's way, but the untimely deaths of your Father and Mother, is a bitter challenge of my faith. Let me say, your father was one of the finest men that ever walked this earth, devoted to God, his family and his country. Your dear sweet mother, no man could beg for a better wife, mother or friend to share his life in this and in eternity.

I wish I could be there to comfort and hold you during this so mournful time. It is not to be, but if my thoughts bring me near to you then I am with you every breath I take.

Lizzie, I want you to know, I will survive this war. These days will end. I will return home to you, even if I must drag myself to your doorsteps one bloody bone at a time. Therefore, I will not worry you with the trials we are all facing here. It is unimportant; I am numb to the suffering, for I am a man living in the future and floating on the wings of love.

Lizzie, I want you to go to the house next to mine and speak to Mr. Cagle. He is the keeper of my horses. Tell him I sent you to get a horse. There should be eight to choose from, providing they are all still living. Pick which one you find to be the most manageable, remembering they are high-spirited creatures. Promise me you will do this right away.

Now, I must ask a favor of you. I have written to Dr. William Teeter in Davidson offering the balance of the horses to him for sale. I have taken the liberty to ask him to contact you to negotiate the deal. He knows the quality of my animals and should offer you a fair price.

I must close now for duty calls. I am sorry not to write longer and more often, but paper and stamps are scarce.

With all my love to my little bride in waiting,

Joel

My heart is lifted by his words and I carefully wipe the tears from my eyes so as not to soil the letter. It is a treasure to me and I will read it again many times. This is one sheet of paper Betty Jo will never have the chance to reform.

Next, I take out Fannie's letter. I know she will be heartbroken with my news and I am anxious to hear the news from Charleston.

Dear Lizzie,

I will not say I understand how you feel, for no one can measure another's pain. I can only say I too have lost my own dear family. Time is the only medicine that will heal the hole in your heart. Try for now to think of the sweet memories that not even death can steal.

Much is happening here in Charleston. Sherman has crossed the river and is heading this way. He has publicly stated he holds Charleston responsible for the war, he plans to see how much he can make Charleston and it's people suffer. For the first time, my friend, I am afraid.

If and when Charleston is occupied, Millie and Simon having been slaves will be safe. I do fear for the clinic and I feel it will be safer without me. Even though I am a Negro, I have never been a slave nor do I subscribe to the Union's principals. I fear Sherman and the band of rebellious Negroes that follow him will not look upon me fondly.

I received a letter from Sister Irene last week and she has offered me a position at the Abbey. I feel for all concerned at this time I should return to New York. It is my sincere hope once the war is over, I will be able to return to Charleston. In the meantime, Simon and Millie will be residing in the house. I think you will be happy to hear they had a healthy baby girl born January 10, 1865, and her name is a favorite of ours, Theodosia. Simon is calling her Dosia.

Lizzie, I feel it is tiresome for you that I am always giving you advice. Yet, for some reason I feel I am called upon to do so. Did I mention in my last letter a Dr. James Cotton in Salisbury, North Carolina? He is in desperate need of nurses. I have written him about you and he is willing to offer you a job. Finances are not a pleasant subject to discuss, but I expect it is an area of concern for you.

By the time you receive this letter I will be on my

way to New York. Many of the good people here have already evacuated Charleston. You would hardly recognize our fair city; the last four years of bombardments have left its scars.

Once I arrive, I will write to you. I am sure I can send you some medication for your thyroid condition. I hope you have been following my advice and keeping up your strength. Good-bye for now, my best and dearest friend, but do not think you have seen the last of me!

Au revoir.
Fannie Holloway

Fannie is right; finances are not a pleasant subject these days. It does not take much money if you are not spending much, but we have nothing in reserve. The $11 a month that Sallie receives as Ransom's military pay did not even come last month. One of us will have to take a job, and for sure it will not be Sallie. I will go tomorrow, see Mr. Cagle and hopefully return with a horse. Then Monday, I will go to Salisbury to see Dr. Cotton.

It is late and I am getting tired, but there is time to look over a few newspapers.

I lay them out on the floor, take out my scissors and begin clipping the headlines.

Federals destroy railways south of Petersburg

Attack on Fort Fisher was a Union Failure- Grant blames General Butler

Congress urges President Davis is to appoint Robert E. Lee General-In Chief of all the Confederate Army

Peace talks to start -Vice President Stephens, Senator Hunter and Pres. Lincoln

January 13-15 The South's last remaining port is lost. Fort Fisher is captured following second battle.

Fort Fisher has been captured? Is this where Ransom is stationed? My first thoughts are to go wake Sallie with the news, but perhaps I am wrong and it would cause her unnecessary grief. If something has happened to Ransom she will get the news soon enough. I will remain silent until more news arrives.

CHAPTER 12

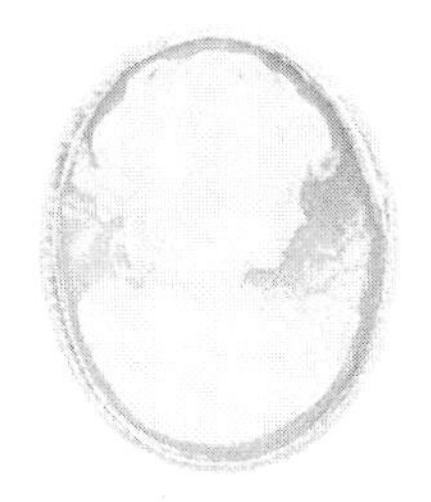

A Gentleman Doctor

March, 1865

From my room in Dr. Cotton's home, I take out pen and paper and compose a letter to Joel. I plan to mail it on my way to work today. Therefore, it will have to be brief.

My darling,

My day's sweetest moments are at dawn, for I awake with dreams of you still in my head. As the light touches my lips, I can almost feel yours upon mine. I imagine your footsteps coming up the walk, but today is the same as the day before. It is only fanciful thinking.

As the first beams of morning sunlight dance across my weary shoulders I cry out, "How can you be so cheery and bright with so much sorrow across our land?"

I know I must be strong and face another day, but tears fill my eyes. Suddenly, a white dove lands upon my window sill. Surely this be the omen that peace is near at hand. Just like the breath of the coming spring, this little dove now brings me new hope. God has heard our prayers and our Southland will flower again.

With all my love and devotion,
Lizzie

I fold up the letter in a handmade envelope and take out one of my three remaining stamps.

Strange how your mind works and thoughts just creep in and out without even being invited. Such is true today as I make up my bed and tidy up the room. I am thinking of the day I found out about Mother and Papa's death. So much has changed since then or has it? The handwriting was on the wall. None of the recent events should have come as a shock to any of us. Yet knowing something is pending is one thing, but the actual occurrence is another.

The peace talks have failed. Lincoln's terms for peace only spell "Union." Even so, President Davis still says Lincoln will soon meet our demands. Much of the South is losing faith in President Davis. Some of our own soldiers are laying down their arms and going home to their families. General Lee is offering the soldiers amnesty and pleads for their return. Yet even the great General fears he is fighting a losing battle.

No one likes to be on the side of the losers. Vice President Stephens has retired to his home in Georgia and the Secretary of War has resigned.

General Lee has appointed Joe Johnson as commander of the Army of Tennessee, giving him but one tall order, "Stop Sherman." Johnson established headquarters in

Raleigh and his army of less than 40,000 troops must stand up against Sherman's army of more than 100,000.

We are quickly being boxed in with no supplies. All Southern ports are lost and our railways cannot be built back fast enough to be destroyed again.

Columbia is a smoldering pile of ashes. Women, children and invalids are left homeless in the night. Sherman bitterly claims Columbia deserves the treatment he bestowed upon them, telling them to thank their courageous General Wade Hampton.

The Southern cities that have not yet faced Sherman's torch are now sitting ducks for his bands of drunken soldiers with matches and muskets.

The stories in the newspapers are enough to melt the coldest of hearts. Still Sherman marches onward in his flame of glory without shedding a tear.

Last night I began reading the letter I received from Simon in Charleston, but I was so exhausted I fell asleep with it in my hand. I glance at the clock. The hour is getting late and I must hurry downstairs or I will miss breakfast. The days at the hospital are tedious, but even harder on an empty stomach. I gather up my things and slip the letter in my apron pocket.

Mrs. Cotton is sitting in her invalid chair out in the sunroom. She says the warm sunshine is comforting to her joints. When weather permits, she takes her breakfast out on the porch. My first thought is to join her, but I am too tired for conversation. I sit down quietly out of sight in the hall and rest my head against the wall.

Even though I have only held this position for a month, it seems like a lifetime. When I wrote to Dr. Cotton, he had two positions he was desperate to fill. One was a full-time nurse for his wife and the second, a nurse to work with him at the prison hospital. As it has turned out, Cindy Lou met his requirements to care for Mrs. Cotton and I as his assistant and nurse. My agreement with Dr. Cotton was I would leave on Friday afternoon and return early Monday morning. It was not to his liking, but the package deal of two nurses was most appealing. The deciding factor, he would be paying Cindy Lou lesser wages.

Dr. Cotton's wife Pricilla, or 'Prissy' as she prefers to be called, possesses an unusually cheery disposition. She is not a southerner, but is from England. I estimate her age to be late 40's. She does not complain of pain and with the exception of weak joints, she appears otherwise healthy. The actual diagnosis of her condition has never been discussed.

She has a studio room where she spends most of the day working on her paintings. I know Cindy Lou is secretly pleased to watch an artist at work. On my next trip home, I plan to bring some of Cindy Lou's drawing for Prissy to see.

I am thankful Cindy Lou and Prissy are getting along. However, I find Dr. Cotton dark and gloomy. He is often short and direct and has very little patience. I tolerate his lack of charm. He is overworked and under more pressure than any human being should endure. I truly believe it is God's practice to turn those hearts in his service to stone. Else, grief would consume them and they could not carry out their duties.

Dr. Cotton is always late for breakfast. I suppose he has the right, but today is Friday and his temperament will be even more sullen. He is never happy on Fridays, knowing I will be leaving.

Cindy Lou does not travel back and forth with me. She has a room of her own, directly across the hall from Prissy's Room. With Cindy Lou's best interest at heart, it is my desire that she finds a permanent home here. Not as a slave, but as Prissy's nurse, earning her own wages. I instructed Dr. Cotton from day one: Cindy Lou is to receive her wages, not me.

Dr. John is Dr. Cotton's son. He also lives here and works at the prison hospital. I think him vulgar and avoid assisting him whenever possible. His father is paying my wages, but that does not give Dr. John the right to stand so close to me. It is degrading and disrespectful the way he looks at me. Lastly, I do not take him to be well learned and I myself have questioned his methods on more than one occasion.

My daydreaming is brought to a close when my ears detect noises coming from the dining room. Cindy Lou and another servant are setting out breakfast. The meals here at Dr. Cotton's house are modest, just as they are on all the tables in Salisbury.

I stand to my feet, feeling a recurrence of an odd sharp pain in the middle of my back. I fear it is a *signal of something worse to come*, but resolve it to be the fault of a poor mattress.

Entering the dining room, I see Dr. Cotton and Dr. John have preceded me and taken places at the table. Dr. John pulls out a chair next to him, inviting me to sit. I pretend not to notice and sit on the end.

Dr. Cotton looks up at me briefly over his spectacles. "Morning, Miss Lizzie," and then he turns his attention back to his plate. Dr. John makes a feeble attempt of bantering with me, opens a newspaper and begins to read:

> *On March 4, 1865, over 2,000 people crowd into the White House to attend the grand ball honoring the second inauguration of Abraham Lincoln. The gates opened at eight o'clock in the evening and the*

mad rush to gain entrance resulted in trampled toes, torn gowns and women fainting.

The President and Mrs. Lincoln arrived at 10:30 p.m. dressed to the nines. The President was dressed in black, with white kid gloves. Mrs. Lincoln wore an elaborate white silk skirt and bodice.

The grand gala included shameful amounts of food, a band on every floor and dancing. The gentleman were encouraged to have their appropriate payment ready when selecting wines and champagnes. Spirits were certainly not dampened, even with prices soaring as high as $5 a quart.

Mr. and Mrs. President made a three-hour appearance, but guests partied into the wee hours of the morning, leaving the room in shambles.

"Well, I for one would have liked to have been on that guest list. What about you Miss Lizzie, Father?" Dr. John asks, looking at each of us.

"No I would not!" I respond, bluntly.

"Ditto," Dr. Cotton says, following my lead.

Undoubtedly perturbed, Dr. John stands up, wipes his face and leaves the room.

Seconds later, we hear the front door slam. Dr. Cotton snickers. "Apparently Dr. John has gone to work early." I am happy for that. Now I will not have to make an excuse for not riding with him.

From what I have observed of Dr. Cotton, he is a creature of habit. As soon as he finishes his last bite, he will remove himself from the table and join Prissy on the porch. He will visit with her for exactly 20 minutes and then go for his morning constitution.

Once the deed is done, in exactly 15 minutes he will be ready to leave. If I am not waiting, he will assume I have walked.

Today is no exception. He pushes away from the table and walks out to the porch. I wait until he is seated before I open Simon's letter. Although Simon was once a slave, he received a second-hand education from his young master. He speaks proper English and can read and write as well as I. This is the first letter he has written since I left Charleston.

Dear Miss Lizzie,

I am sorry to inform you that the letter you sent Dr. Fannie arrived the day after she left for New York. I am sure you know Charleston is now occupied by the Union. I truly believe the day Charleston surrendered was the day the Confederacy surrendered its very soul. I will try to give you an eyewitness account of what transpired here in February.

Since the burning of Atlanta, there has been a steady flow of people evacuating the city. On the 15th, General Beauregard ordered the evacuation of his troops. On Friday the 17th, word came that by tomorrow morning Sherman's troops would descend upon Charleston. In less than an hour, the roads were blocked with wagons, carriages, and people on horseback and even on foot, trying to get out of the path of Sherman.

Late that night and early the next morning General Hardees's troops carried out their orders to leave nothing behind for the Union. Every cotton storehouse, quartermaster's store and the bridge at James Island were burned. Cannons were destroyed, ships and ironclads were sunk and extra ammunition was exploded. Between the fires and the explosions the night became day.

Here my information is still incomplete, so I will have to tell you more or less what happened. From this point, the city was in wild disorder. General Hardee's troops had fled on the last train north, hauling all the rations, supplies and ammunition the train could hold. Word spread they had left behind supplies and provisions. Despite the fires, crowds of starving people rushed into the depot to salvage what they could.

Around daybreak, Millie and I heard another huge explosion that blackened the sky and shook the earth. We were to learn later the Northeastern Railroad depot had been blown up. The counts may be as high as two hundred and fifty men, women and children who were wounded or killed.

After the explosion, the fires spread, destroying residences and buildings much in the pattern as the great fire of 61'. There are still conflicting stories as to who is responsible for the explosion. Some claim it was accidental, that in General Hardee's troops haste to escape they were forced to leave kegs of gunpowder at the station, which later exploded. Others say it was a direct attack by Sherman's army.

When the Yankees entered the city, Mayor Macbeth had no choice but to surrender the city. Sherman hoped to gain a grand prize in Charleston, but after four years of Yankee thunder he has nothing much to boast. Sadly, today as I write this letter the Union flag flies over Fort Sumter.

I tell you Lizzie, it was a sad sight seeing the citizens of Charleston standing in line to take the oath of allegiance to the Union. I am glad you were not here to witness or to partake in this humiliation.

Maybe a better day will come for the South, but it is not likely in my lifetime.

I can only pray our baby girl, Dosia, will see Charleston restored to its glory again.

I will close here. I pray God will keep you healthy and safe until we meet again,

Your friend always,
Simon Sanders

My heart is heavy as I walk down the street on my way to the prison hospital. I feel I have been reduced to the lowest of positions. I know of no one who would trade places with me. As I approach the 16-acre compound, I can smell it from the top of the hill. Just walking in the front gate of the prison compound is repulsive. The water is foul and the sanitation conditions are a threat to the whole city. Every disease known to man lurks inside those tall wooden fences. Death is a reality and to those inside, a blessed escape.

Dr. Cotton says it was not always like this. In 61', the abandoned cotton factory was chosen as the best place for the prison. This was based on the location near the railway, rich resources, fresh waters and the capability of housing up to 2,000 prisoners. When the first prisoners arrived, they found it more like a college campus than a prison. The town's women brought in home-cooked meals and prisoners even formed a baseball team.

As the war progressed and the need became greater, by the end of October 1864 the prison population was over 10,000. This past winter was one of the coldest on record. Over 50 percent of the inmates were without shelter and forced to bare the elements in mud huts and tunnels in the ground. The fighting over shelter, cowpea soup and cornbread was uncontrollable. More guards were sent to help control the prisoners, adding to the numbers of men in the compound.

When I came to work for Dr. Cotton in February, General Johnson had replaced General Gee and the migration was already in place. Most of the officers were gone and all those not too sick or weak were marched to Greensboro, North Carolina, to be exchanged. Sadly, many never made it to Greensboro and died along the road.

Now what is left are the skeletons of men. Dr. Cotton says they are too sick to die. But, they do die and lately it has been at an alarming rate. The blacksmith's house is now called the 'deadhouse.' The dead bodies are stored there until they can be buried. The smell gets in your nose and you must fight to keep from vomiting.

My walk is over and I must enter the gates of hell. The guard recognizes me and allows me to pass. I see a few prisoners in the distance, but overall it is deathly quiet.

When I walk into the main cottage, the halls are bare. I hear the echo of my footsteps as I walk down the hall. There is no one attending the patients, because the beds are all empty. Something has happened. Where are all the people? I must find Dr. Cotton. His office is at the end of the hall. I make a few steps in that direction when I see Dr. Cotton rushing up the hall. "Lizzie, go back to the gate and wait for me!" I hesitate and he calls out with more authority, "Go now!"

I turn around and run out the door. I run pass the dead-house, the mud houses and the cottages until I pass through the gate. My breath has left me and I lean against the wall to regain my strength. Within minutes, Dr. Cotton's carriage pulls up beside me. "Get in!"

I obey and climb inside. He cracks his whip and the horses take off. "Typhoid," he whispers. "Just like a thief in the night."

Not a word was spoken until we arrived at his house. For the first time he demonstrates a gentlemanly manner. He jumps out of the carriage and comes around to help me down. He does not readily let go of my hand. "Lizzie, you must go home. You have a child. Your life is worth more than the few pennies I pay you. I will pay you your wages for the balance of the month, but I will not have your death on my conscience. Leave the Negro girl. She will be fine. Now go on and pack your things."

He stands out in the drive and waits for me to go in the house. I look around for Cindy Lou. What will I say to her? This has all happened so quickly. Will she be all right without me? I understand her and I have always taken care of her.

Slowly I walk down the hall toward Prissy's studio. The door is partially open. I start to enter, but I step back to observe. Prissy is giving Cindy Lou an art lesson. I see the joy on Cindy Lou's face as she dabbles paint onto a fresh white canvas. I step back as not to be seen. God does work in mysterious ways.

Shortly I come back down the steps wearing my old trousers and carrying my worldly possessions. On the table, I see Dr. Cotton has left an envelope with my name on it.

Quietly, I slip out the door and walk toward the barn. I saddle up my horse, but before leaving I open the envelope. There as promised is the balance of my monthly pay and a note from Dr. Cotton,

Dear Miss Lizzie,

It has been my pleasure to have you as my nurse. You have worked above and beyond the call of duty and I wish you the very best.

As for your girl, I will have Prissy explain your leaving. For the time period, it is agreeable. I will keep her in my employment and pay her fairly.

You are always welcome at our house as a guest, but never again will I subject you to the duties of my nurse.

With kind regards,
Dr. James W. Cotton

CHAPTER 13

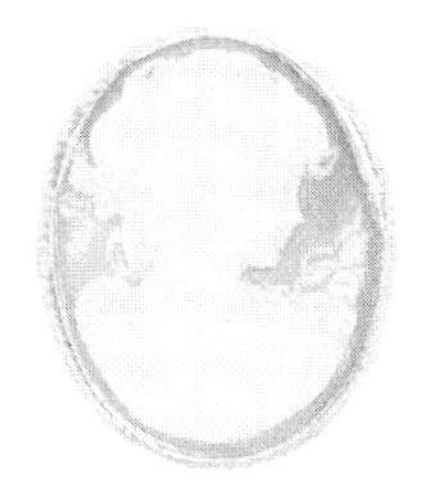

Two Women and Three Children

The ride home is pleasant from Dr. Cotton's home to Sallie's and at a good pace I can make it home by supper. My manly attire of trousers and an old hat is serviceable and attracts less attention than a woman traveling alone.

I have grown to like this horse. Joel had named him Buddy but I just call him Bud. He is an obedient animal, but he prefers to run. I have to keep a tight reign on him at all times.

Today they will be surprised to see me home so early. Sallie reluctantly accepted the job of continuing the lessons for Betty Jo and Hannah Jane. I have the sneaky suspicion she is thrilled to do so and feels she is better qualified. Aunt Martha tends to the children and Mrs. Huneycutt comes to visit.

We are managing. Betty Jo has been a big help and Harper's contract has ended. Soon we will be putting in a garden. It will be crucial this year our garden fares well.

The road leading out of town is often busy, but today not a soul passes. I am glad to have left my troubles behind me and

I could almost fall asleep. I am quickly reminded not to when Bud starts into a gallop. Thinking about the creek on the other side of the hill, I pull on the reigns and redirect him. We both could use a drink and a chance to empty our bladders.

When we reach the creek, I slide down out of the saddle and step off into the woods. When I start to climb back in the saddle, I see two horsemen watching me from the opposite hill. I don't like the feeling of this. My first instinct is to jump on Bud and ride like hell. However, I do not want to draw attention to myself, so I start down the road at a slow even pace. I cannot imagine what business they would have with me. However, I am cautious and nudge Bud to pick up his speed.

After some distance, I look back and discover they are in full pursuit of me. Whatever the reason, this cannot be good. I give Bud a swift hard kick and he opens up. It is all I can do to hold on, but the men are closing in on me.

As we come across the bend, I drop out of site and make the decision to turn down an unknown road. I have no idea where I am heading, but just thankful they have not followed me. After riding hard for a mile or so, I bring Bud to a halt and rest.

There is a farmhouse just up the road a bit. I should report this. What if these men are escaped prisoners? Just before I reach the drive I am accosted by the two men who have cut through the woods and blocked my path. One of the men pulls out his pistol and demands I get off my horse.

The house is in view and I can see two men working in the field. I figure my best option is to get down off my horse and then run toward the house. Only a fool would risk shooting me in plain view.

I dismount slowly, hearing mumbling between the two of them. As the men start down off their horses, I take off running across the field. The briars are ripping open my pants and tearing my flesh. I find myself screaming at the top of my voice to alert the men working in the field.

Running close behind me on foot are the two men. Are they going to kill me right out here in cold blood? I have almost made it to the house when my foot catches on a piece of barb wire and brings me to the ground.

I am caught. One of the men chasing me grabs hold of my arm and jerks me to my feet. The wire cuts my ankle. The other two men walk forward cautiously, holding onto their hoes like weapons.

"What the hell is going on here?" one of the farmers ask.

"We have been on the trail of this deserter for two days. Now it looks like we have finally got our hands on the rat!" The man says, holding tightly to my arm.

"Let go of my arm you fool!" I cry out in pain. Hearing a woman's voice he jerks back as if he has been burned.

I remove my hat and stare at both men. "I am not a deserter as you can see! I am Dr. Cotton's nurse and I am on my way home from my duties."

Both of the men try to make apologies, explaining they are from the Home Guard. In their defense, they tell me I should not have been traveling alone.

"So you think because I am a woman traveling alone you have the right to hunt me down like a wild dog! Now, my leg is wounded and my nerves are destroyed."

Now free, I sit down on the ground and remove the wire from my leg. I am covered with scratches and my leg is bleeding. I am now the object of pity.

The farmers suggest I go inside to rest and the Home Guard offers to take me home, which I bluntly refuse. "You have done enough gentleman! I just want to get on my horse and go home."

I limp back to the road and climb up on Bud and start down the road. Shortly, I hear horses behind me. It is the two men. They are following me, but keeping a safe distance behind me. They continue to escort me all the way to Sallie's house. When I turn in the drive, they wave, turn their horses around and take off.

Leaving Salisbury, I had a plan. I would surprise everyone coming home early, spend time with Victoria and catch up on the news. When I hobble in the house, I do surprise them, but not in the way I had wished.

Victoria seems more or less uninterested in me. I can understand. Mrs. Huneycutt and Caroline and her children are visiting. Victoria is a toddler now and she wants to play with the big children. Martha has brought Betty Jo and Hannah Jane for their schooling with Sallie. Mrs. Huneycutt, Martha and Caroline are in the parlor. I join them, showing them my bloody legs. I begin to tell them about my ordeal. Martha gets so excited and creates a stir. It spoils Betty Jo and Hannah Jane's lesson.

Betty Jo wants me to promise not to go to Salisbury again alone. This is when I explain why I will no longer be working for Dr. Cotton.

Violet, who is standing in the doorway, asks, *"Cindy Lou's she a comin home too?"*

"Not right now. She is going to stay awhile with Mrs. Cotton," I answer, but it is really a misleading lie. I was not up to the full explanation of Cindy Lou. It is best I address that issue with Violet in private.

Betty Jo was happy to see me and went out to the carriage and brought me a stack of newspapers. *"Waits tills you reads all these. I am a telling you fer sure the war is bouts done fer. You are sure enough goin wants to clip these headlines."*

Betty Jo is anxious to show us the papers and spreads them out on the floor. Seeing it must be done right now, I ask Violet to bring my scissors.

Betty Jo and I sit down on the floor and begin to thumb through the papers.

"Sallie, any news from Ransom?" I ask.

"Yes, as a matter of fact I got a letter from him this week. He is not coming home. His regiment was about 16 miles out of Fort Fisher at the time of the first battle. The 42nd had already pulled out to join up with Hoke's Division before Sherman took over Wilmington." Sallie pauses for a moment and looks at Mrs. Huneycutt and Caroline, "And Lord knows where he is now."

"And what about little brother Thomas, any word?" I ask, directly to Mrs. Huneycutt.

"Yes, his letters still show he is in good spirits. How, I do not know, after spending months in the trenches of Petersburg."

In an effort to change the subject I read, "*President Davis approves the draft for Negro Troops*." Violet is back with my scissors and I ask her to bring us some refreshments. She leaves the room quietly.

My eyes turn back to the newspaper. "Betty Jo, here is something you might need to take heed of. *Harpers Weekly has reported that the use of tobacco has been proven to cause cancer.*

Betty Jo picks up the clipping. "*Well, you can't believe everythang in them papers*."

"Now does this not beat all!" I say, trying not to laugh as I read, *"A Wig Hoax: an enterprising man in Augusta, Georgia, is said to have made a handsome profit selling gray wigs to young men hoping to avoid being called into the army."*

Everyone is laughing. Violet comes back with a tray and sets it down on the table, or rather slams it down on the table. Her action gains the attention of everyone in the room. She quickly turns and walks out.

I stand to my feet to go out and speak with her, but Sallie shakes her head. "Close the door, will you Lizzie," she whispers. "Ever since Harper has came back, the two of them are acting so strange. Violet has always been a gentle soul, but lately, I am afraid to leave the children in her care."

Betty Jo is listening carefully. "What about weapons, pistols or rifles?"

I open the door and walk down the hall to the closet where Papa kept his Enfield rifle. It is gone. On my way back to the parlor, I pass Violet in the hall and smile as if nothing is wrong.

"Who is watching the children?" I ask Sallie, as I shut the door.

"Violet is suppose to be."

"She is not, I just saw her walk out the back door."

In a panic, we both run through the house looking for the children. I give a sigh of relief when I see TJ, Minerva and Victoria are sitting at the end of the hall playing with their dolls. "Where is Noah and Robbie?" Sallie asks Minerva.

"They are going to ride Aunt Lizzie's horse," she answers calmly.

Sallie tells the children to stay put and we run out to the barn. We find the two little boys peeking through the stall looking at Bud. Sallie is angry and scolds them both. "Who told you boys you could come down here alone?"

"Nobody told us. We thought it up on our own!" Noah answers proudly. "We were going to ride old Bud to town and get some flour. Didn't you say you needed some flour Momma?"

Sallie was trying not to laugh, when she pulled him off the rail and gave him a pat on his little butt. "Yes, but I think you need to get on back in the house, please."

With the children corralled in, Mrs. Huneycutt announces it is getting late.

Hannah Jane agrees, stating she must get home to fix supper for her new husband, "That man just loves my biscuits."

There are hugs for the children and 'see you laters,' but the topic of the rifle must have been forgotten. Betty Jo lags behind. *"Lizzie, I spect you best lock the doors tonight. I'll be back first thang in the morning."*

I agree and she gives me a flat-handed slap on the back, which I respond to with "Ouch!" She grins and goes out the front door. I start down the hall mindless, without thinking about what she said.

The front door bursts open again. It's Betty Jo. *"Hey, what did I says bout's this door?"*

"All right, Betty Jo. Now go on, scat!" I push the door shut and lock it.

After the children are in bed, Sallie begins telling me about some of the odd things that have been happening. She says at first she did not think much of it when a little food here and there was missing. She figured Violet took extra for Harper, but now the flour barrel is empty. Can goods were missing and a large portion of the seeds we saved from last year's crops were gone. Before Sallie goes to her room, I promise to confront Harper and Violet first thing in the morning or as soon as Betty Jo arrives.

I am wishing for a hot bath and my legs are cut and bruised. Mother comes to mind; she always knew what I needed. Just like the night after the hog killing, she had a hot bath waiting for me. I recall her teasing me. "Lizzie, you have to clean up if you are going to sleep in this house tonight." Then a smile comes to my face, thinking about how mad she got that night when I told her Papa was in the barn drinking brandy.

It is just too hard without Mother and Papa. What I would give for Mother to draw me a bath or hear Papa laughing after a couple of good shots of brandy.

It is all gone, I think to myself, and walk over to the cabinet where Papa kept the brandy. "It is all gone," I say aloud and slam the door.

We are using candles as of late. There is no oil for the lamps. It is hard to see, but I gather up the newspapers and take them to my room. I am hoping to keep my eyes open long enough to read the headlines:

Pres. Lincoln celebrated his 56th birthday on Feb. 12, 1865.

Plot to Kill Lincoln- Thomas A. Clemmons arrested after confessing a plan to assassinate Pres. Lincoln. Same day- actor John Wilkes Booth was ejected from the Capital and questioned.

Scientist say during the period of the war-more rain fall than the past 200 years.

Negro troops enter the newly occupied city of Charleston joyously singing," John Brown's Body."

Union pushes the 13th amendment to be passed- freeing Negroes in the states that have seceded from the Union.

Detroit, Mich. proposing an amendment allowing Negroes to vote.

Anna Dickinson, famed spokeswoman, speaks in New York on female rights-to-vote and equal pay.

Confederate Spy- Belle Boyd is destitute, living in London England. Her husband, one-time federal officer turned Confederate, is captured and held in federal prison.

Newspapers curtailed as more Southern states are occupied by Federals.

Yankees and deserters pillage through empty homes in Atlanta and Charleston.

Sherman takes Cheraw, South Carolina

The South's gloom deepens- Food Shortage

The Union now occupies Fayetteville, Kinston, Goldsboro and Averasboro, in North Carolina.

Battle of Bentonville, North Carolina. Gen. Johnston and Sherman met on the battlefield for what may be the last time. Sherman now holds the upper hand and outnumbers the Confederates three to one. Among the casualties was General Hardee's only son, Willie, age 16, who was killed in cavalry charge.

No matter how far I run, the war seems to have followed me. Soon it will be on our doorsteps again. All I can do is pray.

....

Morning brings Betty Jo knocking at my bedroom door. I stumble to the door and let her in. She bursts in insisting I get dressed at once. "*Meet me downstairs and be ready to ride.*"

I waste no time getting myself downstairs. Sallie and Betty Jo are in the hall talking excitedly. Sallie looks as if she has been crying. "Oh Lizzie, it is so hard to believe. Violet was like family and now she and Harper have packed up and left!"

"Are you sure?" I ask.

"Go see for yourself!" Sallie shouts, pointing to the door.

Betty Jo follows me out back. The cabin door is jammed shut. We use our weight to push the door open and find it has been cleared out. The bed is stripped bare and only one pot hangs in the fireplace. Betty Jo holds her hand over the fire. *"Cold,"* she says. *"Ain't been no fire here all night. I seen some wagon tracks round back, reckon somebody stole your darkies?"*

"No, I don't think so, Betty Jo. I have a good idea what has happened. Let's go inside and talk with Sallie."

After talking to Sallie, I express my theory. "My guess is, while Harper was away working, he was approached by some abolitionists. He got an earful and has been planning ever since to run off."

"That makes sense to me," Sallie inputs. "Thinking back to yesterday, Violet slammed down that tray after she heard us talking about the Negro draft."

"I says we goes after them runaways!" Betty Jo says, jumping to her feet.

Sallie looks at me, "Lizzie, where do you think they will go?"

"I don't know Sallie. But I think they might try to take Cindy Lou with them too. Betty Jo, will you ride with me to Salisbury to Dr. Cotton's house?"

"You bet! Lizzie, the sooner we get on their trail the better. While you gets yourself ready, I'll saddle Bud and we'll be a waitin out front."

"Lizzie, if you don't find them, can we file a report?" Sallie asks.

"Sallie, I don't think it will do any good, not now. We will just have to make do without them. The sad thing is, we can make do better without them than they can without us."

"I think you are right, Lizzie. I feel sorry for them both, especially Violet, out there all alone."

We return home late that afternoon without Violet or Harper. Cindy Lou was quick to confess Violet had slipped in the back door at Dr. Cotton's house early that morning. Violet begged Cindy Lou to go with them. They were traveling with a band of Negroes back to the Charleston Islands. Cindy Lou told her she was content where she was and refused, but she cried knowing she may never see her sister again.

After Betty Jo leaves, the sadness fills my heart. Losing Harper and Violet is like another death in our family. We are now reduced to a household of two women and three children.

CHAPTER 14

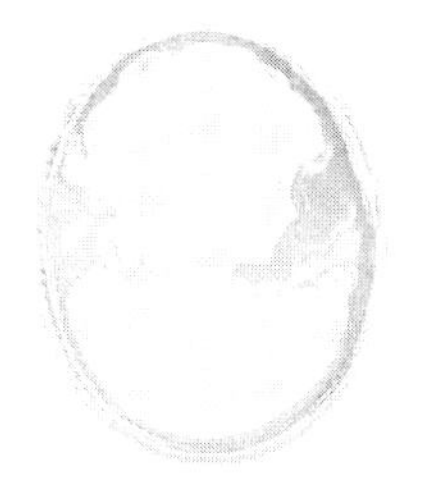

Amazing Grace

Sunday, April 9, 1865

Two weeks ago Betty Jo asked if she could take occupancy of Harper and Violet's abandoned cabin. Sallie and I saw no reason to refuse and every reason to consent. Betty Jo has proven to be worth her weight in gold. She is a good worker and friend. Sallie and I have grown to think of her as a sister.

I helped Betty Jo pack up her things. We loaded up her paper manufacturing business and set it up in our barn. Martha's original mission the day she came to see me was to find the girls a home. However, when we left that day she made us promise to visit often. Martha may appreciate her privacy again, but I think she will miss the girls.

Sallie says with Betty Jo nearby we can monitor her progress. Speaking of the lessons, it is evident we are making progress. Betty Jo will make quite an impression at church today. She is wearing a pretty blue dress with a white lace collar and her hair is nicely arranged. I compliment her and she tells me, *"Shuts your trap."*

I laugh, but as we climb up in the wagon, I realize we still have some work to do. She is wearing her dirty old boots and peeking from underneath her dress are her rolled up trousers. I say nothing about this, but I must demand she spit out the tobacco.

Sallie does not go with us today. After a few trips of taking all three children to church, we decide it is more pleasing to God and the congregation if we leave them at home. So now Sallie and I take turns going to church.

When we arrive at church, I am aware of the admiring looks Betty Jo is receiving, as we take our seats. When we sit down next to Aunt Martha and Hannah Jane, Betty Jo forgets and crosses her legs. I tap her on the knee discretely. She crosses her ankles and picks up her Bible.

Hannah Jane has graduated herself from the charm lessons, claiming she has a husband. The deal is sealed now that she is expecting a baby. When her Herman walks up to the pulpit to begin the sermon, she is all smiles.

I must say Herman Furr does preach a nice sermon. Although he is a nervous sort when engaging in normal conversations, he delivers his sermons with the utmost confidence. However, today he seems unprepared and fuddles with his papers. He looks at all of us, picks up an envelope and walks out to speak to us on the floor level.

Hannah Jane looks around at the reaction of the people. She looks at us and shrugs her shoulders. Herman's hands are trembling. He opens the envelope and takes out the letter. "Ladies and Gentleman, in lieu of the sermon I had prepared, I feel I must share with you the letter I received yesterday evening from my sister in Richmond.

Dear Herman,

It is with heavy heart that I write to you today. I wish I could spare you the agony of this sad, sad news, but you will hear it sooner than later. We heard there had been terrible fighting in Petersburg and Gen. Lee's Army was forced to retreat. As a precaution, Pres. Davis removed his wife and children from the capital over a month ago. Now it is clear. We along with Pres. Davis were holding on to false hope.

We were all aware of the warning signs, yet the events of April 2 came as a great shock. We were sitting in church next to Pres. Davis, when he received a telegram from General Lee. It read: I advise that all preparation be made for leaving Richmond tonight.

At once, Davis excuses himself and immediately issues orders for the Confederate government's evacuation. Soon the word spreads that we were sitting on the eve of our destruction.

Fires were set in front of the government offices to burn important documents; ships and ammunition were ordered to be destroyed. My husband was one of the men put in charge of burning tobacco, smashing bottles of liquor and pouring kegs of whiskey down the drains. Some People tried to stop him, but were quickly discouraged when he reminded them of what a bunch of drunken Union soldiers did in Columbia.

Government orders were for nothing to fall into the enemie's hands. All food and provisions held by the speculators and shop owners must be destroyed. In the people's mind, this would be short orders for we are all barefoot and near starvation. Words cannot explain the rage the people felt when the doors were busted down and they discovered much needed provisions, food, meat and clothing stored inside. Now it was all to be burned as Richmond starves. I say damn those hoarders and their plans to make big profits. I think you will agree it is the devil who will profit from their souls.

It became more maddening after that. Folks were going in all direction trying to vacate the city and grabbing up food and provisions. I must admit to you, dear brother, my husband brought home a small ham. It was the best I have ever eaten. The looting was soon brought to a halt when the arsenal exploded, bursting out windows, overturning tombstones, and tearing doors off their very hinges.

Pres. Davis left that night on the eleven o'clock train. He was one of the last government officials to leave. My husband said he was openly weeping. I can only imagine what a tragic sight this was for him to watch out his window.

The wind continued to spread the fires across the city. By morning, it was reported that approximately fifty blocks had burned. Around seven o'clock, Monday morning, the Union Cavalry arrived; by eight o'clock, the Union flag was flying over the capitol building. The Federals were ordered to put out the fires. Around five o'clock, most of the fires were out and Richmond lay simmering under a dark cloud of despair.

On Tuesday morning, President Lincoln arrived. Brother, it was the eeriest sight I have ever laid my eyes on. Right out in plain view, the Union Cavalry escorted Lincoln down the street to the steps of the executive mansion. The streets were dead silent as thousands of people watched from their windows. Perhaps we were all waiting to see who would plant a bullet in Lincoln's head. Anyone could have done so, even myself.

After his visit there, he set about a sightseeing tour of what was left of our fair city. On the noon hour, a one-hundred-gun artillery salute was fired at all military posts, arsenals and naval bases to proclaim their victory. To the citizens of Richmond, this meant all hope has died.

As to what is in store for the Southern people, I do not know. I must say there is peace here, knowing the struggle is at last over. We must now pray for God to give us guidance to make amends with our fellow countrymen. In God's almighty hands, I place you and your little bride's fate,

Love,
Emily

Herman's eyes are wet with tears as he faces the congregation. "Let us pray," he says in a voice just over a whisper. The church echoes with the sounds of those sobbing at their seats. Herman looks out at his people. He cannot bring himself to pray. His words are lost. He sits down at the altar, cradles his head in his hands and cries. Hannah Jane whispers something to Betty Jo. She looks at her and shakes her head, but Hannah Jane's eyes are pleading. Betty Jo reluctantly follows her to the front of the church. Hannah Jane places her hand on her weeping husband's shoulder. Then as if it has been rehearsed, they begin singing 'Amazing Grace.' I have never heard and most likely never shall hear such fine harmony.

Hannah Jane saved her husband and restored the faith of everyone sitting in the pews. I think back about my statement, "Hannah Jane is not your typical preacher's wife and poor Herman has no idea." No, she is everything but typical and Herman had a good idea just what he was doing.

The members of the church left in a somber mood talking softly among themselves. Betty Jo and I climbed up the carriage to ride home. I allowed some time to pass before I asked, "Now adding to your string of mysteries, who taught the two of you to sing?"

She smiles at me through misty eyes and answer, "Maw."

She changes the subject to our plans to finish the garden. She continued to talk most of the way home about the plow and equipment. My mind was not on her words. I was thinking about Joel. Would he be coming home soon?

....

Tuesday, April 11, 1865

None of us had ever operated a plow. We are relying on Betty Jo's first-hand experience watching her Pa. She said he always said it was important to break in the horse. We put the collar on Bud on Monday and although he pulled the plow around the field, the training was a bit shaky.

Betty Jo claims it will not be much to it and between the three of us we should be able to plow up the whole field by suppertime. Sallie is not fond of the idea, but has agreed to pull her time behind the plow.

When Sallie comes down wearing a pair of Papa's old pants, the children fall on the floor laughing. She has the pants pulled up under her bosom and tied up with a rope. Her hair is knotted on top of her head with a few strands flipping around like a rooster comb. Even Victoria finds this an amusing sight.

We have our day planned. We start across the lot toward the field with three happy little children and a picnic basket. Sallie spreads a quilt on the ground beneath the big oak tree and settles down with the children.

Betty Jo and I have the job of hooking up the horse to the plow. With some struggle and a few scuffed knuckles, we are successful in hooking Bud to the turning plow. I lead Bud and Betty Jo guides the plow out on the field. When Sallie and the children see us out on the field, they begin to cheer and clap their hands. Betty Jo and I take a bow and the procedure starts.

I begin walking backwards leading Bud as near as I can in a straight line. Betty Jo is struggling to keep the plow in the ground. The earth is dry and the field is mostly red clay. The plow is bouncing over the ground like skipping a stone across the river.

It takes us almost an hour to plow the first row and when we look back, it is as crooked as a snake. "Who says the rows have to be straight?" Betty Jo asks.

"I don't know. We don't have to do ours like everyone else. The main thing is that we get the seeds planted," I answer her, and we agree to trade jobs.

It is a warm morning for this time of year and sweat is pouring off Betty Jo's face.

I take hold of the plow and Betty Jo, the lead. I now know why she was sweating. It takes every ounce of strength in my body to guide the plow across the field. Once we complete our second row, we stop to take a break.

I whisper to Betty Jo, "I think a little more weight on the end of that plow might make the going easier. This might be the job for Miss Sallie."

"You better not let her hear you say that," Betty Jo laughs.

We join Sallie by laying flat on our backs on the cool grass. Victoria sees this as a grand opportunity to play and begins climbing up and down my frame. "You're turn, Miss Sallie," I announce.

Noah and Minerva follow Sallie and me out on the field, leaving Betty Jo with the task of trying to hold on to a now screaming Victoria.

Sallie takes hold of the plow and I begin to lead Bud. She says it is jarring her teeth loose and lets go on her first try. "You have got to put your weight into it," I explain.

With a look of disgust, she gives it a second try and we achieve success. We plow the first row and the children follow along behind us singing. They are barefooted, but now it looks like they are wearing little red clay boots. Despite my rude joke, Sallie is doing a good job. She is managing to hold the plow straighter and the work is going a little easier.

I look up and see Betty Jo standing up with Victoria on her hip. She is peering down the road as if someone is approaching. Soon we see Mr. and Mrs. Huneycutt have arrived. The children run off to meet them and Sallie accidentally lets go of the plow. Bud seizes the opportunity to take off for the barn with the plow dangling behind him.

Sallie and I take off running trying to catch Bud. He suddenly turns and starts back toward us. Fearing we may be trampled, we turn and run in the opposite direction.

Soon we see Betty Jo has handed over the care of the children to Mrs. Huneycutt and runs out on the field to help stop Bud. "Spread out!" she shouts.

With Sallie on one side of the field and Betty Jo on the other, Bud stops in the middle of the field. In just 10 minutes, he has destroyed our day's work. I walk slowly toward him. He is snorting and kicking his feet, but he does not attempt to run. He allows me to take hold of the reign and walk him back toward the barn.

"Enough of this today!" I call out to Sallie and Betty Jo.

We are three exhausted women and we agree. Sallie goes to see what is the nature of the Huneycutt's visit and Betty Jo and I unhook the plow and put up the horse.

When we come up over the hill, everyone has gone inside. Betty Jo and I pull off our dirty boots and walk barefoot through the house. We freeze in the hall hearing Sallie crying. Betty Jo catches my arm. "Ransom?"

Slowly we walk to the door of the parlor. My instincts tell me it is not Ransom. From experience, I know Mr. and Mrs. Huneycutt would not have come alone to deliver that kind of news. Sallie looks up at me. "Lizzie, General Lee has surrendered!"

CHAPTER 15

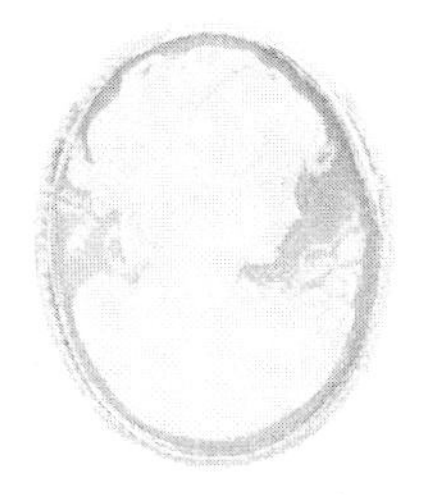

Do You Smell Smoke?

April 12, 1865

After General Lee's surrender at Appomattox Courthouse on April 9, everyone in Stanly County is anxiously hoping to see their loved ones at the door. Sallie is the worst of them all. These past three days, she has been on a rampage to clean the house and get things in order for Ransom's return. I have tried reasoning and begged her to lay down the broom and get back behind the plow. This morning it is the same old argument.

Today she and the children are wearing their Sunday best. Betty Jo comes in the back door to have breakfast, takes one look at her and starts laughing. "*Sallie, I have rode with them soldiers and I can tell you how they think. Ransom ain't goin give a cow's tit about how you look or even how you smell when he gets home. He is goin take you back in that there bedroom and get his last four years out of you. Then he is goin to sleep fer about twenty-four hours. When he wakes up, he is goin to want to eat. If you want to impress him, show him you can put dem vittles on the table.*"

Sallie's eyes widen. "So you think it will be in that order, do you?"

"Pretty darn sure of it," she says, winking at me.

We laugh. The children are sitting at the table and they start laughing too, even though they have no idea why. Innocently, Noah thinks he can make a joke too, and mocks Betty Jo. *"Pretty darn sure of it."*

Betty Jo doubles over laughing. Sallie yanks off her apron and stomps upstairs. While I finish feeding the children, Betty Jo tells me she must go to Salisbury to pick up mail and make the delivers to her paper customers.

On Betty Jo's way out, she says she will help me hook up Bud. When we step outside, she stops and looks up at the sky. "Do you smell smoke?"

I take a deep breath, "No, I don't think so."

She stands still and looks off in the distance for a few seconds. As we walk toward the barn an uneasy feeling comes over me. I would like to ask Betty Jo not to go today, but there is no need to say anything. Betty Jo is an independent sort and she will do as she pleases.

Bud neighs at us when we walk in the barn. "I think he is getting used to his labor, don't you Betty Jo?"

"I spect so. It is better than being shut up in the barn all day." Since we only have enough seeds for one field, Betty Jo agrees I can finish up on my own.

It is almost noon before I see Sallie and the children. She spreads out the quilt on the ground in the usual spot. Then she comes to the edge of the field and waves at me. "I have some lunch for you, sister!"

I have long been without my breakfast and Bud and I both could use a break.

When I join her, she is in a pleasant mood. I am thankful to see she has come dressed prepared to work.

She hands me a boiled egg, a fried potato pancake and a jar of water. "Enjoy sister," she says. "This is the last of the potatoes."

I look at her sincerely. I know what she means by the last potato. We are running out of food. The Yankee's visit cost us all our soup and Violet and Harper stole a large portion of our reserves.

I unwrap the potato pancake and Victoria reaches for it. I break off a bite for her and her greedy little hands reach for more. Minerva and Noah look away, but I know they would like some too. Sallie sees me divide the cake in three pieces and shakes her head, "No Lizzie, you eat it."

She is too late. I have already doled it out to the three little eaters. However, when I take out the boiled egg they do not beg for it. We are all sick of boiled eggs. I gulp down the jar of water, hoping it will fill the balance of my empty stomach. Sallie gives me a sad smile. We have grown accustomed to our insides nagging at us.

I stand to my feet and stretch out my back. "Shall we, my dear?" I ask, flirting with Sallie.

"The pleasure is all mine," she replies, standing to take my hand.

We begin dancing across the yard as Sallie sings. The children are delighted. It is these little distractions that help us keep our sanity. We instruct the children not to get out of sight and Minerva is to mind Victoria.

Sallie and I have only made one sweep across the field, when a horsefly bites me on the neck. "Damn," I say, giving it a swat. It is then I look up and see Sallie's children have climbed up in the tree. Victoria is nowhere in sight. I wave at Sallie and we turn and run, leaving Bud standing alone in the field.

"Get down out of that tree!" Sallie screams. As they are scrambling to the ground, Sallie demands to know where is Victoria.

"She was right here a minute ago," Noah cries.

Scanning over the landscape I scream "Victoria!" at the top of my lungs.

All three of us are in a panic looking for her and we fear the worst. "I see her!" Noah shouts and starts running toward her.

"Wait Noah, stop where you are," I caution him. My heart skips a beat seeing Victoria has climbed up on the ledge of the old well. She is leaning down looking in the hole. I do not dare call her name for fear I will startle her and cause her to fall in. Sallie holds back the children and slowly, without making a sound, I approach from behind and with one quick stroke I pull her into my arms. As soon as Sallie sees she is safe, she exchanges only a few words with her children and gives them both a spanking.

Now with Victoria on my hip and Sallie's two following behind her, we resume our job. Poor Bud is waiting patiently in the field. I give him a pat on the nose and close my eyes for one quick second.

> *Dear Lord, forgive me. I damned the horsefly. Yet, without doubt, you sent it to warn me Victoria was in danger. May I never again curse your creatures.*

Sallie calls out to me. "Before this day ends, that old well is going to be boarded shut."

"Amen to that sister, amen."

We had much to be thankful for that evening. While boarding up the well, we discovered a patch of tender poke salad, Sallie's children had not fallen out of the tree, Victoria was safe and last but not least, the plowing was done!

Long after the children had gone to bed, Sallie and I wait up for Betty Jo to come home. The only sound in the house is the ticking of the clock and Sallie's knitting needles clicking together. "Perhaps she decided to spend the night at Martha's," Sallie resolves.

"Sallie, if that was her plan, it looks like she would have said so."

"I bet she stopped off to visit and it just got late on her," Sallie says reassuring. "Lizzie, what time tomorrow are you to meet that Dr. Teeter about Joel's horses?"

"His letter said he would arrive at Joel's house around four in the afternoon. I was planning on Betty Jo going with me."

"She will be home by then, I am sure. I don't think we have much to worry about. Betty Jo can take care of herself." Sallie stands up and yawns, "Time for bed, Lizzie. Don't forget to lock the door."

Even though I know she is most likely right, I am still worried. I blow out the candle and look out the window one last time. No sign of Betty Jo and the cabin is dark.

....

April 13, 1865

"Morning, Sallie. No Betty Jo."

"Lizzie, did you check the cabin? Maybe she is sleeping."

"Yes I did. She has been gone all night. I suppose I will have to go alone to meet Dr. Teeter. Sallie, Betty Jo knew I was depending on her to go with me today. This is not like her. I am really starting to worry."

"If it will ease your mind, why don't you stop at Martha's on your way to Joel's?

"Good idea."

With another stop on my route, I will be on the road shortly. Sometimes I feel guilty leaving Sallie to care for Victoria. She never seems to mind, nor does Victoria. Hurrying up the steps, I am plagued with a twinge of jealousy. Victoria may not care or even know who is her real mother.

I debate on how I will travel to meet Dr. Teeter. If I go on horseback, it will insure I will arrive on time. However, if I present myself wearing trousers with tousled hair, I will surely appear more common. Papa always said it is best to be a little aloof in business affairs. Taking the carriage is the best option, even if I have to be mindful of my time.

Looking over my pitiful wardrobe, I select the green traveling suit I wore on the train when I came to North Carolina. It is faded and because of a repair, I am forced to wear the skirt backwards. I dress and stand in front of the mirror. Not bad with all things considered.

I find it is good therapy for my nerves anytime I have the opportunity to travel down these country roads, just listening to the horse's hooves. Today, I do not relax and I am unable to shake the worrisome feelings.

To lift the dark cloud hanging over my head, I begin singing a few hymns. It is somewhat helpful. I reason with myself Martha will surely be able to put my mind at ease about Betty Jo.

When I arrive at Martha's, I see there is a carriage pulled up in front. I secure my rig behind the first one and go to the door and knock. After a few minutes Martha opens. "Lizzie, nice to see you," she says, looking over my shoulder. "Betty Jo with you?"

"No, Martha. Actually, that is why I am here. I was hoping you have heard from her. She went to Salisbury yesterday morning and we have not seen her since."

The door opens wider and she motions for me to enter. "Lizzie, follow me in the parlor," she says, concerned.

Once I enter the room, I see two elderly men juggling cups of tea in their hands.

"Lizzie, allow me to introduce my brothers, James and Charles," she says, pulling out a chair for me to sit.

James is obviously more youthful of the two as Charles is bent over and feeble in appearance. Nevertheless, they both stand to their feet and shake my hand.

"I am afraid my brothers have come to deliver some very disturbing news. Now with what you tell of Betty Jo, I find it even more upsetting." She sits down next to James. He gathers up her hand in his.

In a soft raspy voice, Charles turns to me, "When we got word that Stoneman's Raiders were heading toward Salisbury, some of the folks packed up and headed South toward Gold Hill. The Confederate troop's orders were to load up supplies and get on the next train out of Salisbury.

The remainder of us men tried to form up, but the best we could raise was a sad lot of sickly soldiers, a few recruits from the federal prison, young boys and old men like myself. I reckon it was about daylight when we heard the first guns. In no time, they were on us like flies, thousands of Yankees coming from all directions.

It would have been pure suicide for our pitiful army to go up against them. Surrender was the only option. As the Confederates tried to escape, the Yankee Calvary raced down the streets at breakneck speed in pursuit. In the midst of the flying missiles, the cursing and yelling, the Mayor stood right out front of the hotel. He held up the flag of truce, only to have a Yankee whip out his sword and cut right though it. They later set fire to most of the government buildings. As to what all has been destroyed, I expect we will not know until the smoke clears.

The balance of the day, Union soldiers went from house to house busting down doors. When they came to my house, they held my poor wife back as they pillaged through our drawers, closets and pantries. I cannot tell you how degrading it was knowing all I could do was stand there and let them carry off our food, liquor and the few valuables we had left. Dr. Cotton and a long list of citizens were arrested and held prisoner for the day.

Stoneman's Raiders set up camp that night down by Murphy's woods, but none of the citizens slept that night, fearing what else might happen. This morning, about four blocks of military and civilian supplies were laid out on the streets and set afire. It was a sad sight seeing people rumbling among the fires hoping to carry off what they could.

Lastly, the Yankees exploded the magazine as they rode out of town. But the joke is on them if they think they hurt our feelings when they burned down the prison compound. Best I could tell as I rode by it this afternoon, all that is left is one big pile of stinking ashes."

"Any casualties?" I ask, hoping not to hear Betty Jo's name mentioned.

"Captain MacNeely is the only name I have heard so far. I guess we should consider ourselves fortunate, in comparison to Columbia."

I hear the clock strike and I turn to look at the time. "Oh Lordy, I must be on my way. I have a business meeting and now I fear I may be late."

Lizzie, please reconsider and go straight home. I don't

know who you are to meet today, but your party surely will be understanding," Martha pleads.

"Oh, yes indeed, Miss Lizzie, do go straight home," mocks Charles. "It is too dangerous for a woman traveling alone with no protection."

"Oh, I have protection," I say, patting my pistol in my purse.

Martha walks me to the door with a heavy look of distress on her face. "If I hear from Betty Jo, I will tell her you stopped by. Now hurry on. Make sure you are home before dark."

Once I am on the road to Joel's, I take out my pistol and place it on the seat next to me. Now that I have heard the news about Salisbury, I can only hope that Betty Jo had the good sense to spend the night at one of her customer's homes. However, I know her. She was more likely right in the middle of the fight. At least Charles did not mention her name.

I have only been to Joel's a couple of times and I slow down being careful to not miss the drive. I spy a large dogwood tree and a small overturned wooden sign reading "Simpson."

"This is it," I say, pulling back on the reigns to turn Bud down the drive. I recall the house being a fair distance off the road. Most of the houses are wooden in Stanly County, but Joel's house is stone. He told me he had the stone hauled down from the Uwharrie mountains. On my left is a pond covered in water lilies. Bud halts and I allow him to stop for a drink. I am early enough, so I get out to stretch my legs and comb my hair before I meet Dr. Teeter. Over my head, I see a shadow. I duck down in fear as a large screech owl comes in for landing by the pond just in front of me. He takes a quick drink, turns and looks directly at me.

How odd. Mammy always said seeing a creature doing something against its nature is an omen or warning. I cannot recall ever seeing an owl in the daylight hours. I slowly walk toward the bird. The owl turns his head from side to side as I approach. I am almost certain he is going to allow me to touch him, but he takes flight and circles the pond several times before he disappears into the trees. It is a mystifying sight and I am ill at ease as I approach Joel's house.

The house sets up on a hill and reminds me of an English cottage one might see in a painting. The grounds are badly in need of attention, but scattered here and there are daffodils and spring flowers in bloom. Some of the grasses are nearly as tall as the carriage and are intertwining in the spokes of the wheels.

When I pull up in front of the house there are two horses tied to the front railing.

Odd, I was only expecting to meet with Dr. Teeter. Perhaps he has a traveling companion.

When I step up on the porch, I recognize one of the saddles. It is engraved with Joel's brand. Joel must be home! Almost too nervous to walk, I step in the house through the partially opened door, fully expecting to see Joel standing there smiling at me.

Instead, the house is bare and the furniture is still covered up. I walk across the keeping room, hearing my heels hit the plank floor and echo across the room. The bedroom off the hall is undisturbed, but the dining room drawers are standing opened.

There is a soft low vibration, but I am not sure if it is voices. Walking back in the hall, I elect to take the stairs. But first, I pull out my pistol.

I am halfway up the stairs when suddenly a man steps

out on the landing. He is dressed in a ragged uniform. I do not have to reason. He has a bundle under his arm. He is looting. "Well, so nice for you to visit, young lady," he calls out to me, with a smile of evil intentions.

It is at this split second I must make the decision. Shall I raise my pistol and take this man's life? From somewhere inside my head a voice calls out to me, "Pull the trigger!" I raise and point my pistol at the man. When I see the fear in his eyes, I hesitate and start backing down the stairs. I am ever so careful to keep my pistol pointed directly at him with my finger on the trigger.

Just as I make it to the bottom of the stairs, I hear the door open behind me. The intruder's eyes leave my face and there is an explosion. I fall against the stair rail. I feel something hot running down my back. I can hear men's voices, but I cannot see their faces. The room begins to spin and I collapse on the hard wooden floor. I try to lift myself off the floor and submerge my hand in red sticky liquid. I think to myself, "get up you fool and run." Still my body lays helpless on the floor. I try to scream out. "I have been shot!" but I cannot. I feel my pistol and my purse being lifted from my hand. The door closes behind me and the room grows dark.

CHAPTER 16

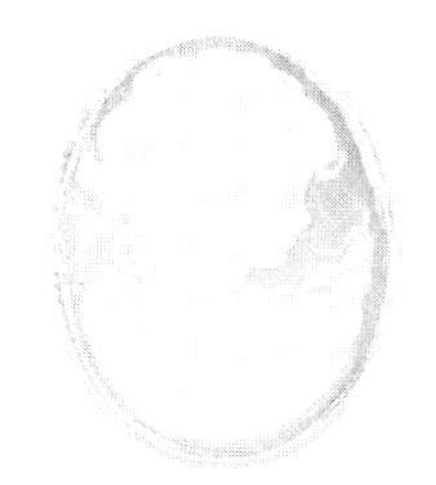

A Bouquet of Black-Eyed Susans

Looking back to the morning of April 12, Betty Jo had detected the smoke and the thunder of distant explosions almost as soon as she left home. Even with her short stint in the army, there are some sights and sounds that never leave the mind. She knew the city of Salisbury was under attack.

Her intended stop was the Post Office, but once she approached the city she realized this would be impossible. She loaded her pistol and took the back streets to Dr. Cotton's house. It was then she learned both Dr. Cotton and Dr. John had been arrested. Feeling that Mrs. Cotton and Cindy Lou needed her, she spent the night.

The next day when the Federals rode out, she left Salisbury, planning to check on Martha before returning to Sallie's. She arrives there shortly after Lizzie had left to go to Joel's. In the excitement, she had forgotten about promising to ride with Lizzie to meet Dr. Teeter. If she hurried, she could meet her there and then follow her home.

When Betty Jo arrives at Joel's house, it is just past four o'clock. There are a number of horse tracks, but only Lizzie's rig is parked out front. She ties up her horse, walks up on the porch and knocks. There is no answer. She knocks again and the unlocked door pushes open. *"Hello,"* she calls out. *"Liz, is you in dar?"*

Fearing something may be wrong, she cautiously enters the house uninvited. She sees Lizzie lying on the floor in a pool of blood and kneels down beside her. Within seconds she discovers she has been shot in the back. Betty Jo begins frantically calling out Lizzie's name and praying *"Dear God in heaven help me!"*

"Pressure, apply pressure," she recalls the field doctor saying. "You must stop the bleeding." Mimicking only what she has seen, she doubles her hands and presses against the wound. By the grace of God the bleeding stops.

The front door is standing wide open and she sees two men riding up. Even though Betty Jo fears it might be the gunmen returning, she is more afraid to lift her hands and allow Lizzie to bleed to death. She looks around the room, thinking about pulling Lizzie out of sight, but the men have already dismounted. She hears them talking as they walk up on the porch. Keeping one hand on the wound, she reaches under her jacket and tries to reach her pistol, it is too late.

"Stands back, I have a pistol!" Betty Jo warns.

"What in God's name has happened here!" shouts the younger of the two men.

"I am a warning yous, I am a gettin this girl out of here to a doctor and if you try to stop me I will fill you both full of holes."

"I am a doctor; please let me help!" says the other man.

"Dr. Teeter?" Betty Jo asks.

He does not answer, but drops to his knees to examine Lizzie. He lays his head to her chest and then calls out, "Joel, go get my bag!"

Joel returns with the bag and Dr. Teeter begins to work on the wound. "It is pretty serious Joel, but I don't think it has hit any major organs and her breathing is pretty stable. I need to get this bullet out and stop the bleeding. Help me lift her up and we can lay her out on the table."

The two cradle Lizzie's frail body and she begins to gasp for air. Her eyes open and she looks briefly at the man holding her head. In a weak voice she whispers "Joel."

"Yes, darling, I am here. You are going to be just fine," he answers, as the sweat drips from his handsome face.

She lifts her hand and attempts to stroke his face, but her eyes close and her hand drops limp.

"Lizzie!" Joel calls out in terror.

"She's in shock, Joel. Don't try to bring her to. She is best unconscious, at least until I get this bullet out of her."

Dr. Teeter says he will need some boiling water and clean sheets. Joel gives Betty Jo instructions and he goes to heat the water. Within a few minutes, Betty Jo returns with the sheets. As she enters the dining room, she sees Dr. Teeter close up his medical bag. She stops cold in the door-way and begins to weep. Joel comes running and Dr. Teeter turns his back to Lizzie's half-naked body lying silently on the table.

"I have done all I can do." he says. "It is a miracle the bullet did not hit her spinal cord" Here it is," he says, extending his hand flat, revealing a small bullet. "It looks like it was hand forged; my guess made at the prison. If it had been a .44-caliber bullet, it would be a different story altogether. I am afraid she has lost an awful lot of blood. Even so, the odds are good she will recover. We must be careful infection does not set in and that she gets plenty of rest. I have given her something to help her sleep. Where shall we take her?"

Joel motions to the bedroom across the hall and Dr. Teeter looks back at Lizzie on the table. He smiles at Betty Jo. "I told you I needed some clean sheets. Go get the bed ready while I dress the wound."

"Well what bouts the hot water?" she asks.

"Pour it on the stain on the rug," he says, giving Betty Jo a tender pat on the shoulder.

Then Dr. Teeter asks, "Joel, you got a nightshirt we can dress the girl in? Might as well do away with this dress."

After Betty Jo prepares the room, Joel and Dr. Teeter lay Lizzie out on the bed.

Joel hands Betty Jo the nightshirt and turns to leave the room.

"Where you goin, you's best help me," Betty Jo, says sternly.

"I...it don't seem right," he replies.

"Well, I bets she ain't worried bouts her modesty. Help me gets her undressed," Betty Jo demands.

Joel walks over to the bed and gently raises Lizzie's shoulders. Betty Jo lifts the bloody chemise over Lizzie's head, exposing her bare breast. Betty Jo expects Joel to turn his head, but he does not.

Once the patient is resting comfortably, Dr. Teeter asks, "Joel, you got any liquor in this house?"

"I might if those scallywags did not take it," he says, as he walks across the room and opens a cabinet. A bottle of whiskey is setting on the shelf. He pulls the sheets off the furniture and we all sit down. Joel pours a glass for Dr. Teeter and one for Betty Jo, but she shakes her head. Joel downs the glass himself.

"I spects someone ought to go let Sallie know what has happen," Betty Jo announces.

"Yes, I am sure she will be worried," Joel says. "I suppose I will ride over there now." He looks across the hall at the bed where Lizzie lays.

Dr. Teeter says, "These first 24 hours are crucial. I'll stay with her tonight, but you need to arrange for someone to sit with her for the next week or so."

Betty Jo stands to her feet. *"No, Joel. You stay here and I will go to Sallie's. I'll be back first thang in the mornin, prepared to sit nurse with her."*

Dr. Teeter looks at Joel. "If she is awake tomorrow she will be asking to go home. They always do. Joel, you will have to be the judge of that, but I would not move her until she can at least sit up on her own."

Joel smiles. "Dr. Teeter, she is home. This is the girl I was telling you about, the one I plan to marry."

Betty Jo nods at the two men and exits the door. Once she is outside, she is slow to mount her horse. She stops and kneels down on the ground and looks closely at the tracks left by the horses of the gunmen. She rides off, looking down at the road. She heads north, away from the direction of Sallie's house. She has a good idea the men who shot Lizzie might have escaped from the Federal prison. They will be looking for a place to camp.

After riding for less than an hour, she sees a small campfire down by the creek bed. Two men are busy bathing themselves and their clothes lay on the bank. Betty Jo ties off her horse, takes out her pistol and creeps down through the woods.

They are clearly in her view, but they cannot see her for the underbrush. One of the men steps out of the water exposing his gaunt naked body and calls out to the other man. "I sure wish you had not killed that gal. She was easy on the eyes and we could have at least got some good out of her. "

The man in the water comes splashing out of the creek, "If you want her, go back and get her. She'll be just as good dead." He walks over to the bank, takes a drink of whiskey and passes the bottle on to the other man.

Betty Jo watches as he takes something out of a bundle off the ground. It is Lizzie's purse. He hooks it over his arm and begins prancing around naked. "Look at me, I am a Southern Belle."

Now the only question in Betty Jo's mind is, are the men deserters or Yankees? Either way, they are thieves and murderers.

The two drunken men are laughing without the slightest knowledge they are being watched. "Fools," Betty Jo says under her breath, as the first bullet leaves her pistol.

....

April 14, 1865

The next morning Betty Jo is slow to arrive at Joel's house with two other horses in tow. The doctor and Joel are sitting on the front porch. It is a warm sunny morning and the front door to the house is standing open.

Joel calls out to her. "Where did you come by the horses?"

Betty Jo does not answer his question, but calls out *"How do. Hungry? Miss Sallie sent over a cake of cornbread and a jar of molasses."*

She slips down off her horse and opens up her saddlebag. First, she sets down the jar of molasses and the cornbread on the edge of the porch. Then she turns back to her horse and tosses a large bundle on the porch next to Joel's feet. She goes back for another bundle. *"How's Liz?"* she asks.

"Her vital signs are stable, but she has not yet regained full consciousness," the doctor responds.

Betty Jo drops the second bundle and looks directly at Dr. Teeter *"Bad or good?"*

"She is responding as I would have expected. No signs of infection or fever. Her body needs time to recover. Sleep is the best thing. I suspect by this afternoon, she should be coming around."

"Sleep," Betty Jo comments, shaking her head. She begins to open up the bundles and Joel stands to his feet with a look of question on his face.

"Recognize any of this?" Betty Jo asks.

Joel squats down next to the bundles. "Yes, most of it is mine."

Betty Jo picks up Lizzie's purse and places her pistol back inside. "*Yep, I don't take too kindly to thieves and murderers*."

"Betty Jo did you...?" Joel starts to inquire, but Betty Jo interrupts him.

"Let's just say when I fired into them, they took off a runnin through the woods like shit runnin out of a goose."

The two men are speechless as they watch Betty Jo sorting through the bundle of items on the blanket.

"Hey, is that coffee in that can?" Dr. Teeter asks.

Betty Jo opens it up and smells it. *"I do believe so,"* she says smiling.

"Well, what are you waiting for. Put a pot on for us." Dr. Teeter says.

They enjoy the muddy coffee and the cornbread. Afterwards, Dr. Teeter prepares to leave, giving instructions for Lizzie's care. He suggests we attempt to wake her this afternoon. If she is in much pain, we are to give her the laudanum he left for her. He and his sons will be back on Tuesday the 18th to pick up the horses he purchased from Joel. He expects to see Lizzie sitting up and eating. If anything seems out of the ordinary, we are to send for him.

Betty Jo agrees to sit with Lizzie for the balance of the day. This will allow Joel to start on his own garden. Around the noon hour, Joel knocks and brings Betty Jo some beans and dried bread. He sits down in the chair next to her, but his eyes are on Lizzie. After a few minutes, he begins to speak. "I was up there at Appomattox with Lee when he surrendered. We were all doled out some seeds, corn and food rations. Our orders were to take nothing but our personal property, get on our horses and go home."

"Just like that the war is over?" Betty Jo asks.

"Oh, it is not over yet, but it will be soon. There are still some skirmishes going on. You just cannot put out a fuse like this with one blow. General Johnston has not officially surrendered yet, but he will. He has no choice."

Before either of them could say more, Lizzie begins to stir. Her eyes flutter and she moans. Joel jumps up, takes her hand and strokes her head. "Lizzie, can you hear me?" Her eyes open and she tries to speak, but within minutes her eyes close again. "Do you think we should at least try to get some water in her?" Joel asks.

"*I spect so,*" Betty Jo answers.

Joel leaves the room and returns with a ladle filled with fresh water. He sits down on the bed next to her. "Lizzie," he calls, gently shaking her arm. Her eyes open and she squints at them as if she does not know them. "Please take some water," he says gently, lifting her head, putting the ladle to her lips. She takes most of the water, but she soon chokes and begins to cough. Joel lowers her head and her eyes close again. "At least that is something," he says. "We need to keep forcing water and by tomorrow, maybe a little soup."

When evening begins to fall, Joel insists Betty Jo go home and rest for the night. Betty Jo is hesitant, but she agrees. Sallie will want an update.

Shortly, Betty Jo is on the road home. Being a backwoods girl, it did not take her long after moving to Stanly County to learn all the shortcuts. If she cuts through the woods and follows Bear Creek, it will take at least a half hour off her travel time. She weighs out the situation. She figures most people would not risk being off the main road these days, but again she is not like most folks.

Her ride is uneventful. She reaches the narrow end of the creek and is just about to cross over when a horse comes flying up behind her. Not knowing the rider's intentions, she makes sure her pistol is in reach. A voice calls out from behind. "Hey there soldier, heading home?"

Betty Jo realizes the rider has mistaken her for a soldier. Her hair is stuffed up in her hat and she is wearing her old army coat. She is cautious not to reveal her identity and answers in a deep voice, *"Yep, headin home,"* and cuts across the creek.

The man crosses the creek and shouts out, "Hey fellow, are you in a hurry to get home too?"

Betty Jo does not look up and urges her horse to speed up.

"Wait, we can ride in together," he says, speeding up alongside of Betty Jo. "What regiment are you with?" he asks.

The voice sounds familiar and Betty Jo gives him a sideways glance. It is Thomas! She wonders how in this great big wide world their paths have crossed again." Fearing he will recognize her too, she kicks the side of her horse and takes off with breakneck speed toward Sallie's. Thankfully, he does not try to follow her.

....

April 15, 1865

The next morning Betty Jo is preparing to return to Joel's to sit with Lizzie.

Betty Jo is understanding that Sallie is anxious to see her sister. She agrees to go to the Huneycutts to arrange for them to tend to the children. Even though it is a short ride, it will delay her. She is worried Joel will need her.

Betty Jo does not wait for breakfast, but jumps on her horse and wastes no time. If they agree to keep the children, she will then go back home and wait with Sallie for the Huneycutts to come for the children.

When she knocks on their front door, she is hoping they will be able to leave immediately. After several attempts, she is unable to get anyone at the front door.

Thinking they may be around back or in the barn, she walks around the house.

As she comes around the house, she sees a shirtless young man bent over working on the plow. His back is turned and he is unaware she is watching. "Dang old hunk of rusty metal," he says, giving the plow a sharp kick.

Betty Jo stops dead in her tracks. Suddenly he turns around and Betty Jo finds herself face to face with Thomas. "Betty Jo?" he asks, softly in disbelief.

"What are you doing here?" she asks.

"I live here!" he says in a defensive tone. "Huneycutt, you know, Thomas Huneycutt. Did you forget my name so soon?" he says, giving her a flirtatious smile. He throws down his hammer and moves toward her. "Well, I sure ain't forgotten about you," he says in a soft seductive voice.

"Oh, fer sure I ain't forgot how you ratted me out. You low down son-of-a bit..."

Thomas interrupts her. "Betty Jo, you know it was for your own good. A battlefield is no place for a woman."

Betty Jo spins around and nearly knocks Mrs. Huneycutt flat on her face.

"Hey there girl," Mrs. Huneycutt says, putting her hands up to protect herself.

"Mrs. Huneycutt, I have come on the behalf of Sallie to ask if you will come get the children while we go sit with Lizzie."

"Of course dear. Rueben and I will be right on over," she says. But she cannot help noticing the sheepish grin on Thomas' face. "Uh, Betty Jo, have you met my son Thomas? He is just home from the war."

"Yep, we've met," Betty Jo calls back as she is on her way to her horse.

Mrs. Huneycutt calls out to Betty Jo as she rides off, "Tell Lizzie we've been praying for her."

As soon as the Huneycutts arrive, Betty Jo helps pull Sallie up behind her on the horse. The carriage is still at Joel's and they must double up, which is surely going to increase their travel time. Without asking for Sallie's approval, Betty Jo takes the short cut through the woods. Sallie says nothing, but it is certainly not to her liking.

When they arrive at Joel's, Betty Jo knocks once and goes straight in. Joel comes out of the bedroom. He looks tired.

"How is she?" Sallie asks.

"Perhaps a little better. She has been in and out, but she does not seem to know me or what has happened to her. She did take a little water and broth; at least that is encouraging."

"Please take me to her," Sallie says, as the tears form in her eyes.

Joel walks across the hall and Betty Jo and Sallie follow. Sallie goes immediately to Lizzie and takes her hand. "Lizzie, it is me. Can you hear me dear?"

Lizzie slowly opens her eyes and looks directly at Sallie. "Mother?" she moans.

In Sallie's wisdom she replies "Yes dear, I am here." Lizzie gives Sallie's hand a little squeeze. Sallie is sitting on the bed next to Lizzie talking to her softly when Joel and Betty Jo step out of the room.

"You reckon I ought to ride up for Dr. Teeter or go to Salisbury and fetch Dr. Cotton?" Betty Jo asks.

Joel does not answer right away. He sits down on the edge of the sofa and cradles his head in his hands. "Dr. Teeter said she should be sitting up and eating by Tuesday. I have seen men lay like this for over a week, but she is different. I don't know..." His voice begins to crack and he starts to weep.

While Betty Jo is searching for the right words, there is a knock at the door. Joel stands to his feet, takes out his handkerchief and wipes his face. Betty Jo quickly recognizes the voice. "We have just found out what happened. Joel, I am Reverend Herman Furr and this is my wife, Hannah Jane. She and Betty Jo are sisters."

Joel invites them in. Hannah Jane embraces Betty Jo and for the first time, Betty Jo breaks down. Hannah Jane has only seen Betty Jo cry twice in her life: the first time, when their mother died, and now here, standing in Joel's living room. Although she has come on behalf of Lizzie, this display of emotion by her sister is heartbreaking and she joins Betty Jo in weeping.

Herman puts his arms around them both. "Ladies, pull yourselves together. This is in the hands of the Lord."

Herman turns to Joel. "May we see her?"

"Yes, of course," Joel answers, and everyone follows him across the hall to the bedroom.

Sallie sees them entering the room. She steps back from the bed so Herman can approach. He looks down at Lizzie tenderly and places his hand on her head. *"Mark 16:17: As believers we can lay hands on the sick and they shall be healed,"* he says softly, looking up at us. "If any of you are in disbelief of these holy words, I must ask that you leave. I am here to do God's work and I need the help of those that stand on his promises."

Every eye meets in passing and every head nods. "Very well, please lay your hands on our dear sister's body and join me in prayer. *"Dear Heavenly Father you are the great and only true physician. We are weak, but you are strong. We ask that through our humble hands you send your glorious gift of healing to this woman. Give us the power to restore her, not to her former self, but as a new creature devoted to your will. With her gift of healing, may her faith be renewed and may she serve as a witness to all, the power of your undying compassion and love."*

Herman turns to Joel. "Go prepare her something to eat, she will be hungry."

Joel looks down at Lizzie, who is lying motionless. Herman gives Joel a little nudge and smiles, "We have asked God, now we must act on faith."

"Ladies," Herman says cheerfully. "Prepare her toilet. Heat water to bathe her and lay out a fresh nightshirt. She will want to comb her hair and brush her teeth. Hannah Jane, open that window and let the sunshine in. This room is dark and gloomy."

Before he leaves the ladies with their duties, he stops for a moment. "I remember on my way in seeing a patch of black-eyed susans blooming down the road. Pardon me while I go collect a bouquet for our patient."

When he returns, Lizzie is freshly dressed and sitting up in bed. Sallie is carefully feeding her a bowl of soup. Herman does not seem the least bit astonished, as if miracles of this sort happen every day. "Hey Joel," he calls out. "Do you have a vase for these flowers?"

Chapter 17

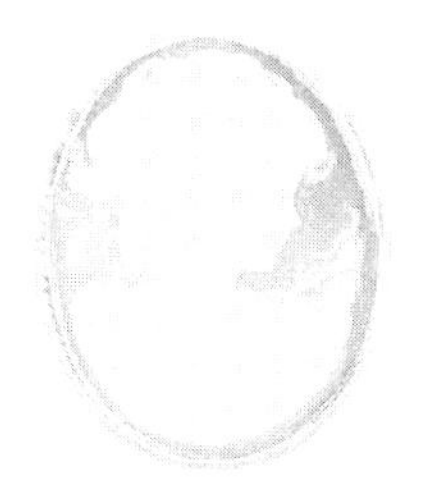

Old Friends Come Home

"Lizzie!" I hear someone calling my name. The sunlight coming through the window hurts my eyes as I open them. The room looks unfamiliar to me and I do not know what day it is.

"Lizzie," comes the voice again from the hall. The door opens and it is Betty Jo.

"How is our patient today? I bet you are hungry enough to eat a bear," she says in an unnaturally cheery voice. "Well, we ain't got no bear meat, but how bouts some eggs and salt pork?" she says, and sets a tray down next to the bed.

"Betty Jo, where am I?" I try to sit up and a sharp pain runs down my back. "Oh my God, where is Victoria?"

"Lizzie, you just calm down, Victoria is fine. She is with Sallie. Now, tell me what is the last thang you remember." she says, and sits down next to me.

"It is like a bad dream. It was so cold. There was pain, great pain. I can still see the faces flashing in my mind and voices calling to me. Betty Jo, I even thought I talked to Joel."

"Lizzie, do you remember goin to Martha's on Thursday."

Her words jar my memory, "Yes, I was looking for you!"

"That be right. Now think real hard, what happin after you left Martha's? Where was it you were a headin?"

I look at her face and I am frightened. "I don't know!" I say, starting to cry.

"Lizzie, don't you remember last night? You were awake and ate a whole bowl of soup."

My eyes roam the room and sitting on the dresser is a vase of black-eyed susans.

"Yes! Yes, I do! There were people standing around me. I think they were praying. Yes, I know they were praying. You were here! Sallie, Herman, Hannah Jane and Joel!"

The door opens and standing in the doorway is Joel. I am not sure if this is reality or I am still dreaming. I struggle through the pain and try to lift myself off the bed. I suddenly feel Joel's arms around me. This is real, he is real and so is the pain. I feel faint and I cannot stand. Slowly he lowers me back down on the bed. "What has happened to me?"

Betty Jo looks at Joel and then again at me. Joel takes up my hand and begins to explain. I am able to recall leaving Martha's and traveling to Joel's to meet Dr. Teeter. I can remember seeing two horses out front and walking through the open door. But after that it is all lost.

"Just as well," Joel says. "Once you are healed, we will think of it no more."

I am thankful Joel is home, but this was not how I wanted it to be. I had imagined a much more romantic setting. Now I can barely stand or hold him in my arms. My thoughts grow dark, but I quickly remind myself how lucky I am my life was spared.

"What is the date?" I ask.

"Easter Sunday, April 16," Joel replies. He then informs me he will be gone most of the day, even though it is Sunday. He has pressing business that cannot be delayed any longer. He says he will escort Betty Jo as far as Martha's house and then stop to collect her on his way back.

"I don'ts need nobody to escort me nowhere, I done and told you that Joel," Betty Jo says firmly.

"And I heard you, but this is my house and I outrank you. I will ride with you and you will wait for me, understood?" he says firmly, but he is smiling.

I detect a hit of flirtation in his voice. I wonder what has transpired over the last four days. I listen as the two of them engage in conversation like old friends. Just a moment ago I was the center of attention. Now they are acting as if I am not even in the room.

I begin to feel weak and I find I am drifting off to sleep again. I am not sure how much time has passed, but I am awakened by a knock at the door. Sallie enters the room and she is smiling ear to ear. "Hello, my dear sister." She runs across the room and embraces me. She stands back and looks at me. "I am so glad you are feeling better. I brought you a nice dressing gown, your toilet items and some ribbons for your hair. We cannot have you looking so drab now that Joel is home, can we?"

For the first time, I give thought to my appearance. "Sallie, do you have a mirror?" She reaches in the bag, hands me a mirror and I look at my face and gasp. I am pale as a ghost, my hair is matted with dried blood and my lips are dry and parched. I am embarrassed to think people have walked in and out looking at me like this, especially Joel.

Something catches my eye out the widow. Betty Jo is holding Joel's rifle and he is standing by her side, helping her aim. Her bosoms are well defined and her red hair is blazing in the sunlight. I watch Joel laugh when she returns the rifle.

"Sallie, you must help me wash my hair. Did you bring my hot iron?"

"Lizzie, I will help you freshen up, but I don't think you should risk wetting your head."

"Perhaps there might be more at stake than my life," I reply, looking again out the window.

"Sallie, please look around this place to see if you can find my dress."

"First, Lizzie, I have a surprise for you. If you are up to it."

"I suppose so, providing it is not painful. I have had enough of that lately," I say, trying to smile. I shift myself up in the bed. She reaches behind me and props a pillow behind my head.

"Wait right here!" she says excitedly and runs out of the room. I close my eyes and laugh. Did Sallie really think I was going anywhere? It is certainly not likely I could jump on my horse and ride off into the sunset.

Seconds later the door cracks open softly. I hear whispering. "Go on," Sallie says, and in walks a face I thought I would never see again.

"Hellos, Miz Lizzie. It's me Violet." She stands there at the door with her hands folded in front of her and her head down, waiting for my response.

"Come here darling!" I call out. She lifts her tear-streaked face and I open my arms to embrace her. "I am so happy to see you. Are you all right? Where is Harper?" I ask, looking at the door.

"We is all rights now, but it weren't like dey said. It wuz awful, jutz awful." she says, now weeping in my arms.

I gently push her off me. "Now tell me what happened!" I say.

"Well, Harper he meets up with des coloreds, and dey says we is gonna bes free. Dey tells him, we ain't pose to works fer yo no mo. Dat Mr. Sherman gonna gives us forty acres and a mule of our own. Alls we is gots to do is comes gets its. We had a map, but its wuz hard travelin. We wuz lost moe dan we wuz found. Four of the coloreds died fer we gotz dar. Harper says it wuz best, we wuz a runnin out of food. Whens we finally gets to da place, we is plum wor out."

"Where was this place?" I ask.

"Its wuz way past de old Charleston plantation. Beaufort wuz wheres we wuz specting to settle, buts dey sends us cross de water to dem islands. I tells yous da bugs wuz awful. Yous couldn't opens yo mouth withouts dem flyin in. We settle in dar with some other coloreds. Dem Union men wuz pose to hep us, but we had nothin. A lots of the coloreds wuz sick with de fever. Da last nights we wuz dar, sum men comes in da camp a shootin at everythang dat moved. Harper and me load up one da mules and leaves dat place, fer good."

"How did you make it back?" I ask, as this seemed nearly impossible to believe.

"Wells we figures to dies on da open road, but anywheres wuz better dan dat place. I reckons its wuz a miracle, sum white folks, wuz headin dis ways and dey gives us food and we follow dem here."

"Violet, will you tell Sallie to come back in? I would like to speak to her alone."

"Yes'um," she says, and closes the door on her way out.

I can hear voices out in the hall, one I am sure is Joel, and the other is Harper. Sallie comes back in and sits down. "Well, what do you think?"

"I don't know Sallie. We can hardly feed ourselves, but I don't like the idea of just turning them out to forge for themselves. "

"Lizzie, I can understand why Harper left. Joel is talking to Harper now. With fields that have not been turned over for four years, Joel is going to need help. He is willing to take Harper and Violet in, providing they agree to work in exchange for a piece of land and a cabin of their own. I think it is a God send and Violet would be of considerable help to you. "

"Very well, send them both in," I say, as I try to sit up as straight as possible.

When they enter the room, Joel is standing behind them. Harper begins to apologize and Violet cries. Even though I can barely hold my head up, they are waiting for me to make a decision which will affect them for the rest of their lives. I am finding it hard to think clearly, especially now that I have a sudden feeling of anger toward Sallie. Here I am practically on my deathbed and Sallie, as always brings the family problems for me to handle.

I gather up my strength to speak, "Harper, Violet, the old way of life is over. As soon as I am able, I will have the paper work drawn up for your freedom. If you can make arrangements with Mr. Joel, it is acceptable with me." I take a deep breath and lay my head back on the pillow and close my eyes. Joel kisses me on the cheek and orders the crowd to leave the room. But before I drift off to sleep, I see Betty Jo and Joel ride away.

When I awake, Violet is sitting in the chair next to me. I inquire about Sallie and she tells me Harper took her home. She informs me Harper and Joel have come to an agreement. Harper will be working for Mr. Joel and she is to care for me.

She said that Sallie had left her instructions to bathe and wash my hair. Once the bath is finished and I am back in bed, I fall asleep again.

The sun has fallen when I am awakened by voices in the hall. I detect the voices of Betty Jo and Joel, but the third I am not certain. I lift myself up, brush my hair and wash my face. Thankfully, Sallie brought my best dressing robe. I have spared it since leaving Charleston. As I slip it on, I am reminded how smooth satin feels against the skin. The rose color is flattering and perhaps when I enter the room, Joel will see me as he once did.

"That's right, John Wilkes Booth," the man says with his back to me. I walk in slowly and sit down next to Betty Jo. When I seat myself, I realize the young man with the newspaper in his hand is Thomas Huneycutt.

"Thomas?" I ask, and he turns to look at me. At once I am taken back to the days of Sandy Ridge when he was in love with my sister Annabelle. My eyes mist over thinking "Oh, if only she could see him now." His round boyish features have been replaced with the sharp angles of a handsome young man.

"Yes, Lizzie," he answers, just above a whisper. He fumbles with the newspaper and hands it over to Joel, who drops it on the floor. Thomas's eyes are on mine and he leaves Joel to pick it up. Thomas kneels down on the floor beside me and kisses my hand. "I am so glad to see you are recovering. If I had been home just one day earlier, I would have hunted down those thieves and blew them to kingdom come."

Betty Jo shifts in her seat and clears her throat. "*Ain't you something Thomas Huneycutt. Always thanking you are da only one fer da job.*"

"Is that so, Betty Jo? Well, you sure felt I was the one for the job when we were in Petersburg."

"Kiss my ass!" Betty Jo says, and stomps out of the room and out on the porch.

"It would be my pleasure, Ma'am," Thomas calls out after her and sits down next to Joel.

"I take it the two of you know each other?" Joel asked.

"Sure do. We were in the same regiment," Thomas answers, trying to wipe the smile off his face. "Even though she was a darn good soldier, she was too pretty to be killed by some Yankee. I was the one that got her and her sister sent home. She was none too happy about it either. I swear, never in a hundred years did I expect to run into her again."

"Looks like she isn't too happy to see you," I poke back at him.

"Oh, she will be," he brags. "I am going to marry that girl."

"You are, are you?" Joel asks, raising his eyebrows at Thomas.

"Betty Jo has a mind of her own and she is not easily persuaded," I add.

"Oh, she can be persuaded alright. Ask her about it sometimes Lizzie," Thomas says, nudging Joel on the arm. This is so unlike the old Thomas I knew.

His words seem to insult Joel. "Well soldier, let's just let dead dogs lie for tonight. We have plenty to talk about other than a pretty face or love's fanciful ways."

I had expected Joel to complement me, but instead he turns and glances back through the open door at Betty Jo leaning against the porch railing. It is almost dark and the moon is casting a soft glow over her slender figure.

"Lizzie, did you hear any of what we were saying?" he asks, looking at me as if I am his business partner.

"I only heard you mention John Wilkes Booth. Isn't he an actor?"

"Yes, Lizzie. It appears Booth has shot and killed President Abraham Lincoln.

"*Shuts ye face!*" calls out Harper, who is standing in the kitchen doorway with Violet.

"I think it is best if I just read to you the newspaper article," Joel says, shaking open the page. "*It appears a conspiracy to kill President Abraham Lincoln, Vice President Andrew Johnson, Secretary of State William Seward and possibly General Grant has been in the works for some times. While others may have escaped a tragic end, it was not to be for President Lincoln.*

According to our sources, the plot was carried out after Booth discovered the President and his wife would be attending the production of "My American Cousin," Friday, April 14, at Ford's Theatre in Washington. General Grant and his wife declined an invitation to sit in the presidential box because the two wives were at odds with each other. Instead, Major Henry Rathbone and his fiancée Clara Harris occupied the seats.

Actor John Wilkes Booth entered the presidential box shortly after 10 p.m. and fatally shot President Lincoln in the back of the head with a .44-caliber derringer. As the President slumps forward in his seat, Booth reportedly stabs Major Rathbone twice. Mrs. Lincoln and Miss Harris were unhurt. He leaps to the stage and his spurs rip through the US Flag hanging below. The audience watches in horror as he raises his knife and shouts, "I have done it, the South is avenged!" How he escaped without injury is unknown.

He then exited through a stage door where a fast horse was waiting. Booth being an expert rider escaped into the *dense forest where he is thought to be hiding in the swampy terrain with his accomplice, David Herold. Both fugitives are still at large and a $100,000 reward has been placed on their heads.*

The paralyzed President was immediately examined by a doctor in the audience and then carried across the street to Petersen's Boarding House where he died early the next morning.

On the same night, an attempt was made on the life of Secretary of State William Seward, who is expected to recover. Booth is known to be in cahoots with a number of others. Possible conspirators and wanted for questioning are John Surratt and his mother, Mary Surratt.

The authorities have also questioned Miss Lucy Lambert Hale, daughter of US Senator John Parker Hale, society belle, and the proposed fiancée of Booth. She denies having any knowledge of the conspiratress or plot to kill President Lincoln.

The Radical Republicans are now pointing a finger at Jefferson Davis and Robert E. Lee, claiming them to have possible involvement and this as an attempt to overthrow the government. There is no evidence, as of yet, that these claims are factual. However, for certain Lincoln's death will breed more hostilities between North and South."

Joel folds the paper up and hands it back to Thomas. We sit in silence. None of us know what to say, until Betty Jo comes back in the house and calls out to Violet, "You gots some supper fer us?" She winks at me or perhaps it was intended for Joel, but she does not look at Thomas.

"Well, I spect I best get on back home," Thomas says, moving a little closer to Betty Jo. "It is going be a lonely ride back home and I could use some company."

"Thomas, stay and have some supper with us," Joel

insists. "For you Miss Betty Jo, you will let Thomas follow you home," he says, sounding like Betty Jo's father.

I hoped for a quiet evening with Joel alone, but that would have to wait. Betty Jo slips out right after supper. Thomas, seeing she has left, takes off after her in fast pursuit.

Violet offers to help me to bed, which Joel encourages. Good night, Sweetheart," he calls out to me, telling me he still has some paper work to do before going to bed.

Once in bed and the light is out, my thoughts begin to race. I miss Victoria. It has been almost a week since I saw her. Will Joel be a good father to her? It is time we make arrangements, if there are to be any. Not once since Joel has been home has he mentioned marriage. He is preoccupied with the concerns of the farm and seems more attentive to Betty Jo than me. I think about his first wife. Was this the bed she lay in, waiting for Joel to come home from working on the railroad? Was she lonely like me?

Chapter 18

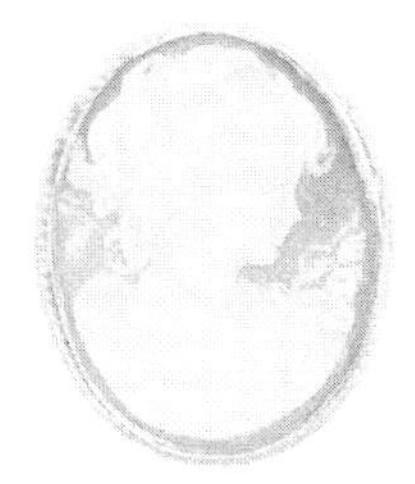

A Victim of Jealousy

It is Tuesday, April 18, and it was six days ago I walked in the front door of Joel's house and discovered the thieves. Six long days Joel has been home and not once has he mentioned our future plans. Truly, I can understand the first three days. However, now I am of sound mind and it is time for such matters to be discussed. Perhaps a man has little time to discuss marriage when he is preoccupied with his business, gardening or a girl named Betty Jo. If Joel Simpson thinks he is going to make a fool of me, he is mistaken.

When Dr. Teeter arrives to examine me and to finalize his business with Joel, he finds I am fully dressed and waiting on the front porch. My few belongings are packed and unknowing to anyone. I am waiting for Harper to arrive with the carriage to take me home.

"Well lookie here boys, will you take a look at my little patient! She is as bright as a yellow buttercup this morning," he calls out. "What a pleasant surprise. I thought I would find you still in the sick bed. I'll take a look at that wound while my sons pick out the horses."

"Joel should be up shortly, Dr. Teeter. Please come up and wait with me on the porch." I stand carefully not showing the slightest hint of weakness. "Wait here, I will have Violet bring out a cool pitcher of water."

When I return, the three men have tied off their horses. Dr. Teeter is sitting in the rocker next to mine. The two boys are relaxing on the steps and we begin to engage in conversation. I am flattered by the attention of the doctor and his sons and thankful I had instructed Violet to bring me my nice dress and bonnet. My plan is to give Joel a vision worth remembering as he sees me step up in the carriage and ride away.

However, when Violet comes out of the house and looks at me suspiciously, I suddenly realize this whole scene may be a stroke of luck. When Joel comes up, and sees me with the two handsome young men at my feet, it is sure to stir his emotions.

Timing is working perfectly in my favor. Dr. Teeter is telling his sons about how he walked in and found me shot, when Joel walks up.

"Did you have a pistol on you?" asked the son named Wilson.

"I am not sure. Yes!" I reply as the robber's face flashes in my mind for the first time. "I see it all clearly now," I say, looking up to see if Joel is listening.

"Oh, don't speak of it dear, if it is too upsetting," Dr. Teeter cautions.

"No, Doctor, I suppose seeing you has triggered my memory. When I saw the horses out front that day, I was a bit suspicious. I recognized one of the saddles as Joel's and I recall thinking how odd. My Papa always said you cannot be overly cautious, so I had my derringer loaded in my purse. The door was open and when I stepped inside a chill ran up my spine. Seconds later, there he stood at the top of the stairs. He was an awful mangy sort. When I saw what he was up to, I took out my pistol and pointed it right at his head. I froze. I could not pull the trigger."

Wilson leaps from the steps and takes up my hand. "Of course not, dear, I just don't see how you could harm a fly."

A voice comes up from behind Joel. *"Well, if she'd laid that bullet to him, she's mights not got one in the back."*

Both young men turn and look at Betty Jo. She is leading up one of Joel's finest horses. She is wearing tight-fitting trousers, her hair is blowing in the wind and her skin is bronzed from the sun.

"What a beauty," Wilson whispers.

"Yes, indeed she is," says the younger son sitting on the steps.

I am not sure if they are talking about the horse or Betty Jo, but again she has stolen my thunder. Within seconds they are patting down the horse and circling around Betty Jo. Dr. Teeter calls Joel to the side to discuss business.

I am wishing I could just disappear when Harper drives up. Again, timing is everything. I pick up my bag and walk down the steps. I am ready to step in the carriage before anyone takes notice.

Joel looks up at me with a puzzled look on his face. My heart is calling out for him to stop me. Dr. Teeter pulls out a roll of money and tugs at Joel's arm. "I think we can come to terms today." Joel turns to speak to Dr. Teeter and I step up in the carriage.

I hesitate to tell Harper to pull off, but I certainly cannot just sit here creating a scene. I have played my card and I must follow through.

"Wait," a man's voice calls out, as Harper starts to pull off slowly.

I am expecting to see Joel at the window, but it is Wilson. "It was such a pleasure meeting you. I am sorry we did not have more time to chat. My father tells me you are engaged to Mr. Joel. Perhaps you will invite us to the wedding."

I look back at the others. Betty Jo is looking directly at me with her hands on her hips. Joel's expression is serious, but he does not approach me. I see the picture all too clearly now. In just six short days, Joel has fallen for Betty Jo. He has publicly made it known that he planned to marry me, but now he is standing there with his regrets.

"Mr. Wilson," I say loud enough for them all to hear me. "It was a pleasure meeting you as well. However, I am sorry to disappoint you. There have been no wedding arrangements made. We will have to finish our chat another time. Good day, sir."

I lean forward to Harper, "Let's go now," I whisper firmly.

Harper lays into the reins and as we head down the drive, I struggle not to look back, although I would like to see the expressions on their faces. One thing I have always appreciated about Harper is he minds his own business. He never initiates conversation and today, of all days, he is wise to hold his tongue.

Several miles into our trip we are alarmed to see a band of soldiers approaching us. They are traveling hard and fast and I instruct Harper to pull over to the side of the road. If need be we will have to abandon the carriage. I pull out my pistol and we wait as they approach. The commanding officer calls for his troops to halt and I am much relieved to see they are Confederates. Three riders approach the carriage. One rides to the rear and one to each side of us. I slip my pistol out of sight.

"Afternoon Ma'am," the soldier on my left calls out.

"Something wrong sir?" I ask, feeling as if my privacy is being violated.

"Mind telling me where you are heading?" he asks.

"Mind telling me why you are asking?" I answer, feeling perturbed.

He looks at the other soldier and he nods his head. "Ma'am, do you recognize the gentleman on the gray horse?"

I am almost afraid to answer for fear I might be mistaken. I take a second look and I am certain. "Yes sir, as a matter of fact I do."

"Well, then I am sure you understand the urgency of our mission. He motions for his soldiers to pass and the man on the gray horse tips his hat as he rides by. Once the party has passed, he calls back to us as he rides off, "Sorry to have delayed you in your travels."

When I arrive home, the children are playing in the yard. Sallie is on the porch and seated beside her is none other than Betty Jo. She must have taken the short cut through the woods and hightailed it over here as fast as she could.

Harper parks out front and Sallie runs to embrace me, calling out to the children, "Look who is here!" Noah drops his ball and they come to greet me.

At once, Noah and Minerva lock their arms around my knees. I look across the yard to see Victoria left out of the huddle.

"Aunt Lizzie, we thought you was shot dead!" Noah says innocently.

"Well, as you can see I am not." I pat each of them on the head and walk over to scoop Victoria up in my arms. She wraps her arms around my neck and cries out "Mommy!" With her in my arms, I am at once healed. Whatever my troubles, nothing is greater than my love for her.

Betty Jo smiles at me innocently. *" Liz, I came aheads to lets everybodies know you was a coming home! Tonight we gonna throw a big party!"*

"Betty Jo!" Sallie shouts. "Don't you know it was supposed to be a surprise?"

"I forgets. Anyways Lizzie, we havin a big home comin party. It's for you, Joel, and I reckons that old Thomas Huneycutt too."

With Victoria in my arms, I walk up on the porch and take a seat. "Sallie, we can't afford to have a party. We have nothing to offer."

Before Sallie could answer, Betty Jo jumps in. *"Oh yes we do! What do you a reckon Joel and me was up to all mornin?"*

"I don't know, Betty Jo. Why don't you tell me what you and Joel were up to all morning?" I answer with a scorching tone to my voice.

"Fishing! What else was you a thinking?" Betty Jo comes back in defense.

"Oh really, fishing. Well, did you catch yourself a big one, Betty Jo?" I reply with even more sarcasm.

"I donts knows whats in the tarnation yous is implying on me Lizzie. Is you a callin me a double crosser?"

"If the shoe fits then wear it Betty Jo!" I sass back at her, while Victoria dangles on my hip. Sallie is at a loss for words, but tries to calm me down.

"Well, I ain't gonna stay arounds heres and hear this kind of talk!" Betty Jo says, and stomps across the yard toward the cabin.

"Lizzie, look what you have done!" Sallie says disapprovingly.

"What I have done? Why don't you ask her what she has done?"

"Oh, I intend to and I think someone is going to have some apologizing to do."

I slowly stand Victoria to her feet. "Go play sweetie so I can talk to Aunt Sallie." I pause and watch her rejoin the other children. I take a deep breath before I speak. "Sallie I wish an apology would fix things, but Betty Jo has ruined my life. Did you not see how they looked at each other? I guess a person cannot help who they fall in love with, but I would never have dreamed Joel would have been so weak or Betty Jo for that matter."

"What makes you so sure? Have you seen them together?" Sallie asks.

"No, but I heard them whispering and I watched them slip off to the barn together. Why do you think he was so quick to get Violet over there to take care of me? He wanted to free up Betty Jo, that's why!"

"Oh Lizzie, have you talked to Joel?"

"No. He has been too busy. All he talked about in his letters was getting married and now not once has the subject come up. I guess four years of war does something to a man's mind. Ransom will be home soon and you will want to rebuild your life. You don't need me here in the way. I am thinking I will take Victoria and go back to Charleston. Maybe I will try to start up the medical clinic again."

"Lizzie, promise me you won't do anything in haste. Give it some time and see if things work out."

"More time for him to make a fool of me? Sallie is that what you want?"

"No, Lizzie, but promise you will wait until Ransom gets home, for my sake."

"Very well, for your sake Sister. I will not leave until Ransom gets home. I have too much to plan anyway."

"Oh Sallie!" Guess who I saw on my way home – President Jefferson Davis! "

"Lizzie, are you sure?"

"One hundred percent sure. I remember meeting him in Charleston. It was him all right. I am sure the Yankees are hot on his trail, for they did not tarry long. I do hope he finds safe haven."

"Me too, Lizzie."

Before we could continue the conversation, Mr. and Mrs. Huneycutt's carriage is seen coming up the drive. When they pull up in front, Thomas helps his mother down and she wobbles up on the porch to hug me. "Oh Lizzie, I was so frighted for you. Did Betty Jo tell you we were all praying for you?"

Thomas and Mr. Huneycutt have trays of food and Sallie tells them to take it around back where the tables are set up. She is planning a real party, but I am in no mood. There is another carriage arriving. It is Herman, Hannah Jane and Aunt Martha. I ease out of the chair and excuse myself to go freshen up.

When I come back downstairs, I see Joel's horse is tied to the front post. How will I react? Then a feeling of comfort comes over me as Mother's words come to my mind, *"The least said, the least to regret."* It was almost as if I could feel her walking alongside of me as I greeted our guests and thanked them for their prayers for my recovery.

The smell of fish frying and the heat is making me feel weak. I take up a chair and pretend to be watching the children. Caroline, Robert and their children are here. I see Thomas talking to TJ. He is her father, but to her he is just a nice stranger. I am happy Thomas is home, but seeing him reminds me of Annabelle's death. Annabelle's death reminds me of Papa and Mother. Thinking of Papa and Mother reminds me of just how alone I am.

TJ quickly tires of talking to Thomas and runs off to play with her cousins. Thomas smiles, but I know he is hurt. His eyes scan over the yard. "Where is Betty Jo?" he asks. I point him in the direction of her cabin, but when he returns he is alone.

The meal is spread out on the table. It is the most food I have seen in over a year. Although I have not eaten since early this morning, I am not sure I can swallow a single bite. People are taking their places at the table and I see Joel coming toward me. He has Victoria in his arms. Is it not enough to mislead me, but my daughter too?

"Here is Mommy," he says, and gently hands her to me. "Come, Lizzie, let's take a seat," he says, taking hold of my elbow. At first I want to jerk away, but I have not the nerve.

Seated at the table is the whole crowd. Joel stands up and waves his hands in the air to cease the talking. All eyes are on him as he prepares to make a speech. "Good evening everyone," he says, and swallows hard as if he has a bone in his throat. "Before the war, life around these parts was slow and predictable. However, over the course of the last four years all of our lives have been uprooted. We cannot expect things to always stay the same, but I for one would like things to at least slow down." He pauses and looks at me tenderly. Everyone smiles as if they know something I do not. "Victoria, I suppose you are the one I should ask," he says, taking her from my arms and holding her up so everyone can see her. "Is it all right with you if I marry your Mommy?"

Victoria looks around at all the faces looking at her. Sallie is nodding her head up and down and smiling. Victoria does the same and everyone claps their hands.

"Well then, Lizzie, seeing as we have no objections," Joel says. "Will you marry me?"

I can feel my face turn red as everyone cheers. This could have been a wonderful moment, but instead I am horribly ashamed of myself. How could I have ever distrusted Joel? I am speechless, but I nod my head yes. Joel leans over, kisses me on the cheek and Victoria on top of her head. "She said yes!" he announces for everyone to hear.

"Well, why wait?" Herman calls out. "There is no time like the present. I can marry you tonight!"

Joel looks over at me and I see he likes the idea. "I am sorry. I am not quite up to it yet. Soon, just not tonight." I answer.

Joel sits back down smiling, but I know he was up for a wedding. All I can think of is where is Betty Jo? I have to find her and tell her how sorry I am for accusing her of the worst possible.

As soon as we have eaten, I find Thomas and ask about Betty Jo. We walk across to her cabin and push open the door. She appears to have packed her belongings and left. Thomas looks at me, "Lizzie, I am afraid this is all my fault."

"No, Thomas, it is my fault." I answer. "Will you do me a favor and go find Joel and tell him I want to talk to him."

Shortly Thomas returns with Joel. They both sit down at the table. I stand to present my case. "Joel, the only way to handle this is to be honest. I have been a fool and I have allowed my own jealousy to hurt and affect the lives of others."

"Lizzie, surely it was unintentional," Joel says, taking up my hand.

"No Joel, it was not. I have been cruel and insensitive. I am ashamed to say I have wrongly accused Betty Jo of engaging in your affections." I bite back my tears. The last thing I want is for them to think I am playing on their sympathy.

Joel stands up quickly and walks out on the porch and Thomas follows him. Their backs are to me and I can hear them whispering. In a few minutes, Joel walks back inside with his head lowered. He pulls a chair out next to me and sits down, but says nothing. I can stand it no longer. "Joel,"

I begin. "I have no excuse to offer. I have wronged you and Betty Jo. I can clearly see Thomas cares for her and now I may have possibly ruined his chances for happiness too. I know my poor judgment has caused you to doubt me. If you do not wish to marry me, I must accept it as my fate.

Joel raises his head. At first the look on his face has me baffled. Then he begins to laugh and Thomas walks through the door laughing too. Do they think I am such a fool that this is a laughing matter?

"Lizzie darling," Joel says, collecting himself enough to speak. "Do you think you are the first woman to be the victim of jealousy? I have to say in your defense I can see how this happened. Betty Jo was there all the time, but she was only trying to help.

"But Joel, since you have been home you never once mentioned marriage to me."

"Lizzie, I did not want to ask you to marry me until I was sure you were able to make a sound decision. What if you said yes and later have regrets?"

"Oh, I have so many regrets," I say crying.

Thomas puts his hand on my shoulder. "Lizzie, my biggest regret is not being here to witness the look on Betty Jo's face when you lit into her. I bet she was some kind of mad."

Thomas and Joel laugh and I suppose I can see a wee bit of humor. Whether I can or not is not the issue. I am just thankful they do.

"But what about Betty Jo?" I ask. "Someone has got to go find her and bring her back. I have got to make this right with her."

"And that will be my job," Thomas says. "I'll talk to Hannah Jane to see where I should start." He winks at me and takes off running toward the house.

I turn to see Joel smiling at me and the mood changes. Suddenly I feel nervous and overcome by his presence. I stand up and walk over by the fireplace. He follows me and looks into my eyes. Then without warning, he takes me in his arms and begins to kiss me. I recall the feeling of our first kiss three years ago. The room disappears and the only thing I am aware of is Joel. I feel as though I might stumble as he pushes his body firmly against mine. Slowly, I am pressed up against the wall. His lips leave mine and he slides them down over my neck. My eyes close as he whispers to me, "Oh Lizzie, why did you not consent to let Herman marry us tonight? I cannot wait much longer to have you."

His breath is hot and his hand is following the form of my breast. I am his and ready to give myself to him.

I am brought back to reality when the door bursts open and I hear a voice say *"Hey, I been gone less than an hour and you a done and turned this place into a brothel!"*

"Betty Jo!" I cry out, pushing a heated Joel off me.

"I was just on my ways to Mexico whens I discover I forgots somethings. Don't mind me. I ain't even gonna be here long enough for your blood to cool off." She walks over to the trunk and fishes out her poncho. *"It is a startin to storm now, so I figure I am a gonna need this here,"* she says in a soft voice, holding up the poncho for us to see.

"I expect so," Joel says, walking over to the window. "Looks like I see some lightning and thunder in the distance now. It stands to reason you might want to camp out here for the night, until the storm passes."

Betty Jo reminds me of a horse that has recently escaped from the corral. If you wait patiently, perhaps she might just walk right back in the fence. If you chase her, she may run and be lost forever.

I smile to encourage her to stay, but before I can speak, I see Thomas is standing in the doorway. "Mexico is a pretty far piece," he says. "I've always wanted to go there myself. Don't reckon you would consider partnering up?"

"I might," Betty Jo answers. Her voice has a soft new quality.

The room is quiet as Betty Jo and Thomas stand face to face. Joel and I are now the intruders. It is Betty Jo and Thomas who have much to talk about.

On my way out the door, I catch Betty Jo's hand and give it a little squeeze. Her eyes brighten and she looks at me with all the forgiveness of a sister. *"You were wrong."*

"I know, I know my friend," I reply.

Chapter 19

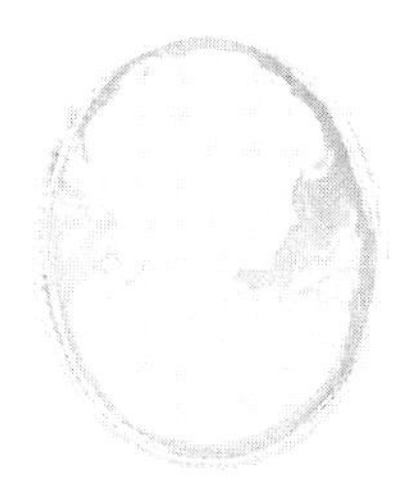

Willie James Burris

After the reunion with Betty Jo, it was late. By the time Joel walked me back to the house it was beginning to rain. It took very little encouragement to convince him to stay overnight, even though the invitation was just for the comforts of the parlor sofa.

I awoke early the next morning and debated how I should dress. Here in North Carolina, I have forgone all the finery. Life here is more about practicality rather than keeping up appearances. What will Joel think if I come downstairs dressed in the old rags I am accustomed to here? Victoria is sleeping and I am careful not to wake her as I sort through my things. At last, I slip on the old trousers, brush my hair and go downstairs.

Joel is sitting on the front porch talking to Thomas. Apparently, he did not go home last night either. I have a strong suspicion Betty Joe offered him a little more than the comforts of the parlor sofa. It is not for us to judge, least of all me.

I open the front door and Joel smiles. His handsome face is lined from the years of war. "Hello darling, please come out and join us." When I step out into the morning air,

I feel alive again. The excitement of having Joel here gives me new hope for my tattered life. I want to run across the green grass, feel the earth against my bare feet and scream up to the heavens with praises.

As I walk past him to take a seat, he grabs me from behind and pulls me down on his lap and kisses me. I struggle to get loose as if I am embarrassed, but I am not. Thomas looks at me and chuckles, "I reckon I better slip on back home before Ma misses me. Got lots of work to do. I'll be back later."

When he comes back on his horse he stops out front. "Hey Lizzie, hold onto Betty Jo until I get back. Don't let her go running off again. She is sure hard to catch." Then with all the speed of the pony express he takes off down the drive.

"I could sit here on this porch just holding your hand forever, Joel Simpson."

"Oh, but Lizzie, there is so much more than holding hands," he says, flashing a devilish grin.

I am just about to make a play on his words when Noah comes bursting out the door. "Aunt Lizzie, Momma went down to the barn. She says you are not able to do chores and I have to wait for breakfast. Is cooking a chore?"

Joel laughs. "Yes, for me it is."

Noah is looking at me anxiously and Joel jumps to his feet. "It is time for me to head home; got them fields to plant."

"Come on little man," I say, taking Noah's hand to go inside. Joel gives me a kiss on the cheek and I turn to leave. I am quickly turned around when I receive a smart little pop to my rear.

"Hey, Miss Lizzie, is planning a wedding a chore?" Joel teases.

"It all depends on what you have in mind," I reply. This playful side of Joel is new to me, but I find it delightful.

Sallie is coming up from the barn with a basket of eggs and Joel stops to look in her basket. "Take a few," she offers. "With spring coming on, I left some eggs for the hen to hatch out. We could use a few more chickens," Sallie says, as if she is a great farmwoman.

"You don't have a rooster, do you Sallie?"

"Not anymore. He died last fall," Sallie, answers.

Joel tips his hat and laughs all the way to the barn. Sallie walks up on the porch and looks back at Joel as if he is crazy. "What do you suppose Joel is laughing about, Lizzie?"

"I don't know, Sallie. Men are a strange breed you know," I reply.

Shortly after Thomas left, I see Betty Jo ride off. She never answers to anyone and today is the same. It is almost dark before she returns and knocks on the back door. She flops down at the table and Sallie asks if she is hungry. Betty Jo nods her head and Sallie unwraps a piece of cornbread, crumbles it up and pours some buttermilk over it.

"Here you go," she says, and sets the bowl down in front of her.

Betty Jo looks tired. I wonder where she has been, until she reaches in her pocket and lays down two letters and a newspaper. Sallie walks over to the table and picks up the letters. One is from Ransom and the other from New York, addressed to me. I am sure it must be from Dr. Fannie.

Betty Jo flips open the newspaper and says *"Well it will all be over soon. The Great War, The War for Southern Independence all lost and nothin to show fer it, but a big pile of dead bodies and starving women and children."*

"What does the paper say?" I ask, standing behind her and massaging her shoulders. I can feel her trembling as if she is angry or near crying.

"*It says right heres in black and white, Sherman and Johnston are working out the terms fer surrender as we speak. Since Old Abe's death, they gots to go to President Johnson for his seal of approval. I don't think he's gonna be too quick to settle.* "

"But wasn't President Johnson born in North Carolina?" I ask.

"*Yep, but he was raised in Tennessee. If he takes our side right now them Yankees are most likely gonna put a noose around his neck."*

Sallie looks at the letter in her hand. "Ransom is in Durham, North Carolina. Is this where the terms are being negotiated?"

"*Read it fer yourselves. I ain't gonna waste no more of my time on this here politics. Ifs you asks me, this whole darn country is going to hell in a hand basket."*

Minerva and Noah are sitting at the table listening to every word. They like Betty Jo. She is anything but ordinary and has certainly broadened their vocabulary, which is not necessarily to Sallie's liking.

"Yes, it is all an unfortunate state of affairs," Sallie confirms.

"Finding an honest man in politics is as scarce as hens' teeth," Betty Jo says, and ends the conversation. She gets up to leave and slams the back door behind her.

About bedtime, Sallie is frightened when she hears a horse coming up the driveway. I look out the window and as I expected it is Thomas. "Go to bed Sallie," I laugh. "I think that boy is going to be paying regular visits at Betty Jo's cabin. You can expect to see him sneaking in by moonlight and riding off by sunrise."

"I don't think much of that kind of behavior," Sallie says, getting up to look out the window for herself.

"Go to bed, Sallie. Surely you have more important things to worry about and I have a letter to read."

I have waited all day to read Dr. Fannie's letter and at last I take it out of my apron pocket.

Dear Lizzie,

I must say if we all live through this April it will be a miracle. I swear I do not know if it is the end of the war or the end of the world.

On a happy note, I am glad to hear you are recovering and that your Joel is finally home. I hope you will be able to be married soon, if that is your desire.

I should not write to you with my distressing news, but I have no one else who cares of my concerns. I am terribly depressed which is not at all like me. I have been working at the Asylum for poor women and children. The hours are long and I am drained for I can provide very little hope for the sick.

Next week, I will be transferring to St. Francis Hospital on East 142nd Street; it is a little closer to my apartment. Perhaps the new facility will be more tolerable, since it will be a change of pace.

There have been a number of horrible fires here

in the City. The old volunteer fire department has now been disarmed. The Metropolitan Fire Department is the new paid force and is said to be better equipped and capable.

I will close for now. I hope you will pray for me while I am here in this God forsaken place. I am hoping to go back to Charleston as soon as things calm down and the railways will have me.

Your friend,
Fannie

....

Thursday, April 27, 1865

Joel was back, with a gift of a fine rooster for Sallie. We were both embarrassed when he explained to us in short: no rooster, no chicks.

Joel also came with news the war was officially over. Johnston had surrendered to Sherman at the Bennett House near Durham, North Carolina. If things played out the same as they did when Lee surrendered at Appomattox, the troops are on their way home.

I would have expected Sallie to be overjoyed, but she stands frozen as if she cannot understand his words. "Don't you know what I mean?" Joel asks. "If all goes well, Ransom could be home in just a few short days."

"It has been almost four years since I last saw him. Up until this moment, I have not given this a thought. He will be a stranger to his own children and to me..." She stops herself in the middle of her sentence and runs upstairs.

Joel sat down beside me and I laid my head on his shoulder. It was as if we were the last souls on earth. The reality of Sallie's words rang in my ears.

After a bit, Joel clears his throat and manages to speak. "Sallie is right. War changes a man. We all are strangers coming home trying to put together the pieces of our missing lives. People say I am one of the lucky ones. I suppose they are right. I have two good arms and legs, but we all have scars. Lizzie, war brands you, clinging to you like a vine. In the daytime, you can keep it shut out, but at night, it creeps in your mind. You wake up screaming with the sweat pouring out of your pores, just like you are living it all over again."

We are interrupted by Sallie's voice. "The Lord is my strength and my shield, Psalm 28:7." She is smiling softly and holding Victoria in her arms. The sunlight coming from the hall covers them with an angelic glow. "There she is," she says, drying Victoria's tears. "Mommy has not left you; she is right here." Sallie walks over and sits Victoria on my lap. Without another word, she leaves us alone.

By the close of Joel's visit, it was decided we would marry the coming Sunday after church. He would talk to Herman in the morning and I would speak to Sallie. It was with the understanding I would not make the move until Ransom was home.

I am glad to retire early with Victoria. I walk up the squeaky stairs to our little intimate room. Even though it is late April, the room is cool and I light a fire. After the room heats up, I ready Victoria for bed. I brush her golden hair and slip a worn gown over her soft skin. Now in her bare feet she wiggles off the bed, goes to the bookshelf that Papa made and pulls out her favorite little book. I gather her up in my arms and begin to read, but soon she loses her battle to sleep. Carefully I lay her down in her little bed and nuzzle my face into her warm body smelling sweet of talcum.

When I first came here from Charleston, the smallness of this room seemed to box me in. Yet, over the past year and a half, this secret little room has proven to be our safe haven. Victoria and I are like little birds sitting high in a tree tucked away from the evils of this world.

When I blow out the light, I stare into the darkness thinking over the last couple of weeks. April 1865 will be a month for my scrapbook. In fact, it may be a month for all of history to remember. So much has happened and I am troubled it is not all over yet.

In just a few days, Joel and I will be married. I am happy in a sad sort of way. There will be no wedding dress, no party and certainly no honeymoon. Worst of all neither Papa nor Mother will be there to witness our vows.

My prayers have been answered, but as I think of Joel and our upcoming life together, I am fearful. My marriage to Edmond Cook turned to agony. Was it all his fault? What if something about me makes a man turn bitter after marriage? I cannot run away again.

Up until now, I have viewed this mundane life here in North Carolina as only temporary. Once I marry Joel, I can never go back to Charleston. Will my memories haunt me and leave me mourning for the social life and finery? As I drift off to sleep, I recall a poem:

The masque is over, the dance is done,
The lights, the music, the flirting, the fun.
Get your hat and pass me my shawl,
Let's make our way home,
before the morning gray.

Sunday, April 30, 1865

On Saturday, Joel and I went into town for the marriage bond. Joel stayed for supper and said he would come in the morning and drive us all to the church. Sallie would not hear of it, holding fast to the old superstition it was bad luck for the groom to see the bride before the wedding.

Joel tries to appease her with his exclamation that the custom went out of style with arranged marriages; when fathers of homely brides hid their daughters under long veils until the final vows were spoken. However, Sallie would not budge. I am sure she felt being the older sister she should take on the role of mother. It was endearing and we both agreed to her wishes.

There were few choices for my bridal attire. Everything I own has been repaired and is faded. It was resolved my blue dress and a headpiece of fresh flowers was the best these times could offer.

Betty Jo drives us all to the church. The children are included this Sunday. They all want to see Aunt Lizzie and now 'Uncle Joel' get married. Even Victoria has begun calling Joel 'Uncle Joel,' which I am strongly trying to discourage.

When we arrive, Joel is sitting in the first row next to Hannah Jane. The people in the pews smile acknowledging their awareness of our pending wedding. I take a seat next to Joel and Sallie and the children sit behind us. It is not to Victoria's liking and a struggle begins between her and Sallie. Victoria wins and crawls up in my lap. Joel pats her on the head, signaling he approves.

The focus of Herman's sermon is on forgiveness and healing for the country. He encourages us as Christians to pray for Mary Todd Lincoln. To pray for the family and soul of John Wilkes Booth who was captured, shot and killed on April 26.

He is praying for Booth's accomplices and asking God to see that they receive a fair trial, when we hear a commotion outside. The door slowly opens and a dozen or so of Stanly County soldiers quietly file in and take a seat on the back pews. Sallie turns to see Ransom among the worn and tattered.

The men stare straight ahead as not to disturb the service. The people begin to stir and whisper. Joel squeezes my hand and I understand that this is no time for a wedding. He goes up quietly and whispers into Herman's ear "Amen!" Herman shouts, "Let us all rejoice in those that God has at last delivered home!"

Sallie jumps from her seat, and runs to Ransom, while Joel and I hold back her confused children. The church is filled with tear-streaked faces of mothers, sisters, wives and fathers welcoming home their sons.

Herman puts his arm around Joel and asks us to walk outside so that he can speak to us in private. As we make our way toward the back of the church, we notice a lonely soldier standing to the side. Herman reaches out to him, "Sir, can I help you find someone?"

"Don't you recognize me, Pastor Herman? I am Willie James Burris. I am looking for my wife, Phoebe."

I watched Herman's shoulders drop and the congregation grow quiet when they heard him say his name. Even a man of God like Herman will surely struggle with words to comfort this man. How do you tell a living man it was written he had been killed, and his heartbroken wife ended her life to join him in eternity?

CHAPTER 20

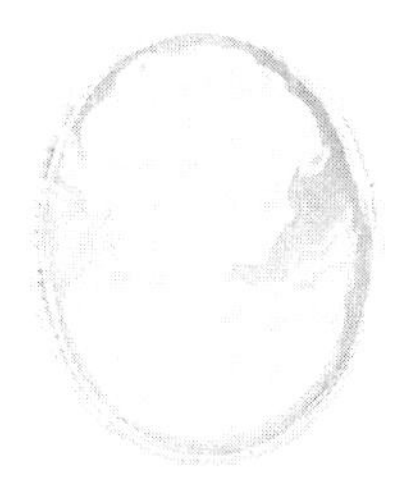

Spring's Glory

Ransom is nothing but skin and bones. His body is covered with sores, cuts and bruises. When he removes his hat there is more sunburned scalp than hair. He has not fared well with war. From the looks of him he is hardly a man able to perform hours of passionate love making, as Betty Jo had predicted. Even if he was able, I can tell by Sallie's eyes his present condition is undesirable.

After church the afternoon was spent sitting on the porch as Joel, Ransom and Thomas exchanged war stories. Betty Jo sat on the steps leaning up against Thomas, chirping in now and then of her own experiences.

I am content sitting next to Joel and watching the children playing in the field. Strange how we always worry about how they will react to change, when it is the adults who are to be considered. If only we could accept things like children. They never really worry about the past or what the future holds. I suppose that is living on faith.

Spring is here, in all it's glory. It's beauty is unscathed by the horrors of war as if it has nothing to mourn. Yet this marks five springs that have bloomed since the first shot was fired at Fort Sumter.

The sun flickers through the trees and shines upon the faces of the men lined up on the porches. Soldiers no more, just ordinary men who, by the grace of God, were spared to tell their stories.

Sallie serves a simple meal of beans and cornbread. The conversation grows thin while the men fill their bellies. Ransom looks at Sallie with tears in his eyes. "This is the best meal I have ever eaten."

"This war has cost us all a great price," Joel says. "What has the Union gained? If they wanted to end slavery, they could have just bought every damn slave and set them free. It would have cost a hell-of-a-lot less money."

"Think of how many thousands of lives would have been saved?" Ransom adds.

"Homes, plantations, business saved, no suffering women and children! Now it will take the rest of our lifetime to rebuild the South, if it can ever be done," Joel says in an angry tone.

Betty Jo is quiet. I have grown to know her ways. She is a listener and is never quick spoken. She is intelligent. When she speaks her mind she is most often right, especially when it comes to politics. "*Write this here down and remembers it. Its will go down in history that we was a all fighting for slavery. A hundred years from now, ain't nobody gonna know it was about states rights and taxes.*"

Thomas looks at Betty Jo strangely. "Who is going to believe a bunch of farm boys would go to war for rich people's rights to own Negroes. That is just plain crazy!"

"Well, you just waits and sees, Thomas Huneycutt," Betty Jo snaps back.

"A hundred years from now we are all going to be dead and gone and who is going to give a damn?" Thomas laughs, and pushes Betty Jo off the steps.

Everyone laughs. Laughter is healing, but the wounds run deep and there will need to be many days of healing before any of us recover.

Around four o'clock, Herman and Hanna Jane pull up in their wagon. Herman carefully helps his little bride with a belly full of baby out of the wagon. Nothing about her now would give the slightest hint she was in the army with Betty Jo. Even though I know it for a fact, I am still having trouble associating this frail little preacher's wife as a fast-shooting soldier.

The sight of them reminds me today was supposed to be my wedding day. I came home quickly, changed my dress and ripped the flowers out of my hair. I have refused it out of my mind all day.

Herman walks up with his Bible in his hand. When he steps up on the porch he looks at Joel. "Sir, did you not promise to marry this young woman today?"

Joel looks up at Herman. "I did, but that was this morning and it is way past morning."

"You best not be trying to weasel out of it. We got laws against that kind of thing around here," Herman says, playing along with Joel.

Joel reaches over to me and turns my head from side to side. "Well, I don't know, Pastor Herman. Let me take one more quick look at her."

Ransom, who is sitting with his legs propped up on the railing, stands up and gives Joel a look. "I say an ugly-looking fellow like you Joel can't be too choosey."

"I spect you are right buddy. I guess she'll do."

"Well, let's get on with it, before you change your mind again and I have to have you locked up," Herman says, and winks at me.

I realize that they are really serious. This very moment! Right here on the porch!

Ransom goes inside to get Sallie and Mr. Huneycutt goes around back to find Thomas and Betty Jo. Moments later, Sallie comes running out of the house untying her apron. She calls for the children, but she gets no answer.

Joel says he has a good idea where the children are. He steps off the porch, gets down on his knees and calls under the house. Shortly, out come three dirty little children and each one is holding a kitten.

Herman lines us up in position for the wedding while we wait for Mr. Huneycutt to return with Betty Jo and Thomas. It is not long before we see Mr. Huneycutt cutting a path across the field from Betty Jo's cabin. When he steps up on the porch he makes a low comment and Ransom shakes his head. "I'll talk to him Pa."

For a brief moment, my mind deceives me as I see two figures running up the hill. It is Thomas and I imagine my dear sister Annabelle following behind. I blink and my reality is restored. It is Betty Jo.

Joel and I join hands and Herman performs a short ceremony, but it is all unreal as if it is happening to someone else. I hear Joel say "I do."

Then I feel their eyes on me. "Theodosia Elizabeth Sanders, do you take this man to be your lawful wedded husband?"

I feel the words pass through my lips, "I do."

The next thing I am fully aware of is Joel taking me in his arms and kissing me. I can hear the others clapping and cheering. He slowly releases me and I look across at the admiring faces. The deed is done and I am now Mrs. Joel Simpson.

By sunset the Huneycutts have left, Betty Jo and Thomas have disappeared and Ransom is waiting for Sallie to prepare his long-awaited bath. Slowly Ransom lifts himself out of the chair, "Ya'll suppose you could watch the children for a bit?"

"Of course, take your time," Joel smiles.

I find myself smiling as I recall the bit of advice Sallie gave me shortly after she and Ransom were married, "Lizzie, men never seem to tire of the experience."

There is a new awkwardness between Joel and I. Nothing has changed, but again everything has changed. The tension grows and he struggles with his words. "Lizzie, this is not the way I would have planned this. You, me on our wedding day. I know this must be very disappointing to you."

I realize this is just one day. We have the rest of our lives to be together. I turn to him and look at him tenderly. "Joel, don't feel badly. I am sure some day when we are old and gray we will look back on this very moment fondly."

He shakes his head, but I can tell he is still in deep thought. "Lizzie, tomorrow morning I could bring Violet and Harper over in the wagon. Violet can watch Victoria and Harper can start hauling some of your things to my house. You and I can ride out to Bear Creek, have us a little picnic and spend the day. What do you say?"

"Sounds wonderful," I reply honestly. At last Joel and I would be alone to talk and plan our life together.

We need no explanation why Ransom had latched the door when he went inside, but the children do. Finding the door latched, Noah and Minerva begin to worry about their mother. I assure them she is fine and for lack of anything else to say, I explain she is washing her hair. They look confused, but Joel's offer to take them for a ride around the pond takes their minds off the situation. Victoria climbs up in my lap and within a few minutes she is asleep.

It is almost dark when Joel rides up with the children. Ransom and Sallie have now rejoined me. Joel helps the children down; they run up on the porch. Minerva climbs up in Sallie's lap and Ransom reaches for Noah. He does not hesitate and climbs up to sit in his father's lap.

"Children know when they are loved," Joel says softly.

"Yes, children are God's greatest gift," Ransom says, appreciating the moment.

Joel suddenly looks out of place, he looks lonely and sad. Joel kisses me softly on the lips and says goodnight. As I watch him ride away, I pray God will bless our marriage with a houseful of children for this man to love.

....

When Joel arrives the next morning, he finds me with a shovel digging a hole by the flower bed. I had hoped to be done with this task before he arrived with Harper and Violet. "Just what is my new bride doing out digging holes so early this morning?" Joel calls out to me, as he climbs down out of the wagon.

I look back at Harper and Violet. I still have not fully regained my trust in them.

"Digging potatoes," I lie.

"*Ain't nos ways, Miss Lizzie yous gots no taters at da end of dat shovel. Dey donts start a comin on till autumn time,*" Harper says, coming over to take a look.

I quickly throw the dirt over my hole and say, "You are right Harper. I have no idea what I was thinking."

Joel knows I am hiding something and sends Harper to the barn to saddle up my horse. Violet, taking a hint, says she will go inside to see about the children.

"Now tell me the truth, young lady," Joel says, looking at me in a fatherly kind of way.

I flip the dirt out of the hole to expose a small metal box and lift it up for him to see. "Papa and I buried this box of valuables. I had almost forgotten its whereabouts until this morning. It came to mind when I thought about Violet packing up my things. However, not all our valuables were in this little tin box. I had these hidden in my room," I say, reaching in my pocket and pulling out a little velvet pouch. Inside are three gold nuggets, three sliver coins and three jewels.

"Lizzie, where in the world did that come from?" he asks.

I smile, "Darling, you have your history and I have mine. We have a lifetime to catch up, but for now where shall we hide this stuff?"

"Good Lord," Joel says, looking around the empty fields. "I agree with you about Harper and Violet. It is never a good idea to tempt a good man."

We see Harper walking slowly up from the barn leading my horse. Joel tells me to take the box and the pouch and wait for him in the parlor.

While sitting in the parlor I think about the attic. It is locked, but I know where Sallie hides the key. When Joel comes in, he agrees the attic will do. He has sent Harper to take care of the animals and assigned Violet the duty of fixing us some breakfast.

Joel and I quickly make our way up the stairs to the attic and I unlock the door. The moment the door opens the sunlight sprinkles particles of dust around the room. There is something magical about an attic and I am reminded of playing in the attic at Sandy Ridge.

I begin looking around for a place to hide the box. "How about here?" I ask, pointing to an old trunk against the wall. Joel does not answer and I see he is intensely looking at something in the corner. He has a strange look on his face, as if he has seen a ghost.

"Did you see a mouse?" I ask, setting the box down, forgetting the task at hand. As I take a few steps, I see he is eyeing the painting Antonio did of me not long after we came to North Carolina.

"Joel, do you like the painting?" I ask. His look reminds me of the first time Papa saw the painting.

"Very much so darling. It is the most beautiful thing I have ever seen. That is excluding the original, of course," he says seductively. He pulls me close to him and starts to kiss me, but halts when we hear a voice calling from downstairs.

"Lizzie, are you up there?"

"Yes Sallie. I was showing Joel the portrait that Antonio painted of me."

"Antonio?" Joel whispers, raising his eyebrows.

"It is a long story," I say, giving him a little smirk.

"Should I hear it before we hang it over the fireplace?" Joel asks, looking a bit jealous.

I only laugh, allowing myself to remain mysterious. We agree to leave the box in the trunk and tiptoe down the stairs. After breakfast, we take off on our honeymoon picnic.

It is a slightly overcast day and the air is soft as it touches my face. This is a perfect day for a ride in the country. We ride slowly, talking of things that have been and things that we wish to come to pass. Whatever doubts I had in marrying Joel have all disappeared. Being with him is as natural as taking my next breath.

When we arrive at the creek, Joel says he has a special place he would like for me to see. We tie the horses off and walk down the bank to a large sandy area next to the water.

Joel spreads out the blanket, lays out flat on his back and closes his eyes. "Listen to the music," he says. "The sound of the birds singing and cool water rushing is better than any grand orchestra. When I was a boy, I used to pretend this was my own private beach. On hot summer days this was just about the coolest spot in Stanly County."

"Yes, it is peaceful here," I add, as I watch a pair of dragonflies dipping in and out of the water.

Then, without warning, Joel jumps to his feet. "I am hungry. How about you Lizzie? Open up that basket and let's see what we have."

The moment I open the basket the smell of real food fills the air. To my delight I unwrap fried chicken, biscuits, a small strawberry pie and a bottle of wine. "Joel!" I exclaim. "This is a feast. How could you afford this?"

Joel bows before me. "Nothing is too good for my queen."

We eat in silence, both of us savoring every bite. The poor chicken that sacrificed it's life for this meal could never have been more appreciated. Sitting there sipping our wine out of a tin cup was the grandest of wedding feasts a bride could ever hope for.

A couple of hours pass and some clouds begin to roll in from the west. Joel suggests we start home or we might be caught in a downpour. I rub across my back, recalling my last ride during a thunderstorm when I lost control of Midnight and landed on the ground. I start to tell Joel the story, but judging by the sky, the story should wait.

We are only on the road shortly when large drops of water begin to pelt the dusty path in front of us. Joel gestures and I follow him up the hill and across the meadow. His lead takes us down a road which has clearly been neglected for many years. There is a pop of lightning in the distance and my horse attempts to rear up in response. We begin to ride faster and harder. We are drenched to the core when Joel stops at a little cabin on the side of the road. "Wait inside. I'll take the horses to the barn."

I step gingerly onto the porch for fear I might fall through the rotten boards. I turn the door handle and the door easily opens. I feel like an intruder, but I can see this place has long been unoccupied. The vines have broken through the cracks and are spreading across the floor. Hanging in the fireplace is a rusted-out pot. There are a couple of broken-down chairs and against the wall is an old rope bed.

I am just about to explore the loft when Joel comes in shaking off the rain. My hair is dripping wet and I am embarrassed by the thinness of my worn blouse. The material is clinging to my breast and I cross my arms, giving Joel the impression I am cold.

Joel looks at me and smiles. "Let's see if any of this wood is dry enough to build a fire." He brought in with him his blanket bundle and haversack. He is lucky to find a box of dry matches. In just a short time we are warmed by a welcoming fire.

I pull up a chair to the fireplace and begin squeezing out my hair, letting it drip onto the floor in front of me. Joel sits down on the rope bed and bounces up a couple of times on the mattress. He then takes out the blanket and covers the bed.

Without asking or warning, he begins unbuttoning his shirt. Outside the sky is darkened by the storm, but the glow of the fire shines on his bare chest. I have never seen Joel without his shirt or even in his bare feet, as he now stands before me. "You know, Lizzie, your clothes would dry off a whole lot quicker if you take them off and lay them out in front of the fire." He leads by example by laying out his shirt, shoes and socks on the chair next to me.

"I suppose," I say. My eyes are on Joel standing before me waiting for me to undress. Slowly he walks over to me and lifts me off my feet. He kisses me passionately and I embrace him, feeling his bare skin under my hands. I am not a child. I have experienced intimacy. Yet alone here with Joel, it is all new. He lays me down on the small bed he prepared. Lowering his body down next to me, he whispers, "*and the two shall become one.*"

For hours afterwards, we lay on that old rope bed listening to the rain beat against the tin roof. There are no words that need to be said. We have found peace in each other's arms.

I am not sure of the time, but the sun has begun to peek through the clouds and shine through the broken windowpanes on our bare skin. The fire has gone out, signaling it is time to leave. As I dress into my dry clothes, I turn to my new husband. "Did you plan this, this way?"

"Aye, you will never know the answer to that my dear," he laughs.

Before we leave, I turn to take one last look around the room and at our marriage bed. "Joel, I want to always remember this place. What shall we call it?" I ask.

"My childhood home, the bed I was conceived in," Joel winked.

CHAPTER 21

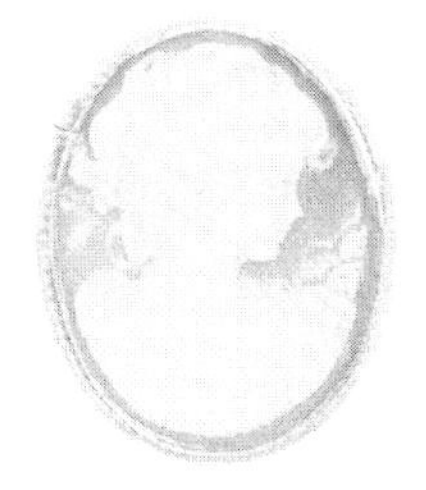

An Uncertain Future

July 20, 1865

I never dreamed the day would come when the sight of food made me ill. Joel is taking me to see Dr. Cotton today. I told him I do not think it is necessary, but he is insisting. I have a very good idea the nature of my illness, although I dare not speak of it so early. This will be the first time I have been to Salisbury since the occupational government has taken over.

Although Joel has never spoken of it, I am certain he, like many of the men, took the *'Oath of Allegiance'* to the Union, or *'swallowed the dog'* as it was unaffectionately called. It was forced upon them in order to receive food or seeds to plant their gardens. I am sure I would not have enjoyed our first chicken meal so much if I had known then what a price he paid for it.

The land is healing faster than our hearts. The peach trees are loaded and the crops are coming on, but holding on to our life-giving land is not an easy task. Just as soon as the Union troops established control, they began to enforce their complicated tax laws, licenses, stamps, duties and fees on us. We have no rights as citizens, but we are expected to pay on every dollar we earn and every hog we slaughter. They even make us pay taxes on our dogs.

The whole war was about unfair taxes the Union was forcing on the South. Thousands of men shed their blood for nothing and now the Union is still bleeding us. How can this be justice? We did not instigate war. We did not go on their soil, seeking to kill their sons and burn their homes. Now we have nothing, but the Union is still standing with its hand out. Why should we help them recoup their war debts?

I overheard Joel tell Ransom he figures before it is all over "a man will have to pay taxes on the number of times he goes to the outhouse."

'Swallowing the dog' was pure humiliation for Joel, but accepting my gold to pay his taxes came with more disgrace. One does not take comfort in knowing others share your suffering, but Joel is not alone. Sallie and I divided the contents of the box that Papa buried in the yard. She was forced to use Papa's gold wedding band to pay the taxes on their farm. *A man's pride is a hard thing to restore, but time takes care of many things.*

We are among the lucky. There are many who will lose everything they own to the Yankee blood-sucking carpetbaggers. They are descending upon us, hoping to make their fortune on our misfortune.

These are fearful and uncertain times. The newspaper headlines are terrifying, telling of poisoned rivers, uprising Negroes and our no-government chaos. What are we to think when the government we now must say grace to just hung a woman? There was little evidence that Mary Surratt was responsible for Lincoln's death, yet the Union was eager for revenge and strung her up like a common horse thief. God only knows what they will do with Jefferson

Davis now that he has been captured. What gives them the right to place him in shackles? How can they say treason when he has done nothing unconstitutional?

People do things in desperate situations. We have had crops stolen out of our fields by homeless whites and Negroes. Joel does not like to leave us alone. When he must, he has no choice but to trust Harper to watch over the fields. Trusting Harper or Violet with our property is one thing, but trusting them with Victoria is a different story. We have heard the horror stories of freed Negroes working in the employment of their former masters. What if they would run off and leave Victoria unattended or worse run off with her?

Harper and Violet appeared to be keeping to themselves these days. Still, it is Joel's decision not to leave Victoria in their keeping while we are not at home. Little Victoria has found a place in Joel's heart and he is not about to take any chances.

Victoria has become a good little traveler. She enjoys riding up front next to Joel and pretending to drive. I have written ahead to Dr. Cotton and he has invited us to stay the night. Joel is uneasy, but it will be a nice break for all of us.

This morning I secretly prepared a bag for our travel and Joel took it out to the carriage himself. As we are leaving, Violet comes out with a basket of food for our travel. "*Whens will yous be home?*" she asks.

"I am not sure, but it might be late. Don't wait up for us," I reply.

Joel and I both agree it would be best not to inform them we will be gone all night. Perhaps they will worry, but best not allow time for them to plot.

Once we are on the road, Joel takes a deep breath. "I guess we are better off to trust the Negroes than Scalawags and Carpetbaggers."

When we arrive in Salisbury, Joel reluctantly agrees to take us into town first. I wanted to do some shopping and mail a letter to Dr. Fannie. At one time Ransom and his father owned the dry goods store. Mr. Huneycutt was forced to sell the store after Ransom went off to war. It was boarded shut during the war, but it has recently been reopened.

Our first stop is the Post Office. I prepared myself for the presence of Union troops and the burned-out buildings, but I was not prepared for the number of amputees and disfigured men I saw on the streets. I turn to look at my husband riding next to me. One hand is holding Victoria and his other hand on the reigns is missing two fingers. It is just by the grace of God that Joel has a hand for me to hold.

Just down the street we see the sign, *"Jones' Dry Good and Mercantile Store."* The windows are richly decorated and the store is full of people. Joel sees us to the door and explains he will just wait for us on the bench out front.

From the moment I walk in the door, the sweet smell of perfumes fills my nose. Slowly I begin to wander down the aisles with Victoria resting on my hip. With such lovely merchandise, it is an effort to keep Victoria's little hands under control.

The store is buzzing with shoppers complementing the quantity and quality of the goods. I stop to admire a lovely piece of calico and debate if I could possibly afford just enough for a new collar and sash. The thought quickly vanishes when I see Victoria reaching for something on the shelf. It is a small china head doll with painted black hair, blue eyes and red lips. I examine it, remembering the dolls I owned as a little girl.

It would be unwise to buy the doll even though I have enough money. I feel sick inside. When I was her age, I had everything. Now I have to question buying my own little girl a penny doll. I am startled by a soft voice from behind me. "Hello Ma'am, may I help you?"

When I turn around, I am face to face with a young girl in her early teens. She has a sweet face and is dressed in the latest of fashion. I am suddenly embarrassed of my shabby attire and quickly tell her I would like to buy the doll.

"Excellent choice," she says, in an educated tone. "And what is your name?" she asks, looking at Victoria.

Something is haunting about the young girl's face. "Her name is Victoria," I answer, slowly, still peering into the girl's eyes.

"Well, it is nice to meet you," she says cheerfully. "My name is Mary, but everyone calls me Ladybug."

"Ladybug!" I say alarmed.

She is taken back by the excitement in my voice. "Yes, it was my father's pet name for me."

"And does your father still call you that?" I ask, even though I know it is rude to ask such a personal question.

"No Ma'am, my father died of smallpox when I was a little girl." She is noticeably uncomfortable and takes a step back from me. "Shall I wrap up the doll for you?"

"Yes of course," I answer. I follow her to the counter to pay for my purchase. I am still trying to put together this puzzle. Jones, Jones, I run through my head. It has to be the right one, but how?

She hands me the package and I thank her. On my way out of the store, I see a dimly lit room on the left. The curtain is only partially drawn. I pause to look at the woman sitting at the desk counting money. When she turns her head to take a sip of her coffee, all my doubts are removed. The woman is Rose, Rose Jones to be exact.

When I rejoin Joel, my hands are shaking. "What is wrong?" he asks, looking around to see if he should be on the defense.

"Joel, let us go for now. I will explain it all later."

Dr. Cotton's home is only a few minutes away, but it seems like a long drive as I try to collect my thoughts. Joel has a worried look on his face.

When he pulls up front, Cindy Lou comes running out of the house to greet us. She comes to my side and pulls Victoria into her arms. *"Dars yous is. Yous is a growin likes a weed."*

Joel carefully helps me out of the carriage. His serious face gives to reason of concern for Cindy Lou. *"Is yous sickly Miss Lizzie?"*

"No, I have just a worrisome husband," I tease, reaching up and pulling Joel's hat over his eyes.

"Thats be goods Mr. Joel. Miss Lizzie sho needs some lookings afters. I worries over her since I beens up heres."

Mrs. Cotton is sitting on the porch in the afternoon sunshine. She calls out for us to bring Victoria up for her to see. As we make our way up the front steps, a young Negro man comes out and offers to bring in our bags. Cindy Lou looks up at him and then back at me. *"Dis here is Homer,"* she says, grinning from ear to ear.

"Homer?" I question, looking up at Mrs. Cotton who gives me a little wink.

"Homer he comes to works heres just afters me." Cindy Lou says proudly.

Homer has the same silly look on his face as he passes by Cindy Lou. It is clear there is more to this story.

"Cindy Lou, go tell Dr. Cotton Lizzie has arrived," Mrs. Cotton asks.

"Yes, Ma'am," Cindy Lou answers and goes inside, but I can tell she is busting to tell me something.

Within minutes Dr. Cotton comes to the door and calls for me. I hand Victoria over to Joel. When she sees me go inside, she starts to cry.

Dr. Cotton's examination is short and he confirms my diagnoses. "Mrs. Simpson, from my findings you can expect the baby to arrive about the middle of January. Shall I give the father the good news while you get dressed?"

"Yes, that would be nice, Dr. Cotton." He leaves me a bottle of tonic and some herbs for morning sickness and slips out the door. Joel jumps to his feet to offer me his seat when I come out on the porch. He kisses me quickly and reaches out to shake Dr. Cotton's hand.

"Why are you shaking my hand sir? It is you that did the work," Dr. Cotton laughs.

"Where is Victoria?" I ask, looking around.

"Oh, Cindy Lou and Homer took her around to show her the fish pond," Mrs. Cotton explains.

When Cindy Lou returns, she sits Victoria down on my lap, steps back and looks at me with that silly grin on her face. Seeing she can no longer contain herself, I ask, "Do you have something to tell me, Cindy Lou?"

She says nothing and runs around the side of the house. When she comes back, she is pulling Homer along by the hand. She is out of breath when she steps up on the porch. *"Miss Lizzie, me's and Homer we's married!"*

Cindy Lou was happy and for that, I was thankful. She and Homer were both free and they had chosen to take on the surname Cotton. She said it was a fitting name, since she was raised on a cotton plantation.

The mention of the cotton plantation brought back memories of Sandy Ridge. I wonder if Cindy Lou ever thinks about the night Mammy died? The next morning smallpox had claimed the lives of almost every slave we owned. I went to find the white overseer Papa had hired. When I saw the barn door flapping in the wind, I soon discovered him and his family missing along with our wagon and all our valuables and gold.

It is not until Joel and I are alone that I dared to tell him about what I had discovered today. Lying in the bed in the dark, I tell him the whole story.

"Yes, Joel, I am certain. It was the girl and I know it was the overseer's wife, Rose. Their names were Jones and that is the name of the store."

"If this is true, you should have a right to walk in and take everything they own," Joel says angrily.

"But how will I ever prove it after all this time? Jones is dead. I guess he got what he deserved. He hated the Negroes and was happy to see them dying. Now they were revenged; smallpox claimed his life too.

"We will go there first thing in the morning and confront them. There is no need to file a complaint. Who will give a damn, the Yankee government?"

Joel's words say it all. There is no law and order to turn to. I am willing to confront them, but the chances of ever seeing any of Papa's wealth again is hopeless.

....

As soon as my feet hit the floor, I follow Dr. Cotton's instructions and take two spoonfuls of the tonic he gave me. So far, my stomach is calm. This will not be a good day for morning sickness.

We dress and go downstairs. Mrs. Cotton, as I expected, is sitting on the porch in her usual spot in the sun. I do not see Dr. Cotton and it occurs to me I have not seen their son,

Dr. John, since we arrived. I think back on the weeks I lived here in this house. Dr. Cotton is such a creature of habit and I wonder how he is managing since the prison hospital was burned. I am not to ponder long, for soon we see Dr. Cotton bouncing down the stairs. "Good Morning, Mr. and Mrs. Simpson, Victoria," he says with a sparkle in his eyes.

We follow him out on the sun porch for a visit. I look up at the clock to see if he will follow his old pattern. In exactly 20 minutes he rises, kisses Mrs. Cotton and goes for his morning constitution. In exactly 15 minutes he is back downstairs, but he comes back and sits down.

He may have noticed I was curious. "Dr. John has opened a medical practice downtown where he now takes his quarters upstairs. He will send a carriage for me shortly. I never know where I am going, but the driver does. I make the home visits and John sees the patients in the clinic. The arrangement suits me perfectly. I am happy for the fresh air. We have all had enough stale air working in the prison, did we not Lizzie?"

"Indeed," I respond. I have never discussed my weeks working with Dr. Cotton in detail with Joel. There are some things just as well laid to rest.

Before we could say more, there was a knock at the door and Dr. Cotton jumps to his feet, "Well, I am off. Lizzie, I would like to see you again in three months. If you have any problems before then, please do not hesitate to contact me."

Shortly after Dr. Cotton departs, we say our goodbyes. Cindy Lou is crying when we leave and I tell her to come and visit soon. Joel is anxious to pay a call on Mrs. Jones. He is hoping we can arrive before the store opens for business.

When we pull out front, there is a light burning upstairs. We assume they are living above the store. I hand Victoria to Joel and tell him I would like to speak to her first. I walk to the door and knock. There is no answer and I knock again.

I turn to look at Joel and he is annoyed. "They are there. I saw her look out the window." Without another word, he marches up to the door and knocks loud enough to wake the dead.

The door cracks slightly and Mrs. Jones peeks out. "What is the meaning of this sir? Can you not read the sign? We open for business at nine o'clock."

"We would like to have a word with you," Joel says, trying not to appear angry.

"Well, you will have to come back after nine o'clock!" Mrs. Jones says, and attempts to close the door. But Joel jars the door with his foot.

Joel motions for me to step in front of the door so that she can see my face. She says nothing and opens the door for us to enter. She is still in her dressing robe and we follow her back to the room where I first saw her. She gestures for us to sit down in a pair of chairs in front of the desk. When I sit down, I am afraid I will fall through and a bit of straw falls to the floor.

Everything about the room is depressing. The only window is covered with a heavy dark drape and I can barely see her face. She reaches across the desk and lights a lamp. The light fully exposes her time-worn face. With one deep breath, she collapses down in the chair at the desk and pushes her thin gray hair out of her eyes. "Alright, what do you have to say?" she asks.

This is not at all what I expected. I thought she would be on the defense, perhaps try to deny the charges, but here she is in front of me like a broken-down horse. I look at Joel and he speaks up, "Mrs. Jones, we want answers. Where is the gold?"

"She smiles and I see a few teeth are missing. "Go upstairs; open the door on the right. There you will find every penny of it sleeping in a satin nightgown."

"What is that suppose to mean?" I ask, bouncing Victoria on my knee to keep her quiet.

"Lizzie, you are a mother. Is there nothing you would not do to provide for and protect your child?"

"I suppose," I reply, running my hands through Victoria's curls.

"Lizzie, when your Pa left and Tom took over Sandy Ridge, he turned into a sort of madman. He was angry and resentful of the things your family owned. He said it was not right for one man to have so much while others had so little. He began to hate your family, but mostly, he hated you. He felt you represented what Mary would never be. I tried to reason with him, but by then it was no use. He even talked about burning the place down. I would have taken Ladybug and run off if I had anywhere to go. Looking back, I wish I had. When the darkies came down with the pox, he blamed them for it.

But when he discovered where you had hidden the gold and valuables, it was no turning back. I begged him not to take it, even tried to stop him." She raised her hair over her ear and I see a piece of her ear is missing. "It was a terrible fight and he slammed me into the door and I cut my ear on the hinge. After that, I loaded Ladybug and we left."

"Where did you go?" I ask.

"Well, Tom was a man not used to money and it had it's way with him. He spent it like water, thinking it would never run dry. The only good thing he did was buy this old store. When he died, I sent Ladybug off to boarding school and worked every odd job I could find to pay for her schooling and save up enough money to open up this here store."

"Does Ladybug know about this?" I ask.

"Not a word. She thinks she went to school on money I inherited from my rich uncle. Lizzie, it would break her heart if she knew the truth. Do with me what you want, but please don't ruin her life. She is all I have."

"Mother!" a voice comes from the hall. Rose looks up at me and bites her lip.

"Oh, there you are Mother," Ladybug says, stopping to look at us.

"Aye... Ladybug, this is Lizzie Sanders and her husband. I am sorry sir. I did not get your name," Rose said in a polite tone.

"Joel Simpson," he said, reaching forward and shaking Ladybug's hand.

I stand up to get a better look at the pretty young girl before me. She reminds me of myself at that age, open and fresh like a page unturned. "Ladybug, we were here yesterday and as I was leaving I thought I recognized your mother. As it turns out, I was mistaken."

Mrs. Jone's eyes are full of tears, "No harm done," she tries to smile.

"No harm done at all," I reply, taking her hand in mine and giving it a little squeeze.

"*Jones' Dry Good and Mercantile* is a nice store, don't you think?" I say to Joel on the way home. "I think it will be my favorite place to shop."

Joel smiles, but he says nothing. In fact, we never mentioned what happened that day again.

CHAPTER 22

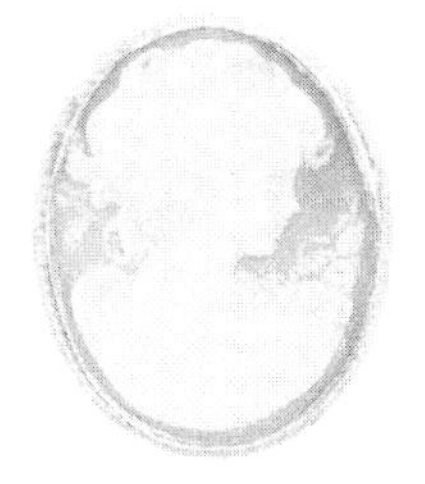

Betty Jo's News

October 6, 1865

I am sitting on the front porch steps showing Victoria how to make a necklace out of clover. Her thick little fingers cannot master the task and she is frustrated. She is wearing two long chains around her neck and one around her wrist when Joel comes from the barn.

"How are you feeling?" he asks.

"Fine," I lie. The truth is my back is paining me again this morning. Dr. Cotton feels it is the pressure of the baby against my spine, very possibly complicated by a sliver of broken bone from when I was shot. He says there is no way to tell for sure and he gave me some Laudanum for the pain.

I am afraid to take it for the baby's sake, especially since what happen with Hannah Jane. Just two weeks ago, her baby was born dead. On two occasions I saw her take Laudanum for her headaches. Dr. Fannie said it was not safe and I have decided to suffer the pain. It is not so bad, just a dull ache. If need be I will address it after the baby is born. The warm sunshine seems to be agreeable.

Today is my birthday and Joel is planning a party for me. I am endeared by his gesture, but I am not looking forward to the commotion. He and Ransom are planning a big day. They are roasting a deer along with some sweet potatoes. Everyone is bringing food, but I am especially looking forward to Mrs. Huneycutt's green tomato pickles.

The guests arrive around noon and the food is spread out. I am thankful my appetite has been restored, but concerned what the effect it will have on my waistline. Joel tells me not to fret. It is of little concern to him.

After the meal, the children are playing in the field and the women gather on the porch to talk. Joel is teaching the boys to play a game he learned while in prison camp. Most of the men that were in the war know how to play "baseball." Thomas and Ransom start up a team and Betty Jo insists on being on the team.

I sit down on a little cane stool with my belly hanging between my legs. I am not the only one expecting a baby. Sallie and Caroline are both expecting too. For Hannah Jane's sake, I try to divert the talk of babies.

"Would you like to see my recent scrapbook?" I ask the ladies. "Betty Jo brought by a stack of newspapers and a Godey Magazine last week." Without waiting for an answer, I strain to my feet and step inside for my scrapbook.

At once the conversation turns to the clippings, t*yphoid fever is sweeping over Yankee Land, Union and England reunite, President Andrew Johnson drops charges against Robert E. Lee, Henry Wirz commander of Andersonville Prison Camp charged with wanton cruelty.*

There were complicated political articles. Stories of Negroes and their Freedman Conventions. Negroes and women demanding the right to vote.

Sallie stands up to stretch her back. "Yes, these are uncertain times. The whole world seems to be angry, everything is changing."

"Mrs. Huneycutt's remark, "I am just thankful here in Stanly County we are tucked away from most of the conflict, " is well received.

I look across at Harper and Violet sitting on a blanket in the yard. Cindy Lou and her husband, Homer, have come to visit. "I suppose you are right. The Negroes, whites, we are mostly the same, just people trying to rebuild our lives."

Sallie brightens up a bit and asks to see the Godey's Ladies Magazine. "We all would like to see the latest French fashions, even if we can't afford a stitch."

The heads nod, but I say I have misplaced it. The truth is, there is an article in the magazine I find most upsetting. I wish my eyes had not seen it and I feel it is not wise to share it with the others. Mammy always said that when a woman is expecting, seeing bad things could mark the baby.

The article told of a woman in Virginia who had a most unusual birth. Two babies born at once, not as twins, but joined together at the hips. They called them Siamese twins, after Chang and Eng Bunker, originally from Siam. The article said the Bunker's now live on a farm in Mt. Airy, North Carolina. They are married and have 21 children between the two of them. There was a drawing of the babies and a photo of the men. I was frightened by the photos. I for one hope that Mt. Airy is a long ways off.

After the ball game, Betty Jo joins us on the porch. It is not a surprise to any of us when she sticks a plug of tobacco in her mouth. "How in God's name do you still have any of that stuff left?" I ask, teasing her.

"Cause I's smart. I mix in bits of dogwood bark to makes it last. Tastes the same," she says proudly.

I was going to comment, but Thomas comes up to her and she hands him a plug too. I can tell Mrs. Huneycutt does not like it, but she turns her head and says nothing. She has to know that Thomas is spending most of his nights in Betty Jo's cabin. She could insist they get married, but then she will have Betty Jo for a daughter-in-law. I think she is wise to let time take care of it.

A carriage drives up and I recognize it as Mrs. Jones and Ladybug. Sallie was not there when Mr. Jones ran off with the gold and thankfully she has never put two and two together. Rose is a lonely woman and I have grown fond of Ladybug.

When they step out of the carriage, Ladybug is dressed like a little princess. I cannot help but notice how ragged Mrs. Jones looks in comparison. Ladybug runs up to me and gives me a big hug. Her face is beaming. "Guess what, Lizzie. Mother is sending me to finishing school!"

"Oh really, where?" I ask, looking over her shoulder at Rose.

"Mt. Pleasant Female Seminary. I will still be able to come home to visit. It is not too far, is it Mother?" she asks, but not at all for my benefit. She is addressing the young boys who have taken notice of her. "We read about it in the newspapers," she speaks up clearly. "They described the school as the very Island of Culture."

"Sounds very exclusive and expensive, I might add." I smile, catching Rose's eye.

"Yes! It is $170 a ..." She is interrupted when her mother takes hold of her arm and shakes her head slightly.

"I hope that school will teach you it is not polite to speak of finances dear. Besides, we are here to give Miss Lizzie her birthday present. Go and fetch it for me, sweetie." Rose comes up on the porch and takes a seat next to me. She watches admirably as Ladybug's blonde curls bounce up and down underneath her silk bonnet.

"Darling young lady," Mrs. Huneycutt remarks.

"Thank you, she is my joy," Mrs. Jones says softly.

Everyone smiles, but it is deeper than that. The girl is her reason for living. She has sacrificed her whole life to ensure the girl has a bright future. I look over at Rose's tired and worn face. Surely Ladybug knows. I think not, but she is not at fault. She has been taught only to receive. Perhaps time will teach her to give.

Ladybug climbs up the steps with a big grin on her face. She drops a large package wrapped in brightly colored paper on my knees. "Here Miss Lizzie, this is for you. Happy Birthday."

She has caught the attention of everyone and they have gathered around to see what is in the box. Joel jumps over the railing to stand next to me. I struggle opening the package and he takes out his pocket knife and cuts the cord.

Once I open the package, I am confused. It is a metal box of sorts with letters on moving keys like a piano. Everyone is whispering and at last someone calls out "Play us a tune."

Ladybug and her mother laugh. "Lizzie, it is a new invention. It is called a typewriter," Rose says.

"A typewriter?" I ask, sitting it down carefully on the table next to me.

"You can compose letters or even write a book and never worry about writer's cramp. Ladybug can show you how to work it."

"Ladybug reaches in the box and pulls out a piece of writing paper and inserts it in the device. Her fingers rest on the alphabetized keys and as she strikes, the key letters appear on the paper. In just a few seconds she has written,

Happy Birthday Dear Lizzie.

Everyone applauds. "Would you look at that." Joel says."What will they think of next?"

Ransom comes up on the porch to take a look at it, "I think we are going to see lots of changes folks. This is only the beginning."

Later in the evening, the men build a fire and we gather around to listen to them play music and sing. Among many of the things I learned to love about my husband is his beautiful singing voice.

When it is Joel's turn to sing, he tells us the story of a lonely soldier who wrote a song after his beloved broke off their engagement. He said his captain had forbidden the soldiers to sing the song, as it made the men too homesick. "Lorena," he looks at the men. "Shall I sing it for you?" They shake their heads for him to sing.

His voice is smooth and tender and he turns to look at me as he sings. *A hundred months have passed, Lorena, Since last I held that hand in mine, And felt the pulse beat fast...*

My eyes are filled with tears as I think of all the lonely hearts tonight. So many hopes and joys are forever buried. For what reason? For what gain?

Joel is sitting here in front of me, singing and holding my hand. He is alive and strong, but even the strongest man is frail on the battlefield. It is a miracle any of them came home at all.

As evening falls, the guests begin to disappear. Betty Jo and Thomas ride off together. Cindy Lou and Homer plan to stay the night with Violet and Harper. Peace falls quietly on the Simpson home.

Late in the evening after Victoria is asleep, Joel and I sit by the fire together. It has come to be our special time. Sometimes he reads to me or I to him. Some nights we say nothing at all; we are just content to be. Tonight is one of those nights.

I am awake long after my husband's breathing turns into the labor of sleep. The fire is burning down, but his body is warm against mine. I think about the events of the day and I wish Mother and Papa had been here. I ask God to forgive me for my mournful thoughts, but nothing will ever fill the void in my heart.

I think back on the night dear Mammy died. Dr. Fannie and I sat outside together on the cabin steps and watched a shooting star blaze across the sky. Dr. Fannie is a special woman. Her words that night have adhered to my heart and have become a part of me. "Lizzie," she said. *"It is a fearful thing when the human soul takes flight. The Bible teaches that we should rejoice, but none of us can rise up to it."*

CHAPTER 23

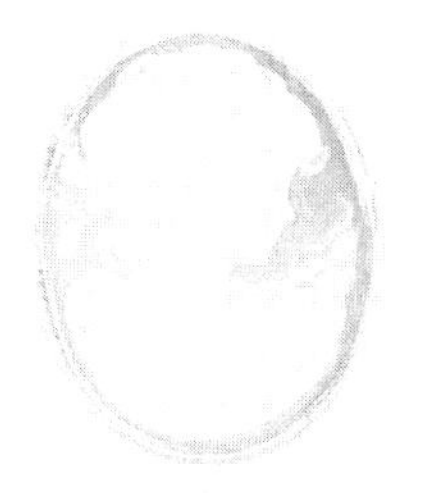

Restored Trust

Monday, January 8, 1866

"No Victoria, it is not a toy!" Joel repeats for the hundredth time. "Come on now and let Mommy finish her letter." Victoria starts crying and the struggle begins for Joel to redirect her attention.

Violet overhears the upset and comes flying out of the kitchen. "*Listin heres Miss Vicky, yous stops dat cowling rights nows. If Mommy and Daddy is a gonna takes yous on a trips yous best starts behavin.*" She sweeps her up in her arms and Victoria quiets down.

For the first time, I realize how much Violet is like Mammy. She has the same voice, the same little bony hands. I don't know why I never saw it before. Perhaps the years have transformed her or it is the hard times. As she carries Victoria up the stairs, I close my eyes. In her voice I can hear the melody of Mammy's voice. I am taken back to Sandy Ridge and thankful for the memory Violet has presented to me today.

From the day the typewriter arrived, it was given a sacred spot in our house. Joel cleared off a small table in the sitting room and provided me with a comfortable chair to work. It took a little time to master the skill, but I am nearly an expert now. I was disheartened to learn the ink does not last forever and must be replenished. Although Christmas has come and gone, Joel promises he will buy me ink and paper while we are in town.

In view of our travel time, Dr. Cotton graciously invited us to stay at his house until after the baby is born. On my last visit, he suggested it would be wise to come the first week in January. We had planned to strike out Monday, New Year's Day, but when we arose, the ground was covered with snow. There are still some icy patches. Although it is terribly cold, the sun is shining today

I look up at the clock and it is almost eight. Joel has gone to the barn to get the carriage ready. I must finish my letter so that I can mail it today.

Dear Dr. Fannie,

I suppose by the time you read this I will be the proud mother of two. Dr. Cotton says the baby is due anytime now. I have not the slightest feelings of anything unusual, except of course the ever-present ache in my back.

I am so glad to hear you are back in Charleston and the clinic is up and running again. I can agree with you, it is better to be on southern soil than on Yankee turf even if we are to starve to death. We too have soldiers straggling in since the rebellion.

In your last letter, you mentioned the disorderly government in Charleston. Yankee Provost Officers

on every corner must be frightening. I know there has been some trouble here too. Joel would prefer I not receive any upsetting news in my present condition, but my friend Betty Jo has not spared me. Most of our trouble with the newly freed slaves is the struggle between white men and Negroes for jobs. There is very little work here and many of the men are planning to go toward Concord for the winter. They are hoping to seek employment at John McDonald and Sons Cotton Mill at Forest Hill.

Joel has a job in Salisbury. He plans to take his instruction tomorrow and will begin work on Wednesday. We have Cindy Lou's husband Homer to thank for the recommendation. His job will be to take census records of the Negroes and their marriages. He will be paid for every new entry he records.

Many of the men refuse to work for the occupational government. Joel says it is foolish. He feels we should take all they will give us. After all, it is by their hand we have lost all we have.

I tell you Fannie these are frightening times. I feel we southerners are sheep among the wolves. The good news; this cannot go on like this forever. Things will have to change. I have heard they are rebuilding the railways. I hope that one day soon I will be able to bring my family for a visit in Charleston. That will be a grand day for sure. Until then, keep me in your prayers and I will you in mine.

Your most devoted friend forever,
Lizzie

PS: Please say a special prayer for my unborn child. I have been uneasy this entire pregnancy. I know I should regard it as nonsense, but I have been troubled by the oddest dreams. First, I dream there is no baby at all and then again it is a boy and he is already two weeks old before I lay my eyes on him.

"Lizzie!" Joel calls, coming in the front door shivering from the cold. "I sure hate to take you and Victoria out in this kind of weather, but it can't be helped. Bundle up the best you can and I will heat some bricks for your feet."

I brace myself and rise out of the chair. Joel shakes his head unhappily. "Next baby I will plan to have in the spring," I joke.

When I get to the top of the stairs, I hear Violet talking to Victoria. *"Yous bes a goods girls whiles yous gone and makes sures you lets yous Mommy gets enough rests. Yous hears." Her voice is hoarse and I can tell she is crying.*

I do not enter the room, but climb back down the stairs to find Joel. He is waiting downstairs and questions why I am without Victoria. "Joel, it is so cold and I am fearful of taking Victoria out. In my heart I feel Violet and Harper will take good care of her. Besides, I have a feeling the baby will be here soon and we will only be a few days."

Joel walks over to the window and looks outside. It is beginning to sprinkle snow. "I suppose you are right, but I am going to have a firm talk with Harper before we leave. Go let Violet know what you expect."

When we left, Violet and Harper were grateful to have our trust again and little Victoria was safe and warm. I felt like I did the right thing for all concerned. The cold was easy to adjust to, but the bumps in the road were troublesome.

We were only on the road for about an hour when I told Joel to pull over so that I could empty my bladder. The moment I step out of the carriage, I feel a sharp pain. I try not to let it show by the expression on my face and pray it would pass. Once we are back on the road, the pain eases.

Joel suggests that I try to nap; it will make the trip seem shorter. I close my eyes and drift off to sleep, but I awaken with pain and pressure in my lower belly. This time I cannot deny the pain. "I think I will be alright Joel, just pull over for a bit and let me out again." His hands are shaking as he helps me out onto the ground. The moment my feet hit the ground a gush of water runs down my legs. "My water has broken, Joel. I am afraid we will not make it to Salisbury."

Joel helps me back in the carriage and we start down the road. He is afraid to drive the horses faster for fear it will bring on the delivery, but if he does not, he may have to deliver the baby on the open road in the cold.

The pains are getting closer together and I look at him and simply say "Hurry." He cracks the whip and the horses take off in full gallop. I am not sure how much time passes for I am in such pain that I am passing in and out of awareness.

In the distance, we see a small frame house and there is smoke coming from the chimney. Joel makes the decision it is not safe for us to go any further and turns down the drive hoping to find help.

He leaves me in the carriage while he goes to the door. Shortly, a man comes out with him to help me inside. It is a small humble home, but it is warm and dry and I am thankful. I can barely stand and Joel carries me to a small room in the back and lays me down on the bed. There is a woman waiting for me.

He leans down over me so that I can see his face. "Lizzie these nice people are going to take care of you until I can get back. I am not going to try to go into Salisbury for Dr. Cotton. The Indian woman that delivered Sallie's baby just lives over the hill and I am going to get her. Do you understand?"

"Yes," I answer, as loudly as I can.

"Good! You just hold on. Everything is going to be alright." He then leaves me in the company of the woman.

She begins to talk sweetly to me and stroke my hair. She wipes off my brow with a damp cloth. I wonder what she knows of delivering a baby. I wish Joel had stayed. He, at least, was not a stranger.

I hear myself scream and I know the baby is coming. "Where is Joel?" I cry repeatedly. The woman is attending to me, but it is I who is suffering the birth. "Help me, oh Lord!"

The pain is over. I must have been asleep. I open my eyes for fear I have died.

"Where am I?" I scream.

Joel is sitting next to me holding my hand. I know something is wrong and I am afraid. "The baby?" I ask. Joel hangs his head and starts to weep. "I could not find Minerva. If only I could have gotten back sooner."

The next thing I am aware of it is morning and the sun is breaking through the window. I can hear Joel talking in the next room. "When she wakes, if she is able, we will start back home. We have imposed long enough on you already."

When Joel enters the room, I am sitting on the side of the bed. "I am ready to leave this place," I say sorrowfully.

We are well on the road before I ask, "What did they do with our baby?"

"Mr. Eudy says our boy was born dead; never took a single breath. He says he buried him around back." Joel was trying to speak clearly, but his voice was cracking.

"Come spring, we can have the body moved and bury him next to your parents if you would like."

"Yes, I would like that," I say softly. "Joel, was it the woman who said our baby never took a breath?"

"No, I did not see Mrs. Eudy before we left. Her husband said she was resting and was awfully upset over what happened."

"But Joel, I heard the baby crying! I know I did!"

"Lizzie darling, it is an awful thing and the mind can play tricks on you. Try to get some rest and we will talk about it later." I wanted to talk about it then, but I was too weak. Joel pulled the blanket up over my shoulders and I fell asleep.

When we arrive home, Violet runs out to greet us. As if Joel's solemn face is not enough to tell the story, my flattened form was. "*Oh Miss Lizzie, Oh Miss Lizzie,*" she says over and over as they help me in the house.

"Violet, where is Victoria?" I ask, suddenly fearing something has happened to her too.

"She is fine, honey pies, juz fine. She is upstairs taking her nap."

I sit down on a little chair in the hall and I start to weep. No, I am wailing. I have lost all control of my emotions. All the years of being strong, Mammy's death, Papa and Mother's are pouring down on me. I am a broken woman. There is no turning back this time. "My baby is dead!" I shout. "Does anyone care?" "My baby is dead."

"Of course we dos Miss Lizzie," Violet says, taking hold of my arm and trying to help me to my feet.

"Stop it! Get your hands off me!" I hear myself saying angrily.

Violet lets go and looks at Joel. He shakes his head. He lifts me up and carries me across the hall. This is the second time he has carried me to this bed near death. This time, I am wishing to die.

Over the next several days, I lay in the bed staring at the ceiling. I demand the curtains be pulled and I refuse to eat. Joel comes in and sits down next to me, but I will not look at him. I don't want to feel his pain. I have enough of my own.

....

Sunday, January 14, 1866

There is a knock on the door, but I do not answer. The door opens and in walks Hannah Jane. She walks in quietly and takes a seat next to me. I am expecting some kind of holy lecture. "Lizzie, most of the talk people gave me when our baby died was just lip deep. How does another person know how you feel? I reckon they meant well, but all the talk in the world cannot do a damn thing for you now. You have lost your own flesh and blood and it is buried in the ground forevermore. You will never get over it and that is the end of it. The only thing you can do now is get your ass out of the bed and live for those that are still living. At least you got Victoria."

It was the old Hannah Jane speaking, not the preacher's wife, and her blunt words cut through me like a knife. "You are right Hannah Jane. Thank you." I reply, looking at her with tears in my eyes. "Enough of this!" I sit up in bed and sling my legs off the side. "I think I owe some people an apology."

She is just about to walk out of the room to let me dress when I catch her arm. "But Hannah Jane, I am certain I heard the baby cry. Joel said they said the baby was born dead and it is just my mind playing tricks on me. But, I heard crying!"

Hannah Jane looks at me. "Then someone might be lying, if you are certain Lizzie."

"Why would they?" I ask.

"I don't know, but I think it is worth checking out. Let me talk to Betty Jo about it. In the meantime, I suggest you not speak to Joel of this. The poor man has had a rough time. He blames himself for what happened."

When I walk out into the sitting room, Hannah Jane is gone. I walk down the hall and hear voices coming from the kitchen. I open the door and the first word I hear is, "Mommy!" My little angel has a mouthful of blackberry jelly and runs to give me a big kiss. "Mommy is back!" she proclaims to Joel and Violet.

"Yes, Mommy is back," I say, barely above a whisper. Within minutes, I am covered with kisses and blackberry jelly. "I am sorry," I announce to both of them.

"*Nothin to be sorry fer, child. Yous best gets working on making another baby,*" Violet says and winks at Joel.

I laugh for the first time in days. Yes, Violet is becoming more like her mother every day. I hope Victoria will learn to love her as much as I loved Mammy.

....

January 17, 1866

Our household has returned to near normal. Joel has gone to Salisbury to break the news to Dr. Cotton. I have just settled down in front of the typewriter to write a revised letter to Dr. Fannie. I kept the old letter for my diary, but the new one will have to tell what has happened since.

I am trying to concentrate and I jump when I hear a knock at the door. I open the door to find Betty Jo standing before me. *"Lizzie, is you in shape to ride*? she asks.

"I suppose, if it is important," I answer.

"Oh, it is important all rights and there ain't no time to kilt. Go get on yous riding britches and I'll saddle you a horse."

Violet looks at me as if I have lost my mind when I ask her to watch Victoria. I dress as quickly as possible. I know Betty Jo and she does not play around. If she says it is important, it is. When I step out the front door, she has a horse waiting for me. "Has something happened to Joel?" I ask.

"No!" she says, and takes off riding. She rides fast and I have to push myself to keep up with her. We are halfway to Salisbury before she slows down. Directly ahead is the house where Joel and I stopped the day I went into labor.

She ties off her horse behind some trees and motions for me to do the same.

"Liz, I donts hows to tells you this. Buts, something ain't right here. After Hannah Jane told me you was certain you heard the baby cry. I thought I'd just come up here and take a look around. I snuck up to the house and looked in the window. There was a woman a nursing a newborn baby. I reckon that's not too strange, but Hannah Jane said you did not mention the woman havin her own baby. Lizzie did you see a baby when you went to that house?"

"No Betty Jo, I didn't see any sign of a baby that day at all."

"Well, what I seen that day sat me to a thinking. I knocked on the neighbor's door, pretending I was taking the census report. An old lady came to the door and tells me

them Eudy's ain't got no baby. She says their backyard is full of dead babies. She said she had not kept count, but she guesses the numbers to be four or five. The last one died too and Mr. Eudy buried it on New Years Day!"

"Betty Jo, what are you saying?" I ask, feeling as if I might faint.

"I am a saying that baby up yonder is yours and Joel's!"

"Oh my Lord," I say, sinking to my knees. "How will we ever prove it?"

"I ain't sure, but we gots to confront them. The man was a packing up a wagon that day and I am afraids they are a fixing to leave town. I can tell you one thing; we ain't leaving without that baby, even if I have to dig up the old one to prove it!"

My heart is racing as we sneak up over the hill. Betty Jo is right on one account. They are packing up to leave. I can see through the window a baby in a basket sitting by the fireplace. Betty Jo tells me to wait and I duck down behind the bushes.

She goes to the door and knocks loudly. Finally, the woman comes to the door.

"How do Ma'am. I need to ask you a few questions."

The woman slams the door in Betty Jo's face. She knocks again and pulls out her pistol. The man comes to the door this time. *"Likes I was a telling your wife, I needs to asks you folks a few questions. I sees yous in a hurry and it won't take long."*

The man steps out on the porch. I see the woman take the baby out of the basket. I run around to the back door. She is climbing up into the wagon. If this is my child, I have to do something. I shout out to her, "Mrs. Eudy, I think you have something that belongs to me!"

She freezes until she sees my face. Then with the baby in her arms, she begins to run toward the woods. "Betty Jo!" I scream.

Betty Jo looks up and sees the woman running across the field. She leaps off the porch and the two of us take off running after the woman. The woman is no match for Betty Jo and she soon has her backed up against a tree. Seconds later, out of breath I join her. "Mrs. Eudy, is that my baby?" I ask firmly.

Mr. Eudy is now standing behind us. "Helen, you don't have to answer that question. Don't be a fool!"

Mrs. Eudy looks at her husband and then back at me. She tenderly folds back the blanket and kisses the baby. "Yes, I do, Emmett. This is not our child and we were wrong to take it. I cannot make this young woman pay for our losses no matter how great they might be."

"Emmett slams his hand in his fist and walks away. Helen steps forward and places the baby in my arms. For the first time I look upon the face of my son.

We walk slowly back to the house. "Do what you wish with me," she says. "It was not Emmett's idea; it was mine. I know I must pay the price for what I have done," she says boldly.

"No, Helen, I understand your grief. How can I be bitter now, when you have given back to me the greatest treasure I could ever imagine?"

I climb up on my horse and Betty Jo hands me my baby. Once I take him to my breast, I am grateful to feel my milk let down. Thank you Lord, thank you Lord.

When we arrive home, Harper is angry when he finds out what happened, but Violet's emotions are more of my own. Victoria now thinks babies arrive on horseback. I will have some explaining to do later on.

It is after dark when I hear Joel's horse coming up the drive. I am sitting in my chair next to the fireplace. He will be expecting to find me here. He comes in the front door and I see him hang up his coat and hat. He sits down to remove his boots and the baby starts to whimper. I see him look up with a puzzled look on his face.

He sees me, but the baby is nuzzled to my breast hidden away. Slowly he approaches me and I uncover my surprise. "Sit down, husband, I have much to explain."

At first he is overjoyed, then he is angry, and then he is overjoyed again. I hand him his son and he kisses him.

"Daddy, your boy needs a name," I smile at Joel.

"And I have a name for him: *Robert Edward Simpson*."

CHAPTER 24

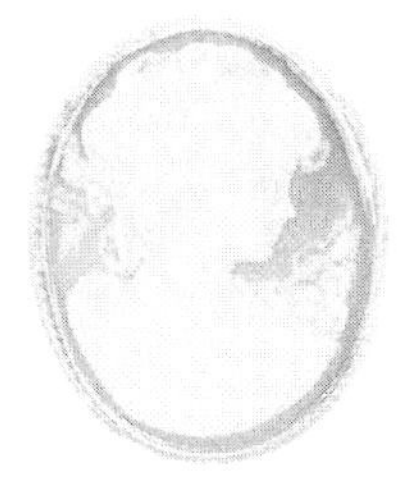

Eileen Fiske

March 21, 1866

I would like to sleep late, but with nursing a baby there is little chance of such. Joel smiles as he passes by me sitting at the typewriter. I have learned to master nursing Robert and typing at the same time. It seems to pass the time for me and the rhythmic sound of the keys striking has become his lullaby.

Joel will be leaving soon. He has taken a job with the census department and is assigned to work the areas of Stanly and Montgomery counties He leaves early and is never home before suppertime.

He says the work is not altogether unpleasant and on nice days he enjoys the ride. However, he says he is often met with resistance. Some people are not too eager to give out information to the Union Regulators.

Just last week Joel said he stopped at a shack down by the creek. He asked a little boy playing in the yard his name. He said his name was Alec Whitley and his Ma's name was Suzanna. But that was all the information Joel got. When he went to the door, Suzanna pointed a gun at him and told him to get off her property. Joel said he felt sorry for the boy and gave him his lunch before he rode off.

We have since learned the woman had a house full of children and no husband of her own. Perhaps she was more afraid of a scornful wife than the Union Regulators. Today he will work his way toward Salisbury, turn in his report to Mr. Henderson at the Register of Deeds and collect his pay. He will then go to Mary Jones' store to buy some provisions – flour, sugar and coffee. On his way home, if time permits, he plans to stop at old man Hinson's house for some of his molasses. If all goes well tonight, we will be eating hot biscuits and molasses. I much prefer that to the raccoon we had for supper last night. Harper trapped the animal and kept it pinned up for several weeks before he killed and cooked it. It is strong-tasting meat and I will refuse it next time it is prepared.

Joel is preparing to leave shortly. I am hoping to compose a reply to Dr. Fannie's letter. If I hurry, he will mail it today while he is in town.

With less than a half page written, I pull the paper out of the typewriter. I am still perplexed by Fannie's recent letter and I take it out to read again.

March 1866

Dear Lizzie,

It was a joy to hear from you. I am glad you are enjoying good health after the delivery of the baby. I urge you to take care and do not overdo until you are done nursing.

I expect your little boy is growing like a weed. What a blessing it was to recover him from the would be kidnappers. I think charges would be in order, but I understand your overwhelming joy outweighed the crime.

You would not like to visit Charleston now. It is a city of anger and uprisings. I believe white citizens would do well to accept the Union and let them do their work. They have promised to rebuild railways and even set up schools for the freedman.

Lizzie, the war is over and a new day is coming for all people. My people are free and I pray for the day of equal rights. However, mountains cannot be moved overnight and violence does not pave the road to peace. We must bury the past and rebuild a new south.

Many of the Negro Union Officers have been placed in high positions, such as judges and clerk men. I fear it is too soon for them to enter into politics. Very few have the education or knowledge to properly fill the position.

I have been assisting my newfound friend and activist, Mary Weston Fordham. She is rallying for the rights of Negroes and women. Hoping to gain equal pay for all and the right to vote. She is a poet and teacher at Saxon School here in Charleston. Like myself, she was born a free woman of color. I would like you to meet her someday. I have enclosed a few lines of her poems for you to sample.

Yours always,
Fannie Holloway

Serenade
Sleep, love sleep,
The night winds sigh,
In soft lullaby.
The Lark is at rest
With the dew on her breast.
So close those dear eyes,
That borrowed their hue
From the heavens so blue,
Sleep, love sleep.

The Coming Woman
For tonight is our Woman's Convention,
And I am to speak first, you know—
The men veto us in private,
But in public they shout, "That's so

Stars and Stripes
Hail Flag of the Union! Hail Flag of the free!
That floats so proudly o'er land and o'er sea.
Thy Stars and thy Stripes, in grandeur doth wave.
O'er hearts that are true and hands that are brave.

I reach over Robert and slip the letter and poems back in the envelope. He is finished nursing and I am sure he needs changing. I look down at him as if he will understand. "Mommy is not going to type today."

No, I will have to think more about the letter before I reply. The first poem was nice, but the second one makes me wonder why a woman would put up such a fight to vote. Yet, the last one can only mean Fannie's allegiance is now with the Union? I suppose after working four years at the war hospital she is entitled to her own conclusion. She is a friend and a good woman. Nothing can change how I feel about her. My better judgment tells me Joel will be far less understanding. Therefore, it is best not to share this letter with him. I struggle to my feet, balance Robert in my arms and with the other hand drop the letter in my apron pocket.

I walk Joel to the porch and watch him ride off to work. Mammy always said that if you want healthy children give them plenty of fresh air. When I see Victoria is in an agreeable mood, I decide to bundle up Robert and take them for a walk.

We have just cut across the field with plans to follow the hay path down to the creek when we see Betty Jo riding up. She drops down off her horse and walks along with us. She has been coming by almost every day lately. I know she has something on her mind. With Betty Jo, it is best not to pry. When she is ready to talk, she will.

Robert is sound asleep when we get to the creek. I am careful not to wake him and sit down slowly on a big flat rock. Victoria runs out to the edge of the water and Betty Jo sits down next to me.

"Mommy, look at the pretty bugs!" Victoria screams out in delight.

"That there's a snake doctor," Betty Jo answers, looking at a pair of dragonflies bouncing along the surface of the water.

Victoria looks puzzled, but does not ponder the answer long. "Look at this pretty bug!" she calls out again, but this time reaches down to pick it up.

"No Victoria!" I shout, waking Robert. Victoria has attempted to pick up a bee and now I have two children crying. Betty Jo jumps to her feet and runs to collect Victoria in her arms. She examines her finger, pulls out the stinger, then reaches in her mouth and places a blob of tobacco on the sting. The poultice calms the sting, but Victoria is no longer interested in exploring.

Betty Jo lifts Victoria up on her back to give her a piggyback ride back to the house and I try to calm Robert. When we step on the porch, Violet opens the door. *"Da wuz sho nough a shorts trip,"* she says.

Victoria sticks out her finger whimpering, "Bee bite."

Betty Jo waits for me to put the children down for a nap so we can have a visit on the porch. When I come back out to join Betty Jo, she is whittling on a little piece of wood.

"You know Lizzie. It is gonna be a long time fer things gets better around heres. The past is too near and the good too weak. But, it ain't so everywheres. They say down in Mexico a body can live like a king with just a pocket full of change."

"Is that so, Betty Jo? Just where did you get this information?" I begin to inquire, knowing she is finally ready to talk about what has been on her mind.

She is just before explaining when we see a couple of men riding up. Betty Jo jumps to her feet and feels for her pistol in her vest. "Wait!" I say. "Let's just see what this is all about before we get antsy."

She sits back down next to me, but I see her hand is under her vest. The two men are riding slowly and I can tell they are looking around at the empty fields and the out buildings, which are badly in need of repairs. They are cautious as they approach and look at us both before either one of them speak. "Good morning ladies," one of the men calls out. "Certainly a delightful morning."

The second man adds, "And a fine day for sitting on the porch. Mind if we ask who owns this property? "

Betty Jo leans over to me and whispers "Yankees." Then in a loud voice she calls out, *"Whats it to yous, Yank?"*

The man attempts to get off his horse and Betty Jo pulls out her pistol. "*I says whats it to you?*"

The man slowly drops to his feet. "I mean you no harm ladies. I was just passing by and noticed that this place was in need of repair. Perhaps I could be of assistance."

"*Yous means to tells us you is a handy mans in that fancy suit?*" Betty Jo laughs.

"No, Ma'am, I was wondering if you are interested in selling. If so I am a perspective buyer," he answers, trying hard to read both our faces.

"*Well, we ain't!*" Betty Jo takes it on herself to confirm. *"And yous best get yous ass back on that horse and gets on downs the roads."*

The man smiles. "No harm in asking is there ladies? My partner and I pay good money for land like this. We have bought at least half-dozen farms here in Stanly County. Some folks see it as a blessing in these hard economical times."

"Wells we ain't one of them!" Betty Jo says, stepping down off the porch to get a closer look at the men.

"Sorry to have troubled you ladies," the man says, looking over Betty Jo's head at me. "If you don't mind, I'll leave you my card in case you change your mind." He hands the card to Betty Jo, but she does not take it. Then he approaches me and extends the card to me. Something inside me says *"Take it."*

We watch the men ride off after a few minutes and Betty Jo turns to me. "*Sees whats I means. Fer long this whole place is gonna be filled with carpetbaggers. Them Yanks ain't looking to pay nobody a fair price for nothin.* "

I study the card and then slip it down my bosom. "Well Betty Jo, people are always going to try to take advantage of people's misfortune. Whether it is here in the South or Mexico, it is just human nature."

I can tell my words did not set well with Betty Jo. She stands to her feet. "*Well, Thomas and me ain't gonna be reconstructed by the Union. I saved my money from my paper business and Thomas has his war pay, we's gonna go to Mexico.*"

I laugh, but I am afraid she is serious. "Will I see you before you ride off into the sunset?"

"Fer sure," she says, climbing up on her horse.

I sit alone on the porch watching her cloud of dust fill the air. She is right. Things will never be the same for our South again. For the moment, I am envious of her. She is young and healthy and is not tied down to anything or anyone. She can just keep on riding until she finds what she is looking for. I hear Victoria calling to me and my vision of Betty Jo riding through the painted desert with the wind in her hair is interrupted. I look out across the land and ask aloud, "Is running away the answer, dear Lord?"

We are forced to make do with the scraps from last night's meal. Joel is late coming home. I justify my concerns with the fact he had a lot of stops to make. He most likely was tied up in town. Once the children are asleep, I light a fire in the parlor and try to read. It is nine o'clock. He has never been this late. I will not go to bed until he is home. I watch the hours pass by and my heart is pounding when the chimes strike 11.

I am certain something is wrong and I feel I must wake Harper and send him out to look for Joel. I dress quickly and start toward Harpers house, but stop when I see a carriage coming up the drive. I have not the slightest idea who is calling or what this might mean.

I walk back to the porch to greet the carriage. Once the wheels stop, I can see there is a woman driving and a man humped over in the seat next to her. In the moonlight, I cannot make out their faces. The woman jumps out of the carriage and calls "Are you Lizzie?"

"Yes," I answer, uneasily.

"Come help me. I have your husband," she replies, running around to open the passenger door.

By the woman's dress, I assume she is a working woman. the sort that worked at Miss Lucy's Brothel in Charleston. I am angry. Even so, I do not hesitate and the two of us help Joel in the house. Joel's speech is slurred and he is having trouble walking. The handwriting is on the wall. Joel has been out with this woman and is as drunk as a polecat.

After getting him in the house, we set him down in a chair in the parlor. Now in the light, I am alarmed to see his head is bleeding and his face is badly bruised. I realize my thoughts have wronged my husband. "What has happened, darling?" I ask.

He straightens himself up in the chair. "I was running late coming out of Salisbury and it was getting dark. I heard folks say the roads were getting dangerous, but I never had any trouble before. I was just about five miles from home when I heard two men riding up behind me. They looked like they were in a hurry, so I slowed down to let them pass. The next thing I knew, one of the men knocked me off my horse. While I was down, the other one roughed me up and stole my wallet and my pistol. I am not sure how much time passed, but when I was able I got up and started walking home. It was not long until I saw the gaslights of a carriage approaching. This time I did not know whether to hide or call out for help. I decided to take my chances and Miss Fiske here was kind enough to bring me home."

"Thank you Miss Fiske," I say, looking at her again. In the light she looks more respectable. She is dressed in evening attire, but it appears to be some sort of costume.

"You are welcome. It was just meant to be. I was on my way back to the hotel from my performance when I saw him."

"Your performance?" I asked, feeling almost ashamed of my first impression.

"Yes, allow me to introduce myself. My name is Eileen Fiske. My husband and I are performers. I should say, my husband and I were performers. We had a number of bookings scheduled when he took ill. After he died, I have tried my best to honor as many as possible. He would not approve of me traveling solo, but I need not remind you these are hard times."

"I do understand, more than you know," I say, reaching out to take her hand. "Please stay the night with us and in the morning you can make a fresh start."

"I do not wish to impose," she says, politely.

"I insist on it," Joel says.

....

Joel was left with a headache the next morning, but other than the sight of him, he was nearly back to normal. Miss Eileen Fiske was late in rising. I instructed Violet to gather the eggs so that we might have a proper breakfast for the actress when she comes downstairs.

In a little notebook, I had carefully reserved Mother's recipe for French toast. I open the book and look over the instructions and ingredients:

Beat four eggs very light,
Stir with them a pint of milk;
Two slices for each of day old bread,
Dip pieces into the egg,
Fry them in a hot pan in hot lard.
Sprinkle with sugar and cinnamon.

I check my cupboards. There is just enough sugar and cinnamon, but I am shy enough bread. I will announce I have already eaten with the children when I serve the meal. I have Violet cut up a few apples and fry them up a bit of pork. I personally want to make the French toast, assuring it turns out just like Mother's.

When Eileen comes downstairs, she is wearing a black and white checked traveling suit and a stylish bonnet poised on her head. The table is set with our best dishes. Violet escorts her to the table with all the manners of our old Charleston life. She then gracefully pours her a cup of coffee. I am hoping she does not notice the coffee is weak, but most of all I hope she does not ask for more than one refill. We have coffee enough for only one small pot this morning.

Soon Joel comes in, takes a seat and inquires about me. Violet quickly tells him I am preparing a special recipe of my mother's. Shortly I come out with a tray of the French toast. I place two perfectly prepared slices on each of their plates. The smell fills my nose and I am afraid my stomach will growl. It is the first time I have prepared it since Mother's death. Violet serves the apples and pork and I take a seat at an empty place setting.

Joel raises his eyebrows and looks at me. "Are you not going to join us dear?"

I am careful not to look at him directly. "The children you know. I have been up for hours. I had my breakfast with them."

"Oh, will you have a cup of coffee with us?" he asks. I am trying to think of a comeback when I hear Robert crying in the other room.

"Sorry, Mother's duty." I smile and make a gracious exit.

I was not to see Eileen again. She was long gone when I came back to the dining room. All that remained were the dirty dishes and an empty pot of coffee. I gathered them up and a sad sort of feeling comes over me.

Dear Lord, let me be grateful for this lesson in humility. Shall I never question your ways or envy the lives of others. For what we take pride in most may be lost tomorrow. In my yesterdays, it was I that ate while others did not. May those days never return. Amen.

CHAPTER 25

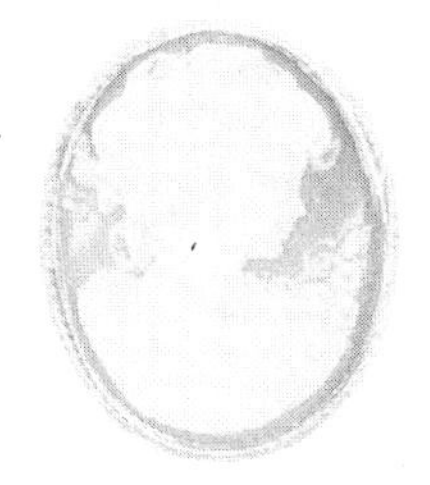

Blessings in Disguise

Sunday, October 6, 1867

Dear Dr. Fannie,

My dear friend, thanks for reminding me I am a quarter of a century old today. Since you have never given us your age, I can never repay you the same courtesy.

Your last letter said you have been doing a great deal of traveling. It is a grand thing you are doing for your people. You are right; there is much work to be done before the Negroes are truly free. However, I can say little for your women's rights issues. I am not so sure taking women out of the domestic circle and placing them in the work force is best for all concerned. Jobs are scarce enough as it is without adding another dimension. But, perhaps that is the old philosophy. You are a free thinker and I admire you for such.

I have little time to ponder such issues anyway. I am knee deep with two children and another one on the way. Joel is overjoyed the baby will come in the spring and not in the deep of winter this time.

I am sympathetic to your description of the difficulties in Charleston over the past year. It has indeed been a rough year for us as well. Farming is uncertain and poor business since the war. Young, old, white and coloreds are all in the same boat, trying to stay afloat. Many have left the county, hoping to find work in cotton mills, tobacco farms or railways. A group of families just left last week heading for the Arkansaws.

We had a fairly decent crop this year, but Joel's job has run out. I think we can make it through the winter fairly well. I have canned until I am sick of it and the men are going to kill a couple of hogs this week.

Our families are growing and the land is forgiving. I suppose we will all survive. My sister Sallie has had another baby boy and she too is expecting again. I laugh often at what you once said to me, "A man ain't good for nothing but filling up your belly with babies." You are right Fannie, but I invite you, before too many more years, to consider a husband for yourself.

Oh, before I close, I must tell you the news on Cindy Lou. Unfortunately, Mrs. Cotton who employed Cindy Lou has died. However, there is good news. She left Cindy Lou and her husband a good deal of money. It appears she is better off than all of us. Who would have thought it?

There is one catch to Cindy Lou claiming the money. Mrs. Cotton was an artist and Cindy Lou had become her student. Mrs. Cotton left strict instructions that Cindy Lou is to continue her studies and become a teacher. She has been accepted to Scotia Seminary in Concord, NC.

Please write often and as always I wish you the very best of luck.

Your forever friend,
Lizzie

It has been over four years since I last saw Fannie. Much has changed since then. I close my eyes and her face beams in my mind, but somehow I fear I will never see her again.

With the years that have passed, few things now take me by surprise, but when Joel came home last week with the news of Rose Jones and Willie James Burris I was shocked. Since Ladybug had gone off to school, Rose hired Willie to help her tend the store. They were both widowed and lonely and the cards fell in place.

The wedding is to take place right after church today. I am hurrying to collect my things, but Victoria is clinging to my leg. "Darling, Mommy will be home soon. Stay here and take care of Robert for me and play with Auntie Violet and Uncle Harper until we get back." I am sorry for her to be upset, but I am truly glad for a day away.

Betty Jo and Thomas are sitting in the second row next to Mr. and Mrs. Huneycutt. Aunt Martha and Hannah Jane are in the front row. Betty Jo is not much of a churchgoer, but her sister Hannah Jane makes up for her. I have heard Betty Jo say "That girl does enough of the Lord's work to save us both a place in heaven."

The church is full and Joel and I take a seat toward the back. The piano is playing as I look across at the faces of the people. Just good honest people. Papa called them God's people. The salt of the earth, he would say.

We are like family. All of us with our joys and our private sorrows. In this church, it makes no difference if you can read or write. The only requirement to enter this sanctuary is that you serve the Lord. Nothing else matters and nothing ever will.

Not a single man, woman or child in this church today is untouched by the war. Many are healing, but none of us will ever be the same. The women hold on to their men, thankful to have what is left of them home. Yet, there are many empty seats next to mothers, wives, lovers and sisters which will never be filled.

Herman begins his service. "My service today is about change. From the moment we enter this world to the day the Lord calls us home, life is about change. The earth changes with the season, children grow up, the government is changing and Lord knows a woman changes her mind!" He must pause briefly to let the men take a laugh. "Yet, the one thing we fear most is change. Why? Because we are not listening to the word of God. His word is settled and unchanging. The grass withers, the flower fades, but the word of our God stands forever: Isaiah 40:8."

At the end of the service, Hannah Jane leads us in singing the closing hymn, *Standing on the Promises*.

Herman then turns and asks us all to stay and be witness to not one, but two weddings.

I could see Thomas shift in his seat and Betty Jo clears her throat. Herman smiles down at Rose and Willie. "Let us take age before beauty," he says teasing.

Joel pokes me and says "I would not have made that choice. Betty Jo is likely to bolt out the back door if he doesn't hurry." Joel begins to laugh at his own joke.

I scold him. "Shh, that is not funny." He is pleased to see that he is not the only one laughing.

Rose and Willie's ceremony is brief and then Thomas stands up and takes Betty Jo's hand. The dress she is wearing is unflattering and I am sure it belongs to Hannah Jane. I cannot help wondering why all of a sudden she is ready to become an honest woman. Thomas would have married her a year ago, but she would not consent.

After the final I do's, we head toward the rear of the church to get in line with the other well-wishers. When I am finally face to face with Betty Jo, she smiles at me and simply says *"I love him."* She need not say anything else.

I watch her from afar holding onto Thomas's arm. I understand her. When a woman is alone, survival depends on her strength. In time, it is love which will soften her rough exterior.

This October 6th, the climate is most agreeable to the human form. The sun is warm, but the cool breeze gently pulls at your clothes and blows your hair. There is a spread of food and music. The mood is light and Thomas and Betty Jo are dancing as the crowd claps. The only ones in a hurry to get home were Rose and Willie.

When the musicians take a break, Joel is sitting next to me. Ransom and a few men come and sit down on the ground next to him. I am not listening to their conversation until Ransom's voice breaks through and silences the crowd. "Sallie and me, we ain't leaving Stanly County!"

I look at Joel and he looks away. For the balance of the evening the men sit huddled up under the tree. I am worried. My mood has darkened and the sun is setting. I am ready to go home.

It is only a short drive home and I wait for Joel to speak. "Lizzie, like Herman says life is about change. I cannot hide it from you that I am worried. Last winter was tight, but this year is looking to be worse. Now that I have lost my job, I cannot even pay the taxes on the farm."

"Joel, we will make it. What about the cotton we have to sell?"

"Lizzie, do you have any idea how hard it is to harvest enough cotton for profit, especially at today's prices? This is not Sandy Ridge with hundreds of hands. Four hands is all we have: Harper's and mine.

"Violet and I can help. I have done it before!"

"I know darling, but as long as I walk this earth it will never be so again. Lizzie, I don't want you to spend the rest of your life doing without meals so the children can have enough to eat. My heart breaks when I see you day after day in that old gray dress. I know how you like pretty things and I want you to have them."

"It is just material things. Joel, we have each other and the children," I say, gently stroking over the new life in my belly.

"Damn! It is just not fair. Don't you see I have to try?" Joel's voice cracks and I can tell he is just before weeping. He is a man of principal and the war has stripped him of his pride.

"Joel, you know I stand behind you. We have been through too much to give up now."

"Lizzie, I am talking about a fresh start. They tell me that in Concord a man can earn a decent living working in the Cotton Mills. I don't know the work, but I can learn it. I have agreed to go with a couple of men tomorrow to see about the jobs. I might be gone a couple of days."

"But are you speaking of moving?" I ask.

"Let's not put the cart before the horse, Lizzie. I will know more when I return."

The rest of the trip we ride in silence. I have never been to Concord, so how can I say good or bad. The children will adjust wherever we go, but I am worried where Violet and Harper fit into the plan.

Just before we reach the house, Joel pulls the carriage over to the side of the road. He reaches in his pocket and pulls out a little box. "I have not forgotten your birthday, darling."

I open the package and find a lovely pearl necklace. "You should not have," I say honestly, feeling they are way too expensive.

"They were my mother's Lizzie. She would be proud for you to own them."

Saturday, October 12, 1867

Joel has been gone for five days. Betty Jo and Thomas stopped by on Wednesday and Ransom, Sallie and the children were here yesterday. I am expecting Joel to return today.

Betty Jo left me with a stack of newspapers and today I have promised Victoria she can help me with scrapbooking. I lay out my work on the table and Victoria climbs in the chair at the end of the table. She eyes the scissors and is anxious to cut, which tries my patience. I take my eyes off

Robert long enough to remove the scissors from Victoria's hands. Robert is crawling on the floor next to us, manages to take hold of the tablecloth and succeeds in emptying everything on the floor. He is delighted, but I am not so much. I decide it will be best to hold Robert in my lap and let Victoria play with the papers. At four years old, her attention span is short. Soon she will tire of the activity.

Once I have put the children down for their afternoon nap, I am free to my own thoughts. It is a rainy afternoon and the old stone house is damp and cold. I light a fire in the dining room and spread out the paper to attempt my scrap-booking again. I promised Papa I would continue the work, but I am beginning to question why. He said that someday people will want to read about the great rebellion. The scrapbooks, now a total of 20 have became a hodgepodge of my life. It is beyond me who will ever find that interesting. Looking over the newspapers, I begin to clip and paste the headlines onto a piece of Betty Jo's handmade paper.

> *Jefferson Davis out on bond. Horace Greeley post bond of $100,000.*
>
> *United States purchases the Alaska Territory from Russia*
>
> *New Wagon Road cut through the Cascade Mountains.*
>
> *Sailor reports seeing mysterious lights over Lake Erie.*
>
> *Indian wars? Kiowa, Comanche, and Apache.*
>
> *Alabama grants Negroes right to vote.*

Today, I am like Victoria and my attention span is short. I close up my work and wander into the next room. Sometimes when I am alone in this house I feel as if someone is watching over my shoulder. It is not at all frightening, almost comforting. Today is one of those days. I sit down in the parlor and my eyes drift to my portrait, which now hangs over the fireplace. "Antonio," I say aloud, wondering what has happened to him. I stand up, walk across the room and gaze up at the painting. It is truly a beautiful painting, but it is of a girl with eyes that are hollow and sad. I wonder how Antonio would paint the girl that is now a woman.

The front door opens. It is Joel. He walks softly. I can barely hear his leather soles fall upon the old plank floors. I do not turn, but I know he is standing in the doorway looking at me.

My heart is pounding as I feel him near me. I am afraid to look at him for fear things have not gone well. His arms reach around my waist and I turn to embrace him.

His lips meet my mind and he kisses me passionately. His clothes are damp from the rain but his body is warm. "Where are the children?" he whispers, kissing my neck.

"I just put them down for their nap," I answer.

"Good," he replies.

....

Monday, October 25, 1867

Joel was able to find a job and has made an offer on a house for us. The deal hinges on the sale of our farm here in Stanly County. Joel has taken the advice of his friends and today our place will be auctioned off. My greatest fear is that our house and land will not bring enough to buy another home and we are left homeless. Joel says it is a chance we must take. For the last two weeks, would-be buyers and curiosity seekers have dropped in on us unexpectedly to preview our house. Joel said most of them are shysters hoping to steal the property right from underneath us.

Mr. Austin, the auctioneer, has arrived and I watch as they head toward Harper and Violet's cabin. Joel wants to make it clear that their cabin and nine acres are not for sale. Mr. Austen is doing a lot of talking, but Joel is a cautious man. He is listening, but that does not mean he will agree.

The sale is to begin at nine o'clock and already the lot is filled with people looking at our things and pondering over the yard. Violet is crying this morning as she is often doing these last days. I understand. She wants to know what is to happen. What happens today will affect us all. Today everything will change.

Violet and Harper are my last link to Sandy Ridge. It seems like a lifetime ago when we were all just children on the plantation. Our greatest worry was who was going to get the last piece of Mammy's blackberry cobbler.

"Violet, I will need you to watch the children today," I say in a demanding tone. She takes hold of Victoria's hand. Before I hand her Robert, I look into her dark eyes and I see the face of my dearest and oldest friend. "Forgive me Darling," I say. "Will you please watch the children for me today?"

"Yes Lizzie," she replies. For the first time she does not call me Miss Lizzie. It is acknowledgment that she understands what today means.

I walk out on the porch and sit next to Joel. His eyes are fixed straight ahead. In many ways it may have been easier on me seeing Sandy Ridge burned to the ground. I can see the pain in Joel's face as he watches everything he owns being carried away, down to the last pick and axe.

The serious bidders come forth as Mr. Austen announces he will now auction off the house and property.

I ask Joel if he would like to go inside. He shakes his head and walks to the edge of the porch and stands proudly.

I look at the faces of the bidders. I recognize a few of the men. Leaning against the oak tree is a tall well-dressed man who has become the high bidder. He looks familiar, but I cannot place him.

Joel turns to me. "That Yankee is buying up half the farms in Stanly County." I suddenly remember where I have seen the man. He was the Carpetbagger that Betty Jo ran off the day Joel was robbed. I kept his card, but I never showed it to Joel.

"I cannot stand here and watch this any longer!" Joel announces, and turns to go inside. He halts when we see a carriage drive up and park right in front of the crowd. Everyone stops to take a look at the fancy rig. A gloved hand extends out the door and we hear a woman's voice call out, "Hold that bid, Mr. Austen!"

Mr. Austen holds up his hand. "Ladies and Gentleman the sale is not final. I think we have another bid to consider."

A gentleman gets out of the carriage and walks around to let the lady out. We hold our breath waiting to see who the mystery lady might be. When she steps out I hear the crowd start to whisper. I recognize her at once. It is the actress, Eileen Fiske, that brought Joel home the night he was robbed.

In minutes, the bidding war begins. When the hammer drops it is Eileen Fiske who holds the high bid. The amount is more than we could have ever dreamed possible. You could hear a pin drop as the opposing bidder walks up to Miss Fiske. She extends her hand to him, but he refuses and spits on the ground in front of her. Her gentleman friend lunges for him, but Eileen takes his arm and shakes her head.

The crowd breaks up and Mr. Austen leads Eileen and the gentleman up on the porch. She smiles. "Nice to see you again, Mr. Simpson. This time under much more pleasant circumstances, I might add. I have admired this house, ever since the night I stayed here. When my fiancé'e and I saw the place was for sale, we decided it was an omen that it was time for us to settle down.

That night laying in bed next to Joel, I think about the wonder of God's wisdom.

Only God could have known Eileen would be traveling down that road the night Joel was robbed. Who would have ever dreamed that frightening night over a year ago would turn out to be a blessing in disguise.

....

Monday, November, 11, 1867

For the last two weeks, Joel and friends have been hauling our things to Concord. Last night was our last night here in this house. I am sad to be leaving Stanly County and will miss Sallie being just down the road. On Wednesday, I insisted Joel take me to the cemetery. "Concord is not that far, Lizzie," he reassured me. I understood his words, but what if I was never to return? Saying goodbye to Mother, Papa and Annabelle gave me closure, courage and hope for a brighter tomorrow.

Joel tells me the new house is large enough for a big family, has two nice porches and sets right on the main street. It is only a short walking distance to town and his work. With the extra money, he assures me we will be settled in by Christmas.

I can hear my footsteps echoing as I walk through the empty rooms. The cabinet doors are standing open, the halls are empty and our bags are packed.

I hear wagons pulling up and the voices of Eileen and her new husband. Today this will be their home and where new memories will begin.

The bedroom across the hall is calling me to say goodbye. I slowly walk through the door. I feel as though I am leaving an old friend. This is the room Joel carried me to the day I was shot, where we made love and where I laid for days thinking my dear baby Robert was dead. Yes, these walls have witnessed my memories both good and bad. The sun's reflection on the floor catches my eye. Oddly enough the flickering light falls in the shape of a heart

"Lizzie! It is time to leave," I hear Joel calling me.

"Goodbye," I whisper to the room and close the door.

In short order, I have the children ready for the trip. Violet and Harper have come to say goodbye. It was their choice to stay here on the land they have earned. Perhaps they will work for Miss Eileen or perhaps they will not. They are free and their destiny is their own.

We are just about to leave when Joel looks over the fireplace and sees my portrait still hanging. "Look what we almost forgot." He smiles and carries it out to the wagon.

It is the last piece of evidence that I, Theodosia Elizabeth Sanders Simpson, was ever here.

Joel and the children are waiting for me. I pull the door closed, but it swings back open as if it is asking me to stay. "No," I say softly. "It is time for a new story and a new beginning. *We are on the road to Concord!*"

Have you forgotten me?

by Nancy B. Brewer

The bricks I laid or the stitches I sewed.
I was the one that made the quilt; a drop of blood still shows from my needle prick.
Your wedding day in lace and satin, in a dress once worn by me.
I loaned your newborn baby my christening gown, a hint of lavender still preserved.

Do you know our cause, the battles we won and the battles we lost?
When our soldiers marched home did you shout hooray!
Or shed a tear for the fallen sons.

What of the fields we plowed, the cotton, the tobacco and the okra too.
There was always room at my table for one more,
Fried chicken, apple pie, biscuits and sweet ice tea.

A time or two you may have heard our stories politely told.
Some of us are famous, recorded on the pages of history.
Still, most of us left this world without glory or acknowledgment.

We were the first to walk the streets you now call home,
Perhaps you have visited my grave and flowers left,
but did you hear me cry out to you?

Listen, my child, to the voices of your ancestors.
Take pride in our accomplishments; find your strength in our suffering.
For WE are not just voices in the wind, WE are a Living part of YOU!

About the author.

Nancy B. Brewer is from North Carolina, where she attended Carolina School of Holistic Medicine in Chapel Hill. Her grandmother was a nurse and her great-grandmother a mid-wife from Stanly County, North Carolina.

She is also a history reenactor and storyteller, which gives her a window for understanding the emotions and lifestyles of the people she writes about. This combined with fascinating family stories and countless hours of research is what makes her works of historical fiction come to life. The author's immeasurable creativity and soft poetic style will captivate you from page one.

Ms. Brewer is available for presentations and book signings
www.nancybbrewer.com